VIOLENT SPRING

BOOKS BY GARY PHILLIPS

NOVELS

The Jook
The Perpetrators
Bangers
Freedom's Fight
The Underbelly
Kings of Vice (as Mal Radcliff)
Warlord of Willow Ridge
Three the Hard Way (collected novellas)
*Beat, Slay, Love: One Chef's Hunger
    for Delicious Revenge* (written
    collectively as Thalia Filbert)
The Killing Joke (co-written with
    Christa Faust)
*Matthew Henson and the Ice Temple
    of Harlem*

SHORT STORY COLLECTIONS

*Monkology: 15 Stories from the World
    of Private Eye Ivan Monk*
Astonishing Heroes: Shades of Justice
*Treacherous: Grifters, Ruffians
    and Killers*
*The Unvarnished Gary Phillips:
    A Mondo Pulp Collection*

ONE-SHOT HARRY NOVELS

One-Shot Harry
Ash Dark as Night

IVAN MONK NOVELS

Violent Spring
Perdition, U.S.A.
Bad Night Is Falling
Only the Wicked

ANTHOLOGIES

South Central Noir
Witnesses for the Dead: Stories (co-edited
    with Gar Anthony Haywood)
*Get Up Off That Thing: Crime Fiction
    Inspired by the Songs of James Brown*

MARTHA CHAINEY NOVELS

High Hand
Shooter's Point

GRAPHIC NOVELS

Shot Callerz
Midnight Mover
South Central Rhapsody
Cowboys
Danger A-Go-Go
Angeltown: The Nate Hollis Investigations
High Rollers
Big Water
The Rinse
Peepland (co-written with Christa Faust)
Vigilante: Southland
The Be-Bop Barbarians
*Cold Hard Cash: A Martha
    Chainey Escapade*

ANTHOLOGIES AS EDITOR

The Cocaine Chronicles (co-edited
    with Jervey Tervalon)
Orange County Noir
*Politics Noir: Dark Tales from
    the Corridors of Power*
*The Darker Mask: Heroes from the
    Shadows* (co-edited with Christopher
    Chambers)
*Scoundrels: Tales of Greed, Murder and
    Financial Crimes*
Black Pulp (co-edited with Tommy
    Hancock and Morgan Minor)
Black Pulp II (co-edited with Tommy
    Hancock, Ernest Russell, Gordon
    Dymowski & H. David Blalock)
Day of the Destroyers
Hollis for Hire
Hollis, P.I.
*Culprits: The Heist Was Only the
    Beginning* (co-edited with Richard Brewer)
*The Obama Inheritance: Fifteen Stories
    of Conspiracy Noir*

VIOLENT SPRING

GARY PHILLIPS

SOHO
CRIME

This edition first published in 2023 by
Soho Press
227 W 17th Street
New York, NY 10011

Library of Congress Cataloging-in-Publication Data

Names: Phillips, Gary, 1955- author.
Title: Violent spring / Gary Phillips.
Description: New York, NY : Soho Crime, 2023.
Series: The Ivan Monk mysteries ; 1

ISBN 978-1-64129-439-3
eISBN 978-1-64129-440-9

Subjects: LCSH: African American detectives—Fiction. | Los Angeles
(Calif.)—Fiction. | LCGFT: Detective and mystery fiction. | Novels.
Classification: LCC PS3566.H4783 V56 2023
DDC 813/.54—dc23/eng/20231205
LC record available at https://lccn.loc.gov/2023056127

Interior design by Janine Agro, Soho Press, Inc.

Photo of Vermont Ave. in Koreatown by Chloeqpan from
https://shorturl.at/bhiH0
Photo of graffiti by Ricky Bonilla from https://shorturl.at/iBDIX

Printed in the United States of America

10 9 8 7 6 5 4 3 2 1

To my father Dikes, a hell of a man.

Our city is wide open tonight, at the mercy of people who [don't know] right from wrong.
—LA TV anchor, 4/29/92

INTRODUCTION
by Walter Mosley

From the very beginning of his writing career, Gary Phillips brought a few new twists and turns to the term *noir*. He gave the word a collar, a color, a class, a political stripe or two, and a set of purposes that included the struggle against unrelenting oppression. He never worried about the world-weary tropes of a literary crime genre that sought balance (the status quo), resolution (the rock-solid knowledge of who was guilty), or justice (in the sense of the so-called good guys winning out over the bad). He wanted to see past the comforting, if somewhat rough, language that spouted the metaphors couched in a hard-boiled poetry that rarely challenged our awareness of a world gone rotten. That is to say, Mr. Phillips wanted to infuse what we read with what we actually experience, taking that knowledge into the drudgery of the everyday lives of most Americans, and therefore making it at least possible to effect change through our imaginations.

Gary's heroes are much like the writer himself: big, loud, inordinately powerful, and willing to put their shoulders to the wheel day or night, night and day. Where most modern-day genre detectives take on cases that are possible to solve, Mr. Phillips's crime fighters are often doomed even when they win. You might be able to see and hear most of the shamuses that grace the pages of this great genre, but you can literally smell the sour sweat, the hint of bad whiskey, and even the faded cologne of Phillips's heroes. These are men and women that you rub shoulders with on the Number 7 Bus, that you fear walking behind you on an empty street, that you might even want to touch in order to feel what it is to be that alive.

The mystery in Mr. Phillips's work is not what the reader can't see clearly but what she, or he, steadfastly refuses to believe. Gary's work is like the cell-phone camera revealing Cop on Black crime, the belated truth about our *justified* war on Vietnam. In this book, *Violent Spring*, and the many others that come after, we find the DNA that exonerates those we have hated, abandoned, and imprisoned—thirty years too late.

And the crime? The crime is most often murder. This is true throughout the many books that define the many crime genres. But, quite often, blood comes hand in hand with theft. People kill for an inheritance, a life policy, while committing a robbery, when they want to take over or get back. Most of the time we accept the concept of theft because we know what it's like to be without. We've been taught since childhood to fight for our property, or to obtain said property.

These truths are self-evident until you come across Gary Phillips's crime novels. Gary knows that property *is* theft, that ownership is at least in part a felonious enterprise. Crime in his world is defined by the hunger to own more than is needed.

And the beginning of this fairly new branch of crime novel was *Violent Spring*, a book that brings all the lost tribes of Los Angeles together in order to hide the truth. Not who killed but why they killed and how that reason is inextricably intertwined with our hungers and a kind of self-generated blindness that can never be excused.

RETROSPECTIVE
by Gary Phillips

Long ago and far away, I'd written my first book, *The Body on the Beach*. This came about when I took a ten-week extension class at UCLA on how to write a mystery novel taught by Robert Crais. At that time, Bob was transitioning from TV writer to novelist. His first in a long line of Elvis Cole books, *The Monkey's Raincoat*, was just coming out. In class, we examined Robert Parker's first Spenser novel, *The Godwulf Manuscript*.

We were tasked with creating our own set of characters and writing the first fifty pages of an original novel. I came up with my donut-shop-owning private eye Ivan Monk; his mentor, retired LAPD cop Dexter Grant; Lt. Marasco Seguin (named for the town in Texas where my dad was from); and his partner, his old lady—as was the term once upon a time—Superior Court Judge Jill Kodama. After grinding out those initial pages and finishing the class, I kept going and completed the manuscript.

That book never sold. I kept my day job. But my gig as the outreach director for the Liberty Hill Foundation was fulfilling. The Foundation then, as now, funds community organizing efforts toward social change. My role involved meeting with various grassroots groups throughout the city, from sit-downs with former gang members in the housing projects in Watts, listening to grandmothers in a church in Boyle Heights, and talking with the Black-Korean Alliance in South Central, to strategy sessions with other funders in downtown high-rises. Then April 1992 happened. The four Los Angeles Police Department officers facing criminal charges for the brutal beating of motorist Rodney King were found not guilty in a courtroom outside the city.

Prescient of today and police abuse captured on smartphones, their actions along with the actions of other law enforcement personnel had been taped by plumber George Holliday. Local station KTLA Channel 5 was the first to play the footage the following evening. The police showed up to the station and confiscated the recording. There was a copy. The impact was monumental. Soon, the first viral video was being replayed on television sets across the country and the world. It was the grainy black-and-white proof of what many had claimed for decades about how policing was conducted if you were Black or Brown.

When the verdict came down, the Rodney King Riots ... the civil unrest ... Saigu, the Korean term for those troubling, turbulent days and nights, jumped off. More than sixty people perished, and more than a billion dollars of property was destroyed. L.A.'s populace sought to rebuild and revitalize its communities and reform the police.

Having gotten to know all sorts of people in L.A.'s numerous enclaves, including those working to make a difference: What if I wrote a mystery set a year or so after the unrest? One laced with the fraught sociopolitical reverberations of a city trying to figure out how to move forward. *Violent Spring* was the result. The book begins at a groundbreaking ceremony for a new shopping center where the riots started, the cross streets of Florence and Normandie in the 'hood.

My then agent sent the manuscript out, earning a round of rejections from New York publishers. Some editors said get rid of the political backdrop. But that was the heart of the book. I couldn't change that. Eventually *Violent Spring* was published by a small press I was part of, along with friend and fellow crime fiction writer John Shannon—West Coast Crime, headquartered in the Pacific Northwest. This was in the days before print-on-demand. We put in money and sweat equity. We printed and warehoused and obtained distribution. If memory serves, we initially published four books, including John's *The Concrete River* and *Served Cold* by Ed Goldberg, which would win a Shamus Award from the Private Eye Writers of America. We paid Ed $500. Our books got on shelves, even in Costcos.

The rise and fall of West Coast Crime has been chronicled elsewhere. As well as how *Violent Spring* got optioned by HBO, my first of several forays in the Land of Celluloid Dreams. At any rate, by then, John, me, and Ed had been picked up by the same New York publisher. I would go on to write four Ivan Monk novels and several short stories featuring the PI. But *Violent Spring* is my entrée to the hardboiled genre, a moment in time, reflections on my city of tarnished angels.

Now here we are, thirty years after its first publication. While there has been significant change, too many of the underlying factors setting off the unrest in '92 remain. Yet I'm so pleased Soho Crime has brought out this thirtieth anniversary edition and will be reissuing the other three Ivan Monk novels, too.

Who knows, I might well finally write the fifth and last Monk novel one of these days.

—Gary Phillips, Los Angeles

ANATOMY OF AN UNREST

A Timeline of the Los Angeles Riots

- **March 3, 1991**

  Just after midnight, motorist Rodney King is stopped
  by the California Highway Patrol for speeding after a
  pursuit on the 210 Freeway in the San Fernando Valley. The Los Angeles Police Department is also on
  scene. Across the way, plumber George Holliday is
  awakened by the commotion. He retrieves his recently
  acquired Sony camcorder. From the balcony of his
  apartment, he videotapes the scene below as some
  numerous baton blows, kicks, and repeated shocks from
  a stun gun are leveled on King. The video is first broadcast on local KTLA Channel 5 during their 10 P.M.
  newscast the next night, then goes nationwide.

- **March 16, 1991**

  Fifteen-year-old Latasha Harlins is shot in the back
  of the head and killed by Soon Ja Du, whose family
  owns the Empire Liquor Market in South Central. Du
  accuses Latasha of stealing a small bottle of orange
  juice. She hadn't.

- **July 9, 1991**

  The scathing Christopher Commission report is released. Formally known as the Independent Commission on the Los Angeles Police Department, the Christopher Commission, headed by lawyer Warren Christopher, was founded in the wake of the King beating to examine the causes and suggest remedies to the LAPD's history of problematic conduct. Among its findings, the report states that, "There is a significant number of officers in the LAPD who repetitively use excessive force against the public and persistently ignore the written guidelines of the department regarding force. The failure to control these officers is a management issue that is at the heart of the problem."

  Those recommendations in mind, the Los Angeles City Council puts forward a ballot measure termed Proposition F. In addition to other matters, it seeks to remove the police chief's civil service protection and strengthen the already existing Police Commission.

  Amid this, embattled Chief of Police Daryl Gates, staunch defender of the police department, suggests he'll resign.

- **November 15, 1991**

  Soon Ja Du is convicted of voluntary manslaughter by a jury. Judge Joyce Karlin sentences Du to probation instead of prison and a fine of $500. A recall is mounted against Karlin. The recall fails.

- **March 5, 1992**

  After a change of venue to the predominantly white
  and conservative suburb of Simi Valley, the state trial
  of Stacey C. Koon, Laurence M. Powell, Theodore J.
  Briseno, and Timothy E. Wind—the four LAPD
  officers indicted for the beating of Rodney King—
  begins at the East Ventura County Courthouse.

- **April 28, 1992**

  A peace treaty is devised and signed between the Crips
  and Bloods at a mosque in the Watts area of town. The
  leaders of the gang truce also author a "Proposal for
  L.A.'s Face-Lift" setting out broad initiatives to better
  conditions in South Central.

- **April 29, 1992**

  Ten not guilty verdicts are delivered by a nearly all-
  white jury in Simi Valley. The single conviction for
  excessive force against one of the officers is declared a
  mistrial by Judge Stanley Weisberg. The announcement of the verdict comes over the airwaves several
  minutes past 3 P.M.

  - **Evening.** Within hours, the intersection of Florence
    and Normandie in South Central erupts in rage.
    Inexplicably, the LAPD is initially ordered to pull
    back. Live feed from news helicopters captures the
    brutal beating of white truck driver Reginald Denny,
    who is pulled from his rig as he attempts to drive
    through the intersection. Nearby, four Black

folks—Bobby Green Jr., Lei Yuille, Titus Murphy, and Terri Barnett—come to the scene after seeing it unfold on the news. Green, also a truck driver, with Murphy's help, drives Denny's truck and the injured man to the hospital.

Altercations break out between protestors and the police in front of the LAPD's Parker Center, their central headquarters in downtown L.A. Anti-police abuse organizer Michael Zinzun admonishes the gathered to keep cool, to not give the police the excuse to bust heads.

Soon after, Mayor Tom Bradley and other political and religious leaders address an overflow crowd at a "Pray for Peace" rally at the First A.M.E. Church in the West Adams District.

Elsewhere as a mini-mart burns on Vermont Avenue in South Central, across the street Chester Murray stands guard in front of the Southern California Library for Social Studies and Research (SCL), a repository of left, labor and peoples' history housed in a former two-story appliance store. Chester is SCL's building manager and lives in the neighborhood. He talks to the crowds, cajoling them not to burn the building. Along with friends of his and even a local gang member, he would return for the next three days to keep watch. SCL is still in operation today.

- **April 29-30, 1992**

   Rebuild L.A.is formed by Mayor Bradley and Governor Pete Wilson, among others. Its board is a who's who of the city's movers and shakers, though lacks representatives from grassroots level organizations. Rebuild is touted as a public-private partnership to spur economic revitalization in the inner city. Bradley appoints Peter Ueberroth (who oversaw the '84 Olympics in L.A., the only profitable Olympics to date) to head the effort. Over the months to come, the organization will be criticized for making grand announcements as opposed to grand accomplishments.

- **April 30, 1992**

   At 12:15 A.M., the mayor imposes a dusk-to-dawn curfew.

- **May 1, 1992**

   The National Guard rolls in including the 40th Infantry Division (mechanized). Some 6,000 will be deployed along with 3,000–4,000 army troops and marines as well as 1,000 riot-trained federal law officers.

- **May 4, 1992**

   After six days of unrest, order is restored and the curfew is lifted.

Sixty-three people are dead, more than 2,000 injured. According to the Rand Corporation, 36 percent of those arrested are African Americans and 51 percent Latinx. There is approximately $1 billion worth of property damage or destruction.

- **May 7, 1992**

  President George W. Bush leads a delegation through the devastation. He denounces the participants in the rioting as "purely criminal." The upshot is not much in the way of federal aid will be forthcoming toward recovery.

  Carlton Jenkins, managing director of the largest Black-owned bank in the city, states, "They [banks and lending institutions] are walking on the fence and can go either way. Now is the time to step up and put your money where your mouth is." The three Black banks in the city will form an effort to facilitate loans to damaged businesses.

- **June 2, 1992**

  Worries of law-and-order backlash by voters dissipate and Proposition F passes, changing city code to establish civilian oversight of the police department.

- **June 26, 1992**

  Police chief Daryl Gates resigns. At the same time, Amnesty International releases a report that concludes members of the LAPD and the L.A. County Sheriff's

Department routinely resort to excessive force, particularly against Blacks and Hispanics.

In the ensuing months, the Community Coalition for Substance Abuse Prevention and Treatment emerges on the frontlines to help ease tensions among Blacks and Koreans, working to not simply rebuild liquor stores, but also to seek resources to convert them into full-service markets in the South Central food desert. Its founder, former physician's assistant Karen Bass, is later elected to congress, then as mayor of Los Angeles in 2022.

• **April 20, 1994**

Rodney King wins his civil suit against the LAPD.

900 block of Vermont Avenue in Koreatown, 1992

Graffiti on Hollywood Blvd, 1992

ONE

Ivan Monk wondered if he was the only one who got the joke. Standing next to his mother and sister at the groundbreaking of the future shopping complex at the corner of Florence and Normandie in South Central Los Angeles, the private eye remembered the maelstrom this intersection had been not so long ago.

It was one of those significant moments in time, forever etched in the deep cells of his brain. Like the day and the hour he heard this father had died or when he was in grade school and a tearful Mrs. Rogers came in and told the class that President Kennedy had just been shot.

Wednesday afternoon, April 29, 1992 was one such moment. All of Los Angeles had its collective ear glued to radios a few minutes past three as the sixty-five-year-old forewoman of the jury on the live broadcast read the not guilty verdict.

The incredible decision was delivered by a jury of ten whites, one Latina and one Filipina who supported the claim of the LAPD officers on trial for use of excessive force against Black motorist, Rodney King. The four cops were captured in a hazy and brutal cinema verite as they beat the living shit out of King on a Lake View Terrace street in the San Fernando Valley.

Monk stared open-jawed at the radio, his secretary Delilah gripping his arm, hard, in disbelief. Soon they both got that look on their faces one got from being Black in America. That look that said, *Yeah, we been given the short end again, so what's new.*

The city raged red with blood and fury. Reginald Denny, a white working-class guy, a union truck driver, was pulled from his cab at Florence and Normandie and senselessly beaten and shotgunned in the leg by young Black men venting their anger in frustrated and futile fashion. And four other Black people got him to safety.

But having no established avenue of redress—indeed what had the incredible verdict delivered from the white suburb of Ventura's Simi Valley said to them?—the fellaheen sought justice in the streets. Subsequently, in the federal trial of the cops, two of the four were found guilty. And a city short on money and hope was momentarily spared another conflagration.

But the fact that now Monk stood at Florence and Normandie at a groundbreaking site, a symbolic gesture of rebuilding at one of the flashpoints for the riots that ripped his hometown, was not what he considered the joke.

"Isn't that Tina over there next to the mayor, Ivan?" his mother said, disrupting his reverie.

Monk glanced at the dais. The mayor adjusted a sheaf of papers held in his thick hands as he stood at the portable podium. On either side of the solid built man in the blue serge suit were folding chairs. Various city officials, business people and some community leaders sat in them or milled about. Councilwoman Tina Chalmers, an African American woman who represented this district his mother lived in, and Monk's old flame, sat on the stage talking to an older white man in an expensive-looking gray and black-flecked double-breasted suit.

"Yeah, that's her, Mom." Monk studied the man Tina talked with.

He'd only seen him on television and in news photos previously, but you'd have to have been in orbit on a space station not to have seen or heard of Maxfield O'Day. After the uprising, as the rubble and rhetoric piled high, O'Day emerged as the silver-haired man on the white charger. Lawyer, businessman, developer, political insider. A Los Angeles mover and shaker of the first order who played an active role in the election of one of his boardroom peers as the current mayor of Los Angeles.

Maxfield O'Day was appointed, some wags say anointed, by the mayor and the City Council to head the official rebuilding efforts of the city. His task was to pull a consortium of city and business people together in an effort to infuse South Central and Pico Union with new business ventures. "To massage capital, to give it confidence in doing business in the inner city," O'Day was fond of saying. Particularly when there was a reporter around. Of course, Monk concluded, if that meant being lax on things like environmental laws, undercutting the minimum wage, and gutting California's workers' comp program, well, big money was so insecure.

"I thought Jill was coming today," Odessa, Monk's sister, said to him.

"She was, but the case she's trying unexpectedly wrapped up Thursday. She has a meeting with the attorneys this afternoon."

"Isn't it about time you two jumped the broom? You've been going out for three years now." His mother looked toward the front, but her eyes glanced at him peripherally.

"What you really mean, is when are we going to have some kids. 'Course you already have one grandchild."

Nona Monk turned her head, gazing into his goateed face. "Not from the male side of my family. At the rate you two are going, I'd be happy to settle for the kids if not the marriage. You're in your late thirties, Ivan, and even though the good judge fudges her age, we all know she's a couple of years older than you. Y'all better get busy." She smiled crookedly at him.

Monk patted his mother on the shoulder. "Yes, Mother."

The mayor tapped the live microphone at the podium and the crowd of a hundred plus community residents gave him their attention. The electronic and print media halted their meandering about the scene and, like trained bloodhounds, aimed the unblinking metal eyes of their cameras on the dapper mayor.

The mild-mannered public official drew himself up to his full height and began. "We are pleased today to have this historic groundbreaking take place little more than a year after the upheaval that tore our city apart." Monk watched O'Day stifle a yawn. "Even more so at this site that has come to represent the financial and social neglect that has plagued South Central."

"No thanks to you and those other sellouts in city government sucking up to downtown business interests," Odessa mumbled under her breath.

The mayor droned on for ten dull minutes, the crowd shifting uneasily in the afternoon sun. When he finished, O'Day came to the podium next. "Good afternoon," the businessman said in a modulated tone. "I know it's hot out there, so I'll make this sweet and to the point." Several people clapped. The mayor displayed no change of face, save a shifting of his eyes.

O'Day, by comparison to the stodgy, steady delivery of the mayor, was smooth and avuncular in his brief address. He reminded Monk of a cross between a Cadillac dealer and a coffin salesman. One of those guys who could stick you with a knife in the kidney and convince you it was in your best interests.

O'Day left the podium and Councilwoman Chalmers came up. Off to the left and behind her, a bulldozer belched to life. The machine idled on the expanse of dirt where the new shopping complex was to be erected. The earth was level and its hue a rich terra cotta that suggested only good could come from its depths. A bulldozer wasn't used for digging, the most it would accomplish was a shallow hole. Clearly though it was chosen for its size, a more impressive-looking machine than a backhoe Monk surmised.

"Up here you see Korean, Black and Latino representatives of the business and grassroots elements of our community," Tina Chalmers said. "The road to rebuilding, indeed the road to true economic justice in our community, is not easily tread. As Mr. Perry, and Mr. Li and Mr. Santillion can testify to." Chalmers gestured to the men seated behind her.

Sitting to her left, Linton Perry, the executive director of the Black self-help group Harvesters Unlimited, nodded slightly. On the other side of her, Luis Santillion, from the Chicano-based group El Major, grimaced. Sitting next to Santillion, Pak Ju Li, the head of the Korean American Merchants Group, grinned without humor.

Tina Chalmers went on. "We have been through a difficult period these past months. It seemed at times that each ethnic group was willing to be pitted against one another in an attempt to devour what little meat remains on the bone." Perry and Santillion stole wary glances at one another. O'Day smiled broadly. "A bone that old white

men who play golf at restricted clubs throw at us contemptuously."

Applause rose from the crowd. Maxfield O'Day crossed his
legs casually and rubbed the side of his hand across one knee.

"None the less," Chalmers said, "today we begin to make
the effort at rebuilding Los Angeles real. And really, the
effort is not rebuilding, because that would only be reinstat-
ing the same status quo that led to the uprising." Many
people murmured "right on" and "tell it" in the crowd.

"This has to be a new day. A day that makes the banks
play fair in their lending, and the police play fair in the
streets." Applause rose again from the assembled community
residents. "Whether it's the gang truce or the signed contract
in the suites, we all must abide by doing the right thing to
our fellow human beings. For this city, the Council that I'm
on and the other officials must show that a partnership
between the private sector and the public can be achieved.
And not at the expense of community people or their dignity.
Or surely our efforts will be shown to be a hollow exercise
in manipulating public perceptions."

Out on the barren field, the bulldozer bellowed into gear on
cue, its powerful engine drowned by the applause Councilwoman
Chalmers received. Black smoke churning into gray clouds
escaped its vertical exhaust pipe, pumping fumes into the clear
afternoon air. The driver turned the machine ninety degrees
and the scoop front levered toward the sky on hydraulic braces
of tempered steel. The operator brought down the rear ripper, a long hooked device in the shape of a giant saber tooth.

With the ferocity of an attacking scorpion, the ripper
plunged into the tender meat of the clay brown earth. Again
and again it drove its tail into the dirt until a large circle of
moist soil was broken and mounded up. The driver spun the
machine on its tractor treads until the scoop hovered over

the new mound. He brought the blade down and its cutting edge dug into the dirt and lifted out a scoopful.

This the driver deposited in a waiting dirt hauler. He went back to tearing out earth as everyone moved forward to the sawhorse barrier separating the crowd and the field. The bulldozer pivoted once more, and the cutting edge of the blade again gathered a considerable measure of loam.

The crowd and the hosts moved toward the field. Tina Chalmers pulled close to Monk. She said her hellos to his sister and mother, then turned her attention to him.

"Looks like you lost some weight since I saw you last," she said, putting an arm around his waist. "You must be hitting the gym again. Are you still doing your private eye thing?"

"Probably till the day I die. I'm hooked." They kissed one another on the lips, and she withdrew the arm. Monk added, "Racing toward middle age made me realize all my meals can't be at Meaty Meat Burgers."

"Uh-huh," Chalmers said. "Of course it wouldn't have anything to do with your little Asian friend."

"Now, now, behave yourself, there are cameras present."

The two moved toward the sawhorses blocking the field. Old friends unencumbered with the need to fill the silence with aimless chatter. They came to the edge of the field, and Chalmers again put an arm around Monk's waist. "Have you seen Ray at all?"

"No, not lately." Monk placed his arm around her waist. "The last time I heard about him he was staying over on 39th near Denker. I went by one day, but the landlady said he'd moved on."

"Yeah." She shook her head in understanding. "Well, I better get back to the dog and pony show. Look me up sometime, big boy." She smiled at him and went out onto the field to join the other merchants of optimism.

Chalmers, the mayor, O'Day, Linton Perry and most of the remaining official guests were now out on the field, standing near the freshly dug hole. Everyone trying their best to look natural as they roamed about a dirt field with a hole in it. The community residents stood behind the barricade of sawhorses. Casually, the mayor handed out shovels to O'Day and Chalmers. He kept the longest one for himself. No sense being mayor if you couldn't have the biggest stick.

The City Hall photographer, an old rummy named Lucasiks who Monk knew in passing, lurched forward to get the shot. The mayor spaded the earth onto the edge of the pit. He held his body rigid, one foot on the shovel, the other planted on the ground. He bent forward slightly, as Lucasiks got into position. Tina Chalmers and Maxfield O'Day stood on either side of the mayor, their shovels held upright in one hand, the blades barely breaking the surface of the soil. Terrified, Monk reasoned, that if they worked up a sweat they'd ruin their photo op.

Lucasiks took three shots of the pose. The mayor glanced down into the pit, then his head came up slowly. He looked over at Chalmers, then looked back into the pit. The motion wasn't wasted on Monk, who began to move onto the field. The mayor straightened up and motioned for the five Los Angeles Police Department officers, who up until then had been standing around listless and bored, to come onto the field.

They ran up, the crowd instinctively halting itself as the law revved up. The sergeant, a bruiser with a smashed nose, looked into the pit, got down on his knees to take a better look, then got up. He whispered something to the mayor, and the demure man nodded in response.

"Ladies and gentlemen," the mayor said in a loud voice.

"I ask everyone to please stay behind the barricades for their own safety."To underscore his request, the five cops stationed themselves in front of the pit, which only heightened the crowd's curiosity.

"What's in the hole, Mr. Mayor? Is it a possible crime scene you're trying to protect?" one of the news people shouted. A chorus of echoes went up from the other news folks and several of the community residents. The news people prowled back and forth, in and around the crowd. A pack hungry for a sexy story and sniffing its proximity, they weren't going to let the scent go until they landed a kill.

Monk, standing on tiptoe behind several others, couldn't see anything. He looked at Tina, but she would only return a blank stare. His mother and sister were behind him.

"Ivan, what do you think it is?" Odessa asked him, also straining to see.

"I don't know." But he did have a guess.

One of the cops left the field and headed for a patrol car, two broadcast journalists trailing him. A video camera operator clambered onto the roof of his station's news van.

The sergeant noticed it and swore audibly. The camera operator zoomed his lens onto the hole. The cops closed tight around it to block the shot.

"Goddamn. It's a body in there," someone shouted from the crowd. "It's gotta be. That's why they're trying so hard to hide it."

People looked at one another and back to the field. A heated din rose from the crowd like naked electricity. Monk felt himself being pushed forward. Another human's death was a magnet for the living that he'd never get used to. The cops hoisted their batons and advanced.

The mayor glowered at the sergeant, and the two exchanged quick words. The sergeant pulled his men back, their clubs held at present arms rest. The crowd moved in, sawhorses falling away like so much papier mâché.

The four cops didn't flinch, but Monk could feel the tension rise. The news crews maneuvered forward, trying to get a picture. Mics jabbed at the mayor, the councilwoman and O'Day. The cops poked their clubs into several rib cages.

"All right folks, this is now an official police matter. If you don't disperse, you will be arrested," the sergeant yelled.

The crowd slowed its pace, then stopped.

"Please, everybody, just step back and let the police do their job," the mayor cautioned.

The citizenry of South Central glanced at one another, uncertain of how to proceed. Two of the cops came forward, arms up, palms outthrust. Slowly, but forcefully, they eased the crowd back to the edge of the field. The news people protested the loudest, but they too were moved back away from the pit.

Monk could see three patrol cars come south on Normandie and turn onto the dirt lot. The cars sped to where the pit was, billowing flowery plumes of brown dust. Cops exited the vehicles en masse, and some took up their command around the hole. The remaining ones formed a curtain of grim-faced dragoons between that portion of the field and the crowd. Many of the residents were already starting to leave.

"I guess the show's over for today," Nona Monk said. She started to head toward her car, Monk and his sister following behind.

"Yeah, but who did the body belong to? And who put him in his grave?" Monk said more to himself than to his family. He turned various scenarios over in his mind as they walked.

"Take it easy, Boston Blackie," Odessa said, patting his back. "You can't solve all the murders in Los Angeles. Leave a few for the cops to do."

The trio laughed, but Monk couldn't help taking a last look at the field. The sergeant and another cop were down on their knees, doing something with their hands in the hole. Tina Chalmers and the others stood back, their eyes fixed on the cops working in the pit.

Heading for their car, they passed Maxfield O'Day who managed to escape the whirl of events on the field. He sucked on a thin cigar ratcheted in his tight jaw. His eyes smoldered with icy fire. He looked toward the field, and visibly drew back as two TV crews descended on him.

O'Day was standing under the banner that spelled out the name of his organization, an amalgam of private business people, public officials, community leaders and charitable foundations. A grouping that went by the acronym of SOMA, Save Our Material Assets. The logo was a stylized hand—its hue and shape indeterminate of race or gender—with a globe in the open palm emerging from red and orange flames.

SOMA was the name of the drug people took to induce docility in Aldous Huxley's classic book of a corporate future England, *Brave New World*, a book Monk reread two times as he worked his way around the world, and half again when he was an engine mechanic as a merchant seaman.

Truly an inspired title, he concluded, getting behind the wheel of his mother's late model Taurus. Several more news people were now around O'Day, who seemed to have regained his composure. He gestured with his hands making boxer-like thrusts in the air, and threw his head back to explode in quick bursts of laughter. Alexander the Great holding court for the unwashed and unknowing.

Monk brought the car to life. As he drove away, he could see O'Day pointing to the SOMA banner for the camera crews. Maybe he got the joke. Or maybe, Monk surmised ominously, it was his joke on the city.

TWO

The Tuesday after the Saturday of the aborted ground-breaking at Florence and Normandie, the name of Kim Bong-Suh was bandied all over town.

TV commentators, local news anchors, the second column under the fold in the *Times'* Metro section and even a popular radio talk show host on the AM band were focused on the murdered liquor store owner. For it was his decomposed body found in the dirt field at the infamous intersection. A field that once, before the conflagration, had been the site of a check-cashing place and Laundromat.

The deceased Mr. Kim was also the topic of conversation at the Abyssinia Barber Shop and Shine Parlor on South Broadway.

"So you found the body, Monk?" Kelvon Ulysses Little asked him as he sat in the chair to get his haircut.

"I was there when they uncovered it by accident with the bulldozer."

Little draped the black striped white shroud across the front of Monk. "Oh," the barber and co-owner of the shop replied. "Brant said you found the Korean's body." He encircled Monk's neck with tissue paper to prevent loose hairs from falling down his collar. It never worked as far as Monk knew, but who was he to break tradition.

Willie Brant, a fifty-eight-year-old retired postman, leaned forward in his chair, pointing at Little. "That ain't what I said, man. I told you 'fore Monk got here that what I heard was that he was there at the field and saw the body being taken out of the ground."

Monk raised an eyebrow. Willie was bald. Completely without hair on his dome since his early thirties. The only reason he came to the barber shop was to hang out and hear himself talk. "I wasn't there when that happened either, Willie. All I know about this is what I read in the papers same as you."

"Well if you want my opinion," Brant started, aware that few ever did, "I think them Rolling Daltons are behind this."

"Now how do you get to that conclusion?" Old Man Spears said. Spears sat in the corner, as he always did, half-listening to the baseball game on the ancient Philco and half-listening to the conversation.

"Cause this truce thing they initiated with that other gang, them Swans, ain't nothin' but a smoke screen they're usin' to take over all the rackets in South Central. And they startin' by bumpin' off all them Koreeans."

Little deftly passed the clippers through Monk's hair. "Some gray's creeping down there in your roots, Monk," he said loud enough for all to hear. "That fine oriental gal of yours must be wearin' your ass out." A chorus of good-natured laughs made the rounds in the barber shop. Then, Little said, "I think them young bloods is sincere in this truce thing. Man, I believe them when they say they're tired of killing one another and running down our neighborhoods. If there's one good thing to come out of the uprising, it will be them getting together to do a Black Panther number like we saw in the sixties."

"Shit," Brant eloquently replied.

Abraham Carson, who sat one chair down from Brant, put down the copy of the *Sports Illustrated* he'd been reading. "What do you think, Monk?" The self-employed carpenter's voice was quiet in timbre and deep as a well.

"About the truce?"

"About the body in the field."

"According to the paper, this Kim Bong-Suh was last seen a week before the riots of '92. He was a bachelor, and he employed local Black folks in his liquor store." Monk paused, assembling the data in his mind. "I don't think he was killed by the Daltons or any usual stick-up."

"Why you say that?" Brant demanded.

"Look at the facts, Willie. The Metro section states he was found with his wallet still on his body. Ninety bucks still in the thing. And the reporter said he was shot execution-style. Which means in the back of the head, into the neck. Professionals do that so there's no blood splattering on them."

Kelvon Little edged the hair around Monk's ears with the barest touch of the clippers. He said, "So who do you think did this?"

"Damned if I know. But I do know the cops are going to have a lot of pressure on them to solve this thing."

"You mean from the Korean American Merchants Group," Abe said.

"Yeah man," Brant began again, "you gotta hand it to them rice cake eaters. Say what you will, they stick up for their own."

Monk all but rolled his eyes in his head.

IT WAS somewhat of a misnomer to say that Olympic and Kenmore was the heart of Koreatown. Like a lot of the other sections of the city that sprawled from the ocean to the desert, where one neighborhood ended and another began was sometimes not always easy to tell.

In Echo Park, which was heavily Latino, one found left-wing lawyers of various races, long-time community activists and punked-out white kids wearing African medallions mixing along lower Sunset or Melrose at places like the Club Fuck. That part of Sunset also was the beginning of East Hollywood and the gay belt. It ran into Silverlake and enjoyed a seemingly peaceful coexistence with the cholos who prowled the boulevards in their chopped '63 Impalas with McLean wire rims. Off the main drag were streets that wound into the hills of Silverlake and the city officials who lived there and people who worked in the real Hollywood as prop builders, camera operators and the lowest of the low, the writers.

Central Avenue had been the cultural Mecca of Black Los Angeles in the '30s through the early '50s. Joints like the Club Alabam, Jack's Basket and Cafe Society swung to the twenty-four-hour beat of the hip, replete with jazz giants such as Dexter Gordon and Teddy Edwards, or Chet Baker and Ella Fitzgerald.

To make the scene, hep-cats would be draped in Zoot Suits complete with spearpoint collared shirts, fob-chains, satin picture ties and gold pinky rings. Chicks in slit skirts, rodeo jackets and rolled socks would drop in for a set or two then amble down to the Dunbar Hotel—where all the Black entertainers stayed—and juice up in the Turban Room, the bar in the basement of the hotel.

Now Central Avenue was home to mom-and-pop furniture stores with names like Zuniga, and where Jack's Basket was stands a branch office of the Southern California Gas

Company. And at present, there were no signs in the Korean alphabet gracing strip malls along Barrington in the upper-class, white Brentwood part of town. But on the side of a three-story brown-tiled building on Olympic Boulevard just east of Kenmore, blue relief letters in Hangul, the Korean alphabet, announced the building as the headquarters of the Korean American Merchants Group.

"I'm not at all certain that would produce the results we are looking for," Kenny Yu said.

"As opposed to us organizing more protests at City Hall like when we were demanding reparations for our lost stores after the riots." The sarcasm in Pak Ju Li's voice, the president of the Merchant's Group, was lost on no one at the table.

Kenny Yu, a Korean American lawyer in his late twenties, leaned back in his chair. "I'm saying that if we simply offer reward money, just throw it out as bait, we'll have every two-bit hustler in LA phoning in useless tips as to who murdered Kim Bong-Suh."

"Twenty thousand dollars is not a simple price," Li answered in a tone reserved for a teacher to an upstart pupil. "It has been done before in other murders in this godless city."

"I think young Mr. Yu's point is well taken," Park Han-kyoung said. He was the owner of the building that housed the Merchant's Group, which also contained commercial office space, and two hotels in town which catered to visiting Korean business people. "Conversely, I think if we organize a visit to the chief of police's office, making sure it's covered in the white press, that would be effective. It is important for us to demonstrate that we believe that the process of justice must be followed. After all, we don't want a repeat of the Du incident."

Groans went up from some at the table. Soon Ja Du was a Korean grocer who had shot and killed Latasha Harlins, a teenage honor student over a disputed $1.79 bottle of orange juice. Convicted of second-degree manslaughter, Mrs. Du's possible eighteen years in prison was reduced to five years probation and a fine for the gun.

The then-LA County DA, Ira Reiner, had the case reviewed by a three-judge panel, which upheld Karlin's decision. The judges, like cops loathe to break ranks, upheld the original decision. This example of judicial wisdom had come a week before the explosive verdict from Simi.

"This and the ramifications from the Du incident have nothing in common," Li protested. "We have put the unfortunateness of that time behind us. The family of the girl was paid $300,000 from the settlement of the case. The Du's have left town, and this city is in the healing mode."

Yu suppressed a grin. It tickled him when Li suffused his comments with phrases borrowed from American politicians. Hollow wordplay meant to obfuscate and redirect.

John Hong, a grocer who had been a math teacher at a university in South Korea, raised an index finger so as to be recognized. "On the one hand, it is important that it be shown that the Korean community fights for the rights of its own as do the other ethnic communities of this city. But it is also important that what we do in regards to Kim's death be a symbolic move that accomplishes for us a better standing among these communities than we've accomplished so far. We must play the game the Americans play, if in the long run we wish to extend the influence of the Merchant's Group. Look what Linton Perry does with the Harvesters Unlimited. A little fire and a lot of strategy can go far."

Kenny Yu looked at the others around the table. Each

man—and the Merchants Group was all men—stared at one another or at the pads of paper before them. Humor creased his eyes and he said, "When I publicly denounced Karlin's decision I was nearly ostracized from this Board. I drew the parallel of the Vincent Chin incident in Detroit where the Chinese student was beaten to death with baseball bats by two out-of-work white auto workers who mistook him for Japanese. Those two were let off because the judge in that case, like Karlins in the Du case, said that prison would not benefit them.

"I said then, and I say it now, we must find those patches of common ground wherein we can unite with the African American, the Latino and other Asian people in this city and this country. So for different motivations, I agree with Mr. Hong and I have a suggestion."

"Which is," Li interjected, his eyes boring down on Yu. Twin orbs that glinted hard and mirthless in a fixed orbit of a universe only their owner could fathom.

"You recall the guest speaker at our luncheon last month?" Yu said.

"Yes. Judge Jill Kodama spoke on the law and Asians and Asian Pacific Islanders," Hankyoung answered.

"After the luncheon, the judge and I talked briefly. Chit chat about how well I thought her talk went and so forth. I don't exactly remember how it came up, but I recall her mentioning that her boyfriend is a private investigator."

After some moments, Li said in Korean, "We hire this man to look into the death of Kim Bong-Suh. I agree this might be a better use of our money than merely offering a reward. Providing of course this individual has references we can check. Indeed, it might even be cheaper than paying some informant. But how does this accomplish the public relations angle?"

"Ivan Monk, the judge's boyfriend, is Black," Kenny Yu said.

Several heads at the table bobbed up, then down.

DETECTIVE LIEUTENANT Marasco Seguin walked along the hall in the Los Angeles International Airport. He was a dark, taut Chicano in his early forties. The drooping mustache he sported, and the way he carried himself, gave one the impression here was a seasoned guerilla fighter come down from the mountains.

Only airport officials and the head of security knew about this section of one of the world's busiest centers of passenger and cargo commerce. Along the corridor were unmarked steel doors of the same milky gray hue. Most had electronic alarms attached to the wall beside them, a few had triple deadbolt locks. Seguin knew what was behind those doors— divisions of the Drug Enforcement Agency, the FBI, the National Security Agency, and until recently, a satellite of the Organized Crimes Investigations Division of the LAPD.

But a book by a former member of the OCID had detailed how the unit was used more for political intelligence gathering by the then-chief of the LAPD Daryl Gates. He had used the squad to amass files on City Council members, the DA, as well as the likes of closeted actor Rock Hudson. The publication of the book had resulted in the closure of the unit by the new reform-minded chief, Willie Williams. Seguin, quietly resplendent in a teal sport coat and gray flannel slacks, stopped before the door that had housed the OCID. He knocked and waited. The door buzzed and he pushed it open.

"Chief," he said upon entering, nodding slightly.

Seated around the inlaid mahogany table were Chief Williams, four other men and one woman. Two of the four

Seguin recognized as plainclothesmen from divisions other than his, Wilshire Station. He unbuttoned his coat and took a seat.

"This is Roberts from Hollywood, and Haller and Bazeco from Rampart," Williams said. Roberts was a large, heavily muscled Black man with hooded eyes that suggested a hidden intelligence. He wore a gray pinstripe three piece suit and an open-collared shirt.

"Nice to see you again, Seguin," Roberts said.

"Same here."

Bazeco was a slender brunette woman on the tallish side in a dark power suit that looked to Seguin like something his son's second grade teacher wore. Splayed in front of her on the table were large hands that seemed better suited for Roberts than their owner. She said nothing, but kept her eyes on Seguin.

"How you doing, Seguin?" Haller rose to shake his hand.

"Fine. How are things over at Rampart?" Seguin responded, returning the handshake.

"The usual. Wife kills boyfriend with knife in head, drive-bys at the Tommys burger stand and more crack floating around than icebergs in Alaska." Haller smiled warmly. He was medium height, thick in the middle and bore a scar down the vertical center of his nose. Unlike a lot of cops, Seguin recalled, Haller had been to college and was fond of displaying a certain wry perspective about the job. He and Bazeco were white.

"I'm Special Agent Keys and this is Special Agent Diaz." Keys, white, was youngish and dressed better than other FBI agents Seguin had met. He wore tortoiseshell glasses, ostentatious jade cuff links and a red pocket square that offset his royal blue suit. Keys was a hybrid of a lounge singer and an accountant.

Diaz was lighter than Seguin, younger, and wide in the shoulders, slim in the hips. He maintained a crew cut, and he sat ramrod straight. The Chicano version of the *stick-up-the-ass federale*, Seguin concluded. Diaz's mouth shaped itself into a slight smirk for Seguin's benefit, then returned to a straight line.

Chief Williams, the first Black chief of the LAPD, said, "You've all read the report on Kim Bong-Suh. To put it quite simply, the heat is on for us to solve this murder. And I'm not implying this office responds to political pressure, but I am saying that it's incumbent upon us to do what we can to make sure the healing process in this city proceeds smoothly. And a high-profile crime like this, which has the attention of a lot of interested parties, deserves our best effort."

"I'd like to add," Keys began, "that the FBI has an interest in this case not just from the standpoint that it might be a hate crime, but also from the gang angle. As you may know, the Director, in the wake of Democracy's destruction of the Evil Empire, has redirected some of us to deal with this scourge that plagues our urban centers."

Idly, Seguin wondered what white suburb Keys lived in. "Are you saying Kim was killed by gang members? Because the MO certainly doesn't suggest that."

"I realize that, Lieutenant Seguin. But it is the Bureau's opinion that the gangs, particularly the Rolling Daltons who operate in the Mid-City part of town, are making moves to consolidate their power and corner the crack distribution market."

"So what does that have to do with killing Kim?" Haller asked.

Keys said, "Kim's market was located on Pico and Hauser, smack in the middle of the Rimpau Avenue Rolling Daltons territory. The set we believe to be the kingpins in this situation."

"And Kim?" Bazeco asked.

"We'll know that when we find Conrad James, the brother who worked for Kim," Diaz said.

Roberts's hooded lids opened slightly as he swiveled his head in the direction of Diaz. "What do you mean, man?" The voice was a rusty blade scraped across stone.

"What we mean is that Conrad James's cousin is one Antoine 'Crosshairs' Sawyer, the reputed leader of the Rimpau Avenue set," Keys replied in his controlled fashion. "At the time of Mr. Kim's disappearance, Sawyer too became scarce. Maybe it's coincidence, maybe it's more. But that's what we need to find out."

Seguin said, "I don't know about that, Agent Keys. That's also the time some of these gangbangers came together to form the truce. Way I understand it, this Sawyer is one of the ones who helped get it going. A lot of those guys were laying low during the riots.

"Besides, the liquor store that Kim had is still there. It's being run by another Korean family. If he was killed because the Daltons wanted to control his store, say as an outlet, then I gotta believe that the folks there now were put in place by the gang. And I seriously doubt that."

"In the last two years, the Bureau has tracked several smuggling operations that had direct ties with the Daltons. This truce is just a smokescreen to gain the goodwill of opportunistic politicians and headline-grabbing con merchants. The fact remains that both Sawyer and James have become scarce. A gangster is always a gangster."

Seguin figured Keys might think it was a genetic condition.

Chief Williams spoke. "Look, I think we can all agree that the murder of Kim was unusual. He is last seen a week before the riots. He has no family and his body is uncovered in a deep grave after all this time. The ME figures he's been dead at least eighteen months but it could be longer."

"Are you going to meet with the Merchants Group?" Seguin asked Williams.

"Yes."

"Did someone from that group report his absence?" Haller said.

"Strangely, no," Holden responded. "That's something I'll have to ask them. At any rate, after reviewing the FBI's data, I'm also of the opinion this Dalton angle should be looked into. All of you were called in on this because some of you have worked the anti-gang CRASH unit, narcotics, or—and he indicated Seguin—"have a solid record in homicide."

Keys took that as his signal to stand. Reaching for a calf-skin attaché case at the base of his chair, he opened it and produced several legal-size manila folders. He passed one out to each of the plainclothes around the table.

"The contents of these are identical. In them you will find reports on the important movements of the Rimpau Avenue Rolling Dalton lieutenants over the last eighteen months. Along with profiles on Crosshairs and Conrad James, who used to be a student at Trade Technical College." He sat back down, crossing his legs.

"This task force will operate out of this office." Williams gestured to a door behind him. "In the next room are desks, phones, file cabinets and computers. You will be assigned an administrative assistant from our civilian pool, and your day-to-day reporting will be to Keys. Though both he and Agent Diaz will also be in the field with you."

Seguin decided it would be best if he didn't look at the other cops in the room for fear of laughing.

The chief uncrossed his legs and stood. "First and fore-most, you are to work the streets as you always do in garnering information as to who killed Mr. Kim. That is our number one priority."

If that bothered Keys, he didn't show it.

"Secondly, what information comes to light on the Daltons involvement in this, fine, but we're not pursuing phantom suspects. I needn't remind you that in this morning's Metro section Linton Perry had an editorial blasting us. He's gotten wind of the task force and is already calling it unequal justice. Forgetting of course the twenty-five-thousand-dollar reward the City Council put up for the Black mother of three slain at the Jack in the Box drive-in last year."

"Unusual crimes demand an unusual response," Bazeco offered.

"Indeed," Diaz said without the faintest hint of humor.

THREE

Tiger Flowers had been, at various points in his life, a middleweight Golden Gloves champ, a Pullman porter (during that tenure he carved a horrendous gash across a Klansman's chest), a numbers man, a dock worker, a boxing trainer and an Army corporal fighting near Pusan in Korea with Monk's father. But it was in his capacity as a trainer that he'd acquired the Tiger's Den, a boxing gym, sauna and weight room located on West 48th Street in South Central.

Monk completed the third set of forty sit-ups on the inclined bench. Sweat flowed from his forehead like a broken spigot. He swabbed at it with a terrycloth towel and got off the bench. Flowers, still a powerfully built man edging past sixty, glided near him.

"Case, huh?" Tiger was not given to excess.

"I work out steady, Tiger." Playfully, Monk slapped the towel at Tiger's solid midriff. "What makes you think I'm on a case?"

In his rasp of a voice, the old fighter said, "You only do sit-ups when you're training to go the distance."

The two walked past a young Latino furiously pummeling a heavy bag on the way to the sauna room. "You missed your calling, Tiger. Ever think of making some money on the side as a therapist?"

The older man merely leveled saddle-brown eyes on Monk, waiting.

"I'm not even sure it's my case yet. But my girlfriend called me early today to tell me that the Korean Merchants want to hire me. They're coming to see me at my office this morning."

"About this fella they dug up."

"Yeah. Jill and I realize the only reason they want to hire me is to make themselves look good."

"Then why do you want to do it?"

They reached the sauna and the two stopped. Monk leaned on the door, its warm waves penetrating the muscles of his back. "If I find the killer, it could be good for business."

"Get yourself an office at the top of Sunset."

"Have a couple of fine secretaries and do business lunches at the chic Morpheus Cafe," Monk enthused.

"Maybe so."

"Hire some assistants to do the leg work."

"Uh-huh," Tiger responded skeptically.

"Who knows."

"Could be you like to see what makes people tick."

Tiger clapped him on the back and walked back to the young man beating the hell out of the bag. Tiger held up his hand for him to stop, then demonstrated a smooth approach to working the bag through consistent blows that built up their effectiveness rather than going for that one knock-out punch.

"Like I said, you missed your calling, Tiger," Monk said under his breath. He opened the door to the sauna and welcomed the satin cloud that swallowed his body.

PAK JU Li sat rigid in the angular Eastlake staring at nothing. Kenny Yu sat next to him, taking in Monk's office. Jill had tastefully appointed it with a couch of supple indigo Italian leather, the low-slung Eastlakes, wood grain file cabinets—which were empty, Monk kept the files elsewhere—and a massive colonial-style desk for her lover. On one wall hung several masks Monk had collected in his travels in the Merchant Marines. The folk art of Senegal, New Hebrides, Guadeloupe, Thailand, Greece and Madagascar.

On another wall were several black-and-white photos in simple frames. One of them depicted Monk's deceased father in his Army sergeant's uniform. He was a big man in the top like his son, and he stood before a bar made of corrugated metal and left over wood from packing crates. Over the entrance was a hand-lettered sign in Hangul and English, a mischievous grin splitting his face. Another photo showed Monk's last ship, the cargo transporter Achilles.

Kenny Yu turned his attention to the private eye sitting across from him at the large desk. "What do you say to our proposition, Mr. Monk? Will you search for the murderer of Kim Bong-Suh?"

Monk, who had been reading the file folder they'd brought him, looked at the two men. "This information on Kim seems sketchy."

"What does that mean, 'sketchy'?" Li demanded.

"I mean that what you have here," Monk said, pointing at the file, "tells me little about the man. Most of the information here deals with facts and figures about his business on Pico, the Hi-Life Liquor and Minimart. The date when he purchased it, its revenues and so forth."

"Yes," Li said, neither a question nor a declaration.

Monk fixed Li with a blank look. "It would be helpful if

you had information on his likes, his hobbies, hell, you don't even have a home address for him. Was he into tall blonde women, short Latinas, what? Or was he gay?"

Li visibly blanched.

"Or for that matter, what he did before he came to America in '82."

"I can't see why that would be relevant," Li said. "He was murdered here, the killer is from here. Probably someone from the neighborhood."

He stopped talking, but Monk said nothing. Li said, "Ours is a professional association, not a social club. Kim's life outside of his store was not known to us."

"But his murder was odd," Yu added.

"Three shots to the rear of his head. Thirty-two-caliber screw-turn brass bullets." Monk paused, reading more of the firearms identification from the criminalist's report the Merchants Group had obtained. That alone impressed him, it wasn't everyone who could get the cops to release that report to civilians. "There was also the presence of grease on the entrance wounds found on the skull."

"What does that signify?" Kenny Yu asked.

"It means the killer used one of those hi-tech suppressors on his gun. Silencers they call them in the movies. They use an all-weather grease in one of the baffles of the thing that along with O-rings help to dampen the noise a gun makes when fired. That is definitely not the weapon of choice of a street thug."

Irritation set Li's face. "Are you saying that the Daltons or the Swans couldn't get ahold of one of these silencer devices?"

"Oh, I'm sure it'd be very easy for them to."

"Then what's your point?"

"Why don't you have more information about someone

who was a member of your association? You're sending me down the mine shaft with a penlight."

Kenny Yu gave Li a sideways look. The president of the Merchants Group said nothing, then rose from his chair. He gathered the file from Monk's desk and began to walk away.

Yu remained seated. Li paused at the door. "If all you have are silly questions and no solutions, you are not the man we need." Li opened the door, but Yu did not rise. Li looked at the back of the younger man's head, anger twisting his mouth. "Are you coming?"

Quietly, Yu said, "I think you should answer Mr. Monk's question, Mr. Li. The board did vote to hire him after we checked into his background."

Li, his head turned to the side, clamped his mouth shut, closed the door and returned to his seat. He placed the file onto the desk as a peace offering. "Kim was never a member."

"Well, that explains why his disappearance wasn't reported. Why wasn't he a member?"

"I don't know. Every Korean business person is not a member of our group. But like any good union, we have to look out for all the ones who we have common interests with. Especially now when we must demonstrate we are not to be pushed around."

Monk looked at Yu, who shrugged his shoulders. "Sorry, Mr. Monk, but I didn't know Kim at all."

"Gentlemen, the way the murder was done, and the hiding of Kim's body infers a premeditated crime, a planned act that had a hitch."

Li raised an eyebrow at this new unfamiliar colloquialism.

"Why wasn't Kim's body dumped in the ocean, or cut up and burned? Why was he buried, albeit in a deep grave?" Kenny Yu contributed.

"Exactly," Monk said. The previous grading of the field had already removed a significant layer of earth.

Li thrust a palm into the air. "That is for you to discern, I suppose."

"All right. But just because you and I sign a contract, that doesn't mean anything goes."

"What do you mean?" Li said, irritated again.

He seemed to Monk a man constantly upset with others or their situations. "If I uncover information that would threaten my license or my life, I'll turn that over to the cops. Short of that, whatever I find, I come to you first with it."

Li said, "Very well."

"And if there's anything of a more personal nature you can find out about Kim Bong-Suh, I'd appreciate knowing it."

"We agree to your price, three fifty a day plus expenses. But, if at the end of two weeks your reports show no progress, we will terminate the agreement. As to Kim's life, I have no more to give." Li got out of the chair and straightened the knot of his tie.

"I'll see what I can find out for you, Mr. Monk," Kenny Yu said, rising from the Eastlake.

Li glared at Yu but remained silent.

Monk got up, his hand outstretched. "I'll have the paperwork drawn up and sent over to you later today." Both men shook it and exited his office. Monk paced the carpet, absently tapping the file with his fingers. The door opened again and Delilah Shay entered.

She was the secretary/administrative assistant/woman Friday Monk shared with the housing development firm of Ross and Hendricks on the third floor of the refurbished office building in Culver City, two women who specialized in designing low to middle-income housing and rehab work. Delilah was a tall, well-proportioned, handsome Black woman whose straight hair was testament to the Chumash bloodline in her family. At any given time, she had two or three men in thrall, all dangling on a string.

Monk stopped pacing and stared out the window overlooking the street. Delilah came up beside him.

"You in business?"

"It would seem so. I have an assignment for you, doc."

"Should I change into my costume with the red *S*?"

"No need for leaping tall buildings in a single bound just yet. This work will require slyness, my dear." Monk grinned and raised his eyebrows at her in an exaggerated manner. He explained what he wanted and she left.

Monk sat down, picked up the phone's handset and dialed.

The sounds of Ennio Morricone's score to *The Good, the Bad and the Ugly* greeted his ears after the line connected. Then he heard the voice of Dexter Grant say, "State the facts please at the tone."

Monk said, "Call me when you get in, got something I'd like for you to check on." He severed the call. From the middle drawer of his desk he extracted a Cuban Monte Cristo cigar. Monk rolled the cigar between his thumb and the first two fingers of his left hand. He bit off the end, fished a match out of the desk and lit it.

Shafts of late morning light illuminated the chalky vapor rising from the burning cigar. Monk leaned back in his padded stainless steel swivel chair, smoking and thinking. Two hours later, Delilah returned. The dead stump of the cigar jammed into the corner of his mouth.

"Here you go." She handed Monk a computer printout.

"Thank you." He read the paper. "Was it much trouble?"

"Not really. The folks down at the Alcoholic Beverage Control department are quite sensitive in these post-rebellion days to residents' complaints concerning liquor stores. After a little smoke and mirrors on my part, they showed me the liquor license for the Hi-Life Liquor and Minimart. That printout gives its history."

"Including the address for Kim Bong-Suh, who originally took it over from a man named John Collier. And look here," he showed her the sheet. "The current license is under the name of something called Jiang Holdings in Stanton out in Orange County."

"What do you make of that?"

"I be finding out." Monk threw the used cigar away. He asked Delilah to send the contract over to the Merchants Group. He grabbed his brown checked sport coat from the old fashioned coat rack in the corner, left his .45 locked in his desk and quit the office.

The '64 Ford Galaxie 500 had been restored to better than assembly line condition. It was a 289-cubic-inch V-8, four-door hardtop, three-speed automatic, Dearborn-issued muscle, built when the big, gas-guzzling car was supposed to be every American's birthright. It wasn't a practical car, as far as fuel economy or tailing someone was concerned, but rebuilding a classic had been a dream shared by Monk and his dad.

They had discussed and planned which old car they were going to redo, spending weekends awed at custom car shows and searching junk yards for just the right shell. Something of a long, low silhouette that bespoke of the legacy of the glory days of car styling. Fifties fins didn't do much for either Monk, and they'd agreed that early '60s cars, generally a little shorter in their wheel base than their Cold War compatriots and more understated in profile, yet containing road-gobbling mills, was the era for them.

But then in the summer of '69, Josiah Monk suddenly died. And the dream of father and son became a fleeting image for the younger Monk. It would be years later before Monk made the wish reality. In between he'd bombed out as a football player on scholarship, and found himself working under the PI license of ex-LAPD detective, Dexter Grant.

Monk halted his musings as he drove east along Pico Boulevard in the Mid-City area. Nearing Fairfax, the vestiges of the uprising were evident here too. Several lots were still barren of structures, providing mute testimony to the difference between Los Angeles 1992 and Watts 1965.

The wellspring of both unrests had been the same. Police abuse, dead-end or no jobs, and economic and social racism. But while Watts was contained both geographically and racially to African Americans, the spring of '92 jumped off in South Central but spread to this area, the Latino Pico-Union, to Hollywood and parts of the Valley, and even into the gilded edges of Beverly Hills.

Monk passed the Hi-Life liquor store on the Southwest corner of Pico at Hauser. A middle-aged Korean woman, incongruously dressed in a black knee-length skirt with a slit and a white brocaded top, swept the sidewalk in front of the business. Monk turned left on Hauser and continued north. He'd stop back at the Hi-Life another time.

He approached the apartment building Kim had lived in. Interestingly, it wasn't in Koreatown nor out in Monterey Park or Alhambra where some Koreans lived who plied their trades in the inner city. Rather it was in the Mid-City area on Dunsmuir, north of Olympic Boulevard and before Wilshire. The Galaxie came to rest at the curb in front of the Jordan Palms.

The private eye walked to the entrance shrouded by a security gate partially hidden by blooming oleander bushes. He found the button for the manager and buzzed. Momentarily, a feminine voice cracked over the intercom.

"Yes?" it asked.

Monk bent near the speaker. "My name is Ivan Monk. I'm a private investigator looking into the murder of Kim Bong-Suh."

"He's dead, his apartment's been rented for a long time now."

"I know, I just said that. Did you keep any of his things?"

There was a pause. Then the voice said, "Yes, come on in." The gate clicked and Monk entered. He walked toward apartment 2 which the legend indicated belonged to the manager. The door to it opened as he got closer.

The manager was a redhead with her hair piled high in some kind of '60s hairdo Monk used to see on the old show Shindig. Getting closer, he was mesmerized by the heavy sea-green mascara which lined eyes with long false lashes. She had to be somewhere in her late forties but she still had her looks. Maybe she'd been thinner when she was younger, but there was a Rubenesque flair to her now.

"I'm Betty," she said, extending a purple-nailed hand.

"Ivan Monk." He returned her firm handshake and showed her his photostat.

Betty wore a grey V-neck sweater. A radio playing the all-news station could be heard behind her. "Mind if I ask you some questions about Kim?" They stood talking in the doorway.

"Not much I can tell you, honey." She appraised Monk as if he were a prime piece of steak. "He paid his rent on time and kept to himself. Never any trouble." She tilted her head which caused the large hoop earring she wore to bang against the door jamb.

"How long did he live here?"

"'Bout four years or so. I'd talk to him occasionally about the weather or this and that. Nothing important really. Say who hired you to look into his death? I don't watch TV but I heard about them finding his body on the radio. Jesus, living in the city, huh? That's funny that the cops haven't been around to ask me anything."

That occurred to Monk also. It probably meant they were assembling a task force. He told her who hired him then went on. "Did he disappear from here the same week he left his store over on Pico?"

"You know that's the funny part. I read in the papers—I like to keep up on things you know—about how he wasn't supposed to be around a week before the riots—oh excuse me—the uprising."

"But he was still around."

She squinted her eyes, seeing into the past. "Oh yeah. Now, I don't know the comings and goings of all my tenants, Mr. Monk."

"Ivan, please," he said, flirting just to keep in practice he rationalized.

"Ivan," she responded, displaying even teeth. "Anyways, I didn't have any reason to believe he wasn't still running the store until I drove past there, oh, I guess it was a month after the fires, and I noticed it was closed up."

"Did Kim continue to pay his rent on time?"

"Oh yeah. First of the month like always right up until October. And there'd be mornings when he'd leave and come back at night. I think there were several times when he was gone for days."

"Really. You have a record of his last payment?"

She shook her head in the direction of the interior of her apartment. "Come on in, I gotta look it up."

Monk entered the place. It was furnished in preserved vinyl chairs and a sofa done in tubular postmodern lines. There was a bookcase filled with current and past best

sellers as well as a healthy dose of nonfiction books on top-
ics ranging from the S&L crisis to a biography of Golda
Meir. Along the walls were inexpensive prints of Picasso,
Braque and Nagel.

"Did you ask Kim why he'd closed up?"

Betty was looking through her book of receipts on a
neatly ordered desk. "I thought about it. Sure was curious
him paying the rent on time and all but having no visible
means of income. But frankly, I didn't work up the nerve
to." She found what she was looking for and walked over to
where Monk stood in her living room. She gazed at a slip of
paper.

"I made this note to myself. October first was a Thursday
and I collected the rent, and I didn't see Mr. Kim that whole
day." She lifted her eyes off the paper. "I remember now. On
the following Saturday I happened to be up early watering the
plants out front and I saw him come up."

"Walking or driving?"

"Driving. But it was a different car than the one he had
before. It was brown, small, but I don't know from cars. I
asked him about the rent, and he assured me I'd have it that
afternoon. Only that was the last I saw of him."

Monk wrote down the make and license number of the
car Kim had listed on his rent application. "Do you know
what time he left that day?"

"No, I don't."

"How did he seem to you that morning?"

"Like he always was, I guess. I don't mean to be racist or
anything, but Mr. Kim was always pleasant, always composed, like I notice a lot of Asians are. Self-contained you
might say."

"He didn't seem to have anything on his mind?"

"Like I said, Ivan, he just walked up calm like, we

exchanged a few words, then he went on in." She squinted her eyes again. "He was carrying a big—oh, I don't know what you'd call it—but a large accordion file folder with a flap over it and tied up." She pantomimed the size of the file. "He had it tucked under his arm."

"And that was the last time you saw him?"

"Yep. A week went by from that Saturday, and on the following Friday I used my key to let myself into his place. Gone." She did a thing with her hands like an umpire signaling "safe."

"What became of his personal possessions?" There was an anxious edge in Monk's voice.

"I waited two weeks more, then gave his clothes to the second hand."

"Damn," Monk swore.

"Hey, at least I should be able to get a tax deduction for the lost income," she said defensively.

"What about books or papers he had?"

"Threw them out. A lot of them were in Korean." She held up her hands pleading self-defense.

He stared at her intently. "Do you remember anything about them?"

"I leafed through a couple of the Korean magazines. There was a picture of these cops beating people and some others showing people throwing Molotov cocktails."

"This was coverage of what happened here?"

"No, these were Asians, Koreans I guess."

"What about anything in English?"

"Oh, just some *Time and Newsweek* magazines, and some business ones also."

"Listen, you've really been a big help." He handed her one of his business cards. "If you think of anything else, give me a call will you."

"I sure will." She put the card in the hip pocket of the jeans.

"See you around." He started to leave.

"Could be," she said, smiling.

And Monk allowed his mind to wander as he drove to Continental Donuts on Vernon Avenue near Crenshaw.

When Monk signed out as a merchant seaman, being single and having no children, he'd managed to save a tidy sum. He told his friends he wasn't going to do any more bounty hunting, that he wanted to try something different. He thought about opening a car repair place but he'd had enough of engines, save working on his own. Dexter Grant, his ex-boss, told him about the donut shop.

It belonged to a friend of Grant's, an ex-cop like he was, and the guy was looking to sell. Getting up in years, and with a changing neighborhood, the place was more than he was willing to handle. Continental Donuts had been built in 1941, three months before Pearl Harbor. It was an *L*-shaped affair done in Streamline Moderne with a counter, fixed stools and several booths of blood-red leather. On the roof was a plaster donut twenty feet in diameter with the title of the establishment painted on its side.

At least that's how it had looked back then. When Monk saw it, stucco was falling from it like leaves off a tree in the fall. The donut on the roof was missing sections, and the booths bled their cotton stuffing. But Monk thought the joint had promise, so he hired Abe Carson to oversee the redoing of the place.

Yet after eight months of deep frying dough and mastering the fine art of glazing cinnamon rolls, Monk the donut king was bored. He turned the running of the shop over to others, then went back to doing bounty hunting work with a vengeance, mainly working for two bailbonds people, a man named Lasalle and a woman in a wheelchair named McLeash.

He hunted bailjumping burglars with acne-scarred faces and fleeing gang members hefting Uzis with Reeboks on their feet that cost more than their weapons. He searched for runaway daughters, and sought to find what made them run. The detective, like Jesus, walked the walk of thieves and murderers, cheats and liars. But unlike Jesus, the detective had no forgiveness to dispense, no great truth to find, only the hand that pulled the trigger, or grabbed the money from the till, or sunk the blade below the third rib. And what it was that made them do it. After a fashion, Monk settled into investigative work and concluded that was his evolutionary niche. His reason for getting up in the morning.

He parked on the lot the donut shop shared with the gas station. A couple of doors east of the lot were the burned out hulks of more stone victims of last spring's revolt. Monk smiled ruefully at the memory of him and Elrod, the man-ager of Continental Donuts, standing guard on the lot during that crazy time. Monk's .45, Elrod's Remington shotgun and signs stating "Black Owned" on the two structures were all they had against the torrent of frustration that swept through Los Angeles.

He waved to Curtis, the co-owner of the gas station. Using his key, he entered the donut shop through the secu-rity screen in the rear.

Instantly, a shape—was it Mount Kilimanjaro? —blotted out the light from the overhead fluorescents. A hand anviled from wrought iron emerged from the shape and clamped around Monk's shoulder.

"What up?" The voice rumbled.

"Nothin' much, Elrod. Everything okay here?"

The hand returned to its owner. "Same ol', same ol', chief."

Monk craned his neck upward at Elrod. A Cruise missile would have to hit the place directly to faze the six foot eight, 325 pounds of solid mass. "I gotta do a little computer work then I'll buy you a cup of coffee."

"Sure." The big ex-con ambled off to further demonstrate the involved process of making donut holes to the teenager he'd been instructing when Monk arrived.

Turning down a corridor in the *L* shank of the building, Monk unlocked a steel-sheeted door diagonally opposite the employee restroom. He entered the room and closed the door behind him.

The lights in the ceiling hummed to life and revealed a cheap wood-paneled room containing a standing safe, two heavy-duty file cabinets, a cot and an IBM PC on a small table. A folding chair fronted the table, and two more, folded up, leaned against the wall. There was a phone jack currently sans phone. Monk sat at the computer and powered it up.

Tumbling across the black ether of the monitor came yellow phosphorescent text. With two-finger effort and studied concentration, Monk entered his preliminary notes on the case. A knock sounded on the door.

"Yeah?"

Elrod's voice came through the door. "Chief, Delilah just called. Said you better get back to the office quick. Shit's jumpin'."

FOUR

They crowded the rotunda where Delilah's desk and computer sat. Dressed in Calvin Klein and Alexander Julian suits, their ages ranging from mid-twenties to early fifties, the members of Harvesters Unlimited were a GQ version of an occupying army. Monk threaded his way through the phalanx of African American men. Counting heads as he went, he calculated at least fifteen were jammed into the reception area.

Gaining the front, he spied Linton Perry leaning on Delilah's desk, amiably talking with her. Perry turned his head as Monk glided in.

"Brother Monk. We meet again." He held out his hand and Monk shook it. Perry was tall, taller than Monk and fleshly in the body. He was lighter in complexion than Monk, and there was a gray shock cutting a swath through part of his hair. The hand Monk shook had a gold ring on the middle finger and a silver one on the little.

Pointing his thumb behind him, Monk said, "Why the big turn out, Mr. Perry?"

"To impress on you, my brother, that I didn't come here speaking for myself. I came here with these gentlemen who represent various constituencies in our community so you could see we are united on this matter."

A sour taste gathered in Monk's mouth. "And what matter is that?"

"Why, these clients of yours, the Korean American Merchants Group."

"How do you know that?"

"There was a press conference this afternoon in front of their building announcing just that."

Monk swore under his breath. Goddamn thing was already being turned into a circus for everybody's benefit except his. He eyed the room. "And you decided you needed to remind me of how to do my job."

Perry stood up. He was relaxed yet Monk sensed it was all an effort at tight control. A mannerism that hid a volatile nature. Much like what he'd felt with Li. "We came here because we can't have brothers doing things against other brothers. We can't be seen to be working at cross purposes, at least not in the public eye."

Monk rubbed a hand across his forehead. "Come in my office please. Just you."

"I'd prefer it not be just me."

"It's you or I'm out of here. I'm not in the mood to get Mau Maued this late in the afternoon."

A long stretch of seconds passed as they stood looking at One another. Finally Perry said, "Okay, if it's all right with everyone else." He looked at the others in the room who shook their heads in concurrence.

The two entered the office. Monk removed the sport coat he wore over his starched khaki trousers with cuffs, blue-striped button-down shirt and tassled loafers. He hung the coat up and sat at his desk. Perry eased his large frame opposite. He tented his hands, waiting.

"What is it you expect me to do or not do, Mr. Perry?" Monk said testily.

"Are you determined to pursue this matter?"

"I'm going to look into the murder of Kim Bong-Suh."

"Then we hope you aren't going to play their game, brother Monk. We hope you'll be fair and impartial in your investigation."

"How do you mean their game?"

"At the press conference, Li answered reporters' questions. He said it was his opinion that Conrad James, if he could be found, might shed some light on this case. It seems to me that the Koreans want to put the noose around the young brother's neck a little too soon."

"James hasn't been around much. It is logical to want to talk to him. And I intend to. But I'm not naive or a hand-kerchief head, Mr. Perry. I know what time it is. I realize the Merchants Group hired me for PR value and as a wedge to pressure the cops into action."

Perry assessed Monk with new eyes. "It might interest you to know that James was let go by Kim that week. James locked up that Friday, came back on Saturday and there was a note left on the door for him by, allegedly, Kim."

"How do you know this?"

"I keep an ear to the street, Mr. Monk." Perry bowed his head to silent applause. "My understanding is the note instructed James, who was the manager by the way, where he could find the pay coming to him plus another two weeks."

"Did this note say why Kim closed up?"

"As far as I know, it did not."

"And do you have an address for James?" The file given to him by the Merchant's Group lacked that as well.

Perry stirred in his seat. "I didn't come here to do your

work for you. I came here to make sure you aren't going to be the goat for the Koreans."

It was meant to bristle him and it did. Monk fought down a response and remained quiet.

"Bigger things than the death of a Korean shop owner are at stake in this."

"Like SOMA?"

"My being on the board of SOMA is just one means to an end."

"And what are your ends, Mr. Perry?"

"Economic justice for the Black man, Mr. Monk."

"And your way of achieving that is getting your name in the newspapers often?"

Perry rose, brushing imaginary lint from his trousers. "It was a pleasure having this little talk. We'll have another one soon." He smiled warmly and departed.

Night time came and Monk prepared dinner at Jill's house. It was a two-story angular model a la Richard Neutra located on a hill in Silverlake. The view from the window in her study overlooked the Silverlake reservoir. And on Sunday mornings one could find various people, including the judge and a city councilman who lived nearby, jogging around its concrete skirt. Rarely Monk.

He did his best to cut down on red meat—the judge was a virtual vegetarian—and work out regularly, but he'd rather be dragged behind a IROC Trans Am butt naked than endure the ennui of jogging.

Monk brought the plates of steaming yellow rice and shrimp, black beans on the side, to the dining room table. Kodama tossed a salad and poured equal amounts of an especially dry sauterne for both of them. She'd changed from her downtown business suit into form fitting cords and a loose flannel shirt. She was a Japanese American woman of above average height with an intelligent face framed by walnut dark hair of medium length.

They sat, clinked glasses and ate their food, making small talk. Later, they nestled on the couch in the judge's study. The room was done in somber paneling with a large floor-to-ceiling Cherrywood bookcase filled with tomes of all sorts. Wing chairs occupied two corners like silent sentinels, and the judge's desk was a twin of the one in Monk's office. The floor was covered with a rug in bold Assyrian patterns. On the wall were various framed photos including one of Kodama being congratulated at an ACLU dinner. There was also a black lacquer frame around a photostat. It was Executive Order 9066, the law that FDR signed sending Japanese Americans to concentration camps during World War II. Including Kodama's parents.

"You know, Ivan," Kodama began, "this city scares me more now than at any other time."

He caressed her hair. "How so?"

"There's too many trains running. Black leaders like Linton Perry who play the nationalist card when it suits him. And the next week saying how badly he wants to build coalitions with Latinos and Koreans."

Monk said. "And cats like Luis Santillion writing editorials saying in effect that African Americans are incidental when it comes to numbers and therefore why worry about alliances when they have forty-one percent."

She laid her head in his lap. "It's all so depressing. Los Angeles's capitalists trying to desperately leverage this place as the center of Pacific Rim finance and kids going hungry and people sleeping in their cars. And where I've had bricks thrown at my car because Black people thought I was Korean."

"Learning is always a tortuous process, an old ship's captain told me once. All we can do is keep going forward."

"For a cynical private eye, you carry around quite a bit of hope in your back pocket." She looked into his face and kissed him for a long time.

They made love, there in the study, spread out, their hips on the sofa, their legs across the coffee table. They sweated to climaxes while Muddy Waters sang "Baby Please Don't Go" on the stereo, his voice rich as the Delta fields he came from.

In the bedroom, a circle of light illuminated them by the Tensor lamp on Jill's nightstand. She straddled him wearing black lace panties as Monk lay naked underneath her. She bent over him and finished trimming his goatee with the small scissors, then put them on the nightstand. Monk cupped her breast in his hand.

"That's it, isn't it?" she said, rocking to and fro on him.

"Huh."

"You took the job because you want to prove a point. You get off on the idea of out-manuevering Li, Perry, all of them and still find the real killer."

"I'm not that deep, baby. I need the business. You're the one who sits on the bench, keeping the snarling dogs of Aryan fury from being unleashed on us poor citizens."

He pulled her close, and she bit one of his nipples. "You're full of shit, Ivan." She nuzzled his neck. Jimmy Smith, jazz master of the Hammond electric organ, played a steady, driving beat underneath their conversation, "Eleanor Rigby."

Her fingers rubbed a spot over his left rib cage. It was an elliptical section of flesh that had the consistency of a dried orange peel, the legacy of a .22 slug which had fragmented on impact. It took the doctor who worked on Monk more than two hours to dig the pieces out of him. Further up on his torso, a .38-caliber ricocheting bullet had ripped into his collar bone. The result was a bone chip that caused him arthritic inflammation in cold weather. But the wounds, and the ones who caused them, were far from Monk's mind.

She inched her body forward until the 'V of her legs covered Monk's head. Dexter Gordon's wails of urban angst filled the room. The judge turned her body so that she was on her knees over him, taking him in her mouth as he did her. The saxman preened notes, dove in and out of sections as a race car driver might take a raceway.

Afterward, they lay side by side in the bed, each staring at the shifting shadows on the ceiling thrown by the votive candles on the nightstand and the diffused light coming through the curtained bedroom window.

"I was in this Greek village once, back when I was a merchant seaman. It was called"—he searched his memory—"Kilada."

Jill rose up on an elbow to take a sip of her wine. She smiled at him and put her head on his chest.

"We were walking around—"

"Looking for Mediterranean babes."

"Taking in the sights," he continued. "And on some of the clotheslines hung octopuses, or octopi or whatever the plural is, drying in the sun. Later they would be marinated, cooked and served with ouzo. See, a lot of the porches were covered, so these creatures gave off weird shadows across the raw stone of the houses. None of them alike, yet related."

"Like a Rorschach test," she offered.

"Yes. You could see in the shapes whatever you wanted to. But there's always something solid beyond the pattern."

"Is that right, Mr. Monk?"

They both laughed. After a while, Kodama fell asleep and Monk eased out of the bed. Unable to sleep, he went downstairs to the study, got a book and came back to the bedroom. Sitting in a chair in the corner, he switched on a Art Deco wall sconce. He read several chapters from Jim Sleeper's *The Closest of Strangers*. The patterns on the walls shifted as the wicks grew longer in the candles and the curtain swirled about the open window. The shadows of ectoplasm.

FIVE

The room was quiet like a run-down watch. Next to him, Monk heard the rhythmic breathing of the woman he loved. Gazing at her, he imagined what she was dreaming. What do women dream about? What do they see in men like him? Three years. Not long in the annals of humankind, an eon in relationships in the city of dashed hopes.

He scratched his side, got out of bed, and went into the bathroom. Then he trod into the kitchen and started brewing some coffee. He slipped on the jeans he'd left draped over the faux Louis XIV chair in the study. Out front, on the well-tended lawn, Monk picked up the morning edition of the *LA Times*, the folded part moist from the morning dew.

Back in the kitchen, Monk poured two cups of coffee in oversize stoneware mugs. Black for Jill, liberal amounts of sugar and milk for him. Paper tucked under his muscled arm, he strolled back into the bedroom with the hot coffee. He put the cups on the nightstand and sat on the bed, digging the Metro section out of the paper.

Jill moved under her blanket and slid an arm onto Monk's thigh. The covering moved below the middle of her back. "Hey."

"Hey." Monk read the article about yesterday's news conference the Merchant's Group had held.

Jill's hand rubbed his leg. "What time is it?"

Monk glanced at the clock. "Six-forty." He leaned over
and kissed her shoulder blade.

"Would you hand me some coffee, baby?"

He retrieved it as she sat up in bed and handed it to her.

"Thanks. I've got to—shit!" she suddenly exclaimed,
clutching at the blanket and drawing it over her nude torso.

Monk had been sitting on the bed facing Jill. From her
position, she faced the bedroom windows running on the
south side of her house. He spun in that direction. There in
one of the windows was a blonde bush. No, Monk corrected
himself, it was the ash-blonde mane of Kelly Drier, one-time
minor league ball player, currently six-figure sensationalist
hack for the number-two local TV station in town.

Drier knocked lightly on the window and pointed at
the two on the bed. He mouthed something which Monk
couldn't make out. A tight grin pulled his lips back. "I'm
going to go out there and stick my foot way up that
moron's ass."

"As your lawyer, I must advise you if you do, Drier will
have it all over the four o'clock news." Jill calmly sipped her
coffee, eyeing the reporter who continued to gesticulate at
the window. "I think he wants to talk to you, Ivan."

"Uh-huh." Monk went to the window. Drier, a kind of
sun-tanned version of ex Vice-President Dan Quayle, but
with better taste in ties, smiled broadly. Solemnly, Monk
pointed toward the front of the house. The reporter's head
worked up and down as if it were a clown head on a spring.

It occurred to Monk the analogy was not too far strained
as he put on his shirt, tail out. He padded to the front in bare
feet. Opening the door, Drier stood there blow-dry fresh,

his cologne cloying like a woman's. Behind him and to the left stood a minicam operator holding his camera at rest, waiting for the word from the maestro.

"I've never met you before, Mr. Drier."

"But you dug me on the tube, right?" he interrupted.

Monk blinked, hard. "But yeah, I recognize you from the TV. Now why the fuck couldn't anything you have to ask me wait until I was at my office?"

"Because Monk, my man, you're the wild card in this deal. And from what I've read about you, I think you're going to be where the action is."

He hated when people, guys who didn't know him called him "my man." The camera operator hefted his device, adjusting the lens.

"You haven't heard, have you? It was on the news radio stations about half an hour ago."

"What?"

"The cops and the FBI did a raid at a house near Adams and Western."

"Looking for Conrad James, I bet."

"That's right, homeboy. 'Course they didn't find him, but they did manage to roust a mother and her two children out of bed and tear up a chest-of-drawers her grandmother gave her." The microphone, it must have been at his side all along, appeared under Monk's nose. The red light winked red on the minicam. Drier swiveled his coiffured head to the camera.

"I'm here with private eye Ivan Monk who has just learned that the combined efforts of the local police and the FBI, operating in a joint task force, have conducted an early morning sweep for the suspect in the murder of Kim Bong-Suh. A murder Mr. Monk has been hired to solve by the Korean American Merchants Group." The blonde head pivoted back.

"What are your reactions to this, Mr. Monk?"

He mumbled some inanity as a reply. Drier continued for several minutes with questions whose purpose seemed to be to get Monk to pontificate on the state of the cops, the Koreans, Black folks or the universe in general. He was getting edgy with boredom.

"Finally, Mr. Monk, if this murder investigation does indeed turn out to have been done by a Black murderer, do you think the city will explode again?"

Monk clamped his lips and rubbed the back of his neck. "Then he deserves a fair trial by a jury of his peers."

"But you'll admit that's hard to come by for a Black man around here."

Monk knew where it was going, but what the hell. "Yeah, that's right."

"Then the city could go up again if a Black man is arrested?" A lascivious gleam lighted Drier's baby blues. The microphone inched close enough for Monk to shave with it.

"Well I'm sure if that happens, you'll join me in helping to keep the peace, Mr. Drier."

"Pardon?"

"I mean right here and now on live morning TV, I'm joining with you." Monk put his arm around Drier's shoulders. "As a representative of electronic journalists, as a man who has said he believes in activist reporting, I'm asking you to pledge that you'll come with me into the deepest, darkest heart of South Central and together we will meet with the brothers and sisters on the battle lines. They respect you down there, you know."

Drier's glare bored angrily into Monk who remained stone-faced looking at the camera. With practiced fluidity, Drier regained his facile composure. Through thin lips he said, "Bearing in mind that my job is to report breaking events, of course I'll do everything I can to maintain calm if those riotous events should repeat themselves."

"Good, good." Monk clapped him several times on the shoulder. "Now if you'll excuse me, brother Drier, my coffee's getting cold." Monk wheeled about and went into the house, silently closing the door behind him.

THE OLDER man sat in the chair reading a current issue of *Popular Science*, his feet propped up on the semicircular desk. His long legs were clothed in dungarees, and his barrel chest covered in a plaid flannel shirt. A pair of threadbare chukkas shod his feet. On his head was one of those formless fishing hats with a brim like the undulating body of a jellyfish. Beneath the hat, the platinum white hair curled past the shirt's collar.

The office wasn't open yet, it was eight-twenty, and Monk entered, deactivating the alarm after throwing the two dead bolts that allowed him into the rotunda.

"'Bout time you got here," the older man said, not lifting his head from the article he was reading in the magazine. "Back on the farm, half of the day would already be wasted."

"Why don't I just give you a key to the place, Dex?"

"I like to keep in practice, youngster."

Monk crossed to the coffee machine and started it to brewing.

"Says here," Dexter Grant began, pointing at the *Popular Science*, "engineers are working on the fusion angle, using deuterium-tritium to produce energy."

"That's nice," Monk said. He unlocked the door to his office.

Grant rose, stretched and put the magazine back on the small table in the center of the chairs for waiting clients. "They figure it won't be until 2030 when there's an online fusion plant though. Assuming this particular energy source holds up."

"That's fucking fascinating."

"Goddamn, you and Jill go at it this morning?"

The two entered the dark office. Grant flipped the lights on and slouched down in one of the Eastlakes.

Monk angled behind his desk. "How do you know I was with Jill?"

"'Cause I went by your pad before I came over here and the Ford wasn't there. Barring the notion that it had been stolen, and I would have heard about the bodies laying along the avenues if that would have happened, I am left with the irrefutable fact that you were over at Jill's. You don't sleep around, you don't have the temperament for it like some cops I knew."

"Get us some coffee, will you, smart guy."

In a dead perfect imitation of Eddie "Rochester" Anderson, Grant said, "Sure, boss, comin' right up." He left and returned with two cups and set one down on the massive desk. "So what's up?" His body poured back into the chair.

Monk sipped, and regarded the man sitting before him. Dexter Grant was built like an over-the-hill fullback from the era of Red Grange, leather helmets and footballs made of pigskin. He'd been a kid off an Oklahoma oil lease who found himself in World War II. Big shouldered and raw-boned, the young Grant had only made it to the ninth grade when his folks had to pull him out of school to help out on the land. But that hadn't stopped him from reading everything he could get his hands on nor listening to the tales of his uncle Logan when he came to town.

The uncle, through marriage to one of his mother's sisters, had been an organizer for the Wobblies. The Wobblies, the Industrial Workers of the World, had been organized in 1905 by progressives in the labor and socialist movements for the purpose of joining all workers regardless of job type, color or sex.

Uncle Logan had tales to tell a wide-eyed lad who'd never seen more than the rear end of a mule and a pressed shirt for Sunday-go-to-meetin's. True tales of his imprisonment in Folsom on trumped-up charges, and the brawls against the guards he and other Wobblie organizers had to win to survive. Of bloody Ludlow and John D. Rockefeller's goons cutting down striking miners with machine gun fire.

At seventeen, Grant had been signed into duty by his father. It wasn't the elder's idea, but they'd lost the lease, and the younger Grant saw the Army as a way of eating steady and sending something home to his folks and younger sisters. At basic training at Fort Wachuca, it came out that Grant had a pretty fair grasp of written and spoken German, another gift from his uncle Logan, who was of German extraction.

And so the OSS, the Office of Strategic Services, saw that it could use a quick-witted youngster who read a lot and understood the enemy's language.

Monk told Grant about the case and gave him a copy of his notes. "I need you to find out something on Kim. I want to know who he was before he got to the States."

Grant fingered the file before him on the desk. "This is all they gave you?"

"Yeah."

"Do you think the Merchant's Group is purposely holding back on Kim's background?"

"I think some of them in the organization have their mind set on one direction. Find the guilty, and damn the rest. And far as I can tell, Kim was an independent type. He didn't belong to their group."

Grant touched his lips with the side of his index finger. "So they want to set an example, make a point that Korean shop keepers won't get pushed around."

"Exactly," Monk said.

"Yet the only employee they show that worked there is this Conrad James. The two of them couldn't have worked ten to fourteen hours a day, and keep the inventory and whatever else you gotta do to keep a store going."

"I realize that," Monk said testily.

"So why don't they have other people listed who worked there?"

"I'm working on it. I don't even know if anything Kim did before he came here has any bearing on this case. Hell, I'm not sure Kim came straight from South Korea or Steubenville, Ohio. But I damn sure want to find out."

"And since I'm the one with the State Department contacts . . ." Grant let it trail off.

"Come on, I'll let you buy my breakfast." Monk and Grant left the office and walked down the block to the Cafe 77, a retro-fit Chinese joint that served great biscuits and grits for breakfast. Afterward, Grant drove off in his mint-condition '67 Buick Electra deuce and a quarter, and Monk traipsed back to his office. Delilah was at her desk.

"Marasco called for you. Dexter was here wasn't he?"

"Yes he was."

She tapped the cylindrical vase to her left. Sticking out of it, unnoticed by Monk before, was a single fresh cut pink rose.

"Careful, baby. You might blow his circuits if you fool around with him."

"Or he mine," she replied to his back as he entered his office.

Monk had an idea what his friend Lt. Seguin had called

about and he was none too anxious to get into it with him just yet. On the other hand, he couldn't ignore the call. Marasco was a good man, better than okay as far as cops went. But he did work for the LAPD, and when they put their pointed heads to it, they damn sure could land on you with both feet.

Certainly it wasn't a walk in the park for a Chicano straight off the hard streets of Boyle Heights to keep his nose relatively clean, not kowtow to the racism of the department, and still make lieutenant before forty. Added to that, he remained friends with a Black private eye nobody else on the force associated with. But a call from a cop is a call from a cop.

Monk dialed the inside line to the detective's section of Wilshire Station on Venice Boulevard. "Is Marasco there? This is Monk returning his call." A pause, then the line picked up.

"Ivan. Glad you called me back." There was a formality in the voice that raised Monk's antenna.

"Of course. What can I do for you, lieutenant?"

"We'd like you to come down here and discuss this case of yours."

"We being you and the chief?"

"You two can cut it out," a new voice said. As Monk assumed, someone else was listening in. "This is Special Agent Keys, Mr. Monk, of the Federal Bureau of Investigation. As field commander of the task force looking into the murder of Mr. Kim, I'd consider it a professional favor if you'd meet with us."

Jesus, this guy believed in the carrot and the stick in the same swipe. "It's gonna have to be day after tomorrow, Agent Keys. Or Monday."

"Today would be better." Keys's tone was flat, unshaded. The threat hiding in back of it.

"As one pro to another, I'm sure you understand I'm in the middle of things just now."

There was a silence on the line. Finally, Seguin spoke. "It'd be good if you got over here tomorrow, Friday. Around noon."

Just to irk Keys, Monk said, "Two o'clock then." He hung up before either could voice an objection. Monk pushed away from the desk, rubbing his temples. He made three more calls and left the office again.

He drove over to the Culver City DMV and waited in the registration line. Reaching the counter, he was greeted with the apparition of a reed-thin man in a cheap suit way past the need for pressing. The bureaucrat's face was sunken and partially hidden by the thick lenses of his glasses. He stood motionless, waiting for the last customer in the last line on a career to nowhere.

"I've been the victim of a hit and run." Monk said.

The skeleton said nothing. His face a zero of acknowledgement.

"I want to find out who hit me. I have the license number." Monk enunciated each word as a tourist might to a person who spoke another language.

The arm of the man with the build of a stork's leg disappeared under the counter and reappeared with a form printed in blue ink. "Fill this out, including your own license number. Bring it back to this window. You do not have to get back in line again."

Monk filled out the form, putting down the license number he'd gotten from Betty, Kim Bong-Suh's ex-landlady. He returned it to the counter.

The DMV clerk looked at it, said nothing and went away. Presently he returned and said, "That'll be four dollars." He pointed to another counter. "Pay the cashier and bring the receipt back. You don't have to wait in line," he said in his blank slate of a voice. Monk did so and returned to the charmer. The man's bony hand passed a printout to the private eye. As Monk walked away, a woman behind him came up and began shouting at the deathly thin man.

"Why the fuck has my car had one of them boots put on it, huh?"

Without a change of a expression, he produced another form.

Monk read the information on the printout. A certificate of non-operation had been filed on the 1988 Honda Civic DX Kim had driven. It was dated from November of last year. The address on the certificate was in Orange County. He took out his notepad, and sure enough, the Orange County address was the one given for Jiang Holdings in Stanton, the company that now owned the liquor license on Hi-Life Liquors and Minimart.

But a jaunt behind the Orange Curtain was going to have to wait. Monk had other fish to fry for the moment. He got in his Ford and drove east on Washington, away from Culver City, back into Los Angeles.

Reaching Hauser, Monk swung the car left and arrived at the Hi-Life liquor store at the corner of Pico and Hauser. There was a parking stall behind the establishment accessible off of Hauser just north of the intersection. Monk parked in it and walked in the front.

Behind the counter was the woman he'd seen sweeping down the sidewalk the day before. She was dressed in an orange and tan jumpsuit, her hair pulled back in a severe ponytail. In the corner, two kids Monk made to be around twelve or thirteen played on one of the video games. There was a lot of those sounds you hear in dubbed kung fu flicks when the hero is beating the hell out of a dozen bad guys. At each violently loud impact, the two youngsters would laugh and exude 'aghhs,' twisting their bodies as if they too felt the blows.

The woman studied Monk as he approached the counter. He had his photostat out, pushed toward her. "My name is Ivan Monk. Mr. Li of the Korean American Merchant's Group hired me to look into the murder of Kim Bong-Suh."

"Yes," she said, "I saw the news." She gestured at a compact portable TV on the counter. It was surrounded by an open box of Baby Ruth candy bars and baseball cards, near a horizontal rack of polybagged ten-dollars-per-pack for three softcore girlie magazines. The set played a silent soap opera. "I remember your name."

Monk replaced his wallet. "Did you know Mr. Kim?"

Her eyes looked over at the two youngsters, then back to Monk. "No."

"How did you come to buy this business?"

"Why not? It was for sale."

"By who?"

"The Bank. Ginwah Bank. When Kim Bong-Suh leave, payments stop, bank take over. We pay them, take over business."

"How much did the liquor license cost you?"

She didn't miss a beat. "Bank say liquor license belong to Jiang Company, not our concern. We get good rate on store, Bank take care of Jiang."

"Look, Ms. . . ."

"Chung. Mrs. Chung."

A tall clean-cut Korean American young man stepped from the rear of the store through a door next to the beer case. Monk took him to be twenty-two or three, and he wore knee-length baggy shorts and a T-shirt with a giant *X* on it.

"What up, Aunt So?" the new arrival said. He came up beside her on their side of the counter.

"This is the one the Merchant's Group hired." She shook a thumb at Monk. "Answer his questions, I got work to do." She marched off into the back.

"Hi, I'm David," the young man said, extending his hand.

Monk shook it, introducing himself. "I was asking your aunt what she knew about Jiang Holdings."

David lifted a shoulder and an eyebrow. "Who are they?"

"The company that has title to the liquor license of this place."

"Well, homey, that's beyond me. I just work here part time to help the folks out and shit."

That's why your aunt sicced you on me. But Monk said, "Do you know anything about the people Kim had working here before your aunt and uncle bought this place?"

"No. Wait a minute," he said, snapping his finger. "I was in here one day and this chick came in, fine too. Anyway, she said she used to work for Kim and was wondering if we'd heard from him."

"He owe her money?"

"I don't know, man. But I think—" He stopped himself in mid-sentence and pulled out a drawer in the counter. He dug around for several seconds then produced a scrap of yellow, blue-lined paper. This he handed to Monk.

"Can I keep this?" Monk said, shaking the piece of paper.

"Sure. Don't look like we're gonna hear from Kim now, huh?"

Monk handed the young man one of his business cards. "You never know what a dead man might tell you. If you think of anything else, give me a call, will you."

"Sure, Mr. Monk." And they shook hands again.

Monk walked past the action video game. Only one kid played now, his eyes semi-glazed, mouth hanging open. The game was called, "Bring me the Head of Saddam Hussein."

Out at the curb, Monk noticed two young Black men, also in their early twenties, stopped on the other side of Pico Boulevard in a late model, gun-metal gray Blazer with Weld rims. He noticed them because the one in the passenger seat was pointing toward the store. Or him. The utility vehicle pulled away quickly, and Monk wasn't about to rush out in the busy street and try to get the license number. He got in his car and took Hauser south to Adams, then made a left. Deeper into the black belt, the more segregated portion of Mid-City which eventually became the Crenshaw District.

Nearing La Brea, Monk passed a stretch of shoddy motels laid out one against another like fallen dreams. In the gated courtyard of a pink and green stucco model, he spied small Latino children laughing and kicking a ball back and forth. One of them stood at the gate, looking out at the passing traffic, a thumb lodged comfortably in her mouth. In the next motel, with an ungated courtyard, two young men stood under the eaves. Each was dressed in black khakis and black Air Jordans. One of them, short and muscular, had on a purple shirt buttoned at the cuffs and collar, the regalia of the Rolling Daltons.

The other wore a fedora with a feather in its crown crammed low on his head, and he whistled at Monk as he drove past. On the corner where the motels ended, a woman darker than Monk with hair dyed an eye-hurting color that might charitably be called blonde, lolled against the east wall of the building.

Above her, on the roof of the motel was a billboard. It was the logo of SOMA printed in garish colors. In reversed-out letters below the flaming logo were the words THE FUTURE BEGINS TODAY. The woman smiled at Monk, revealing gold-capped front teeth.

He reached Palm Grove Avenue and turned right. Monk

parked the car at a rectangular duplex sitting on a lot of brown grass in the middle of the block. The porch had spots of chipped red paint, and the apartment on the right had a hole in its screen door. The one on the left, the one that Monk approached, had a heavy gauge security door fronting it. He rang the bell.

The inner door opened but he couldn't see beyond the opaque mesh of the screen. "Yes, may I help you?" The voice belonged to a young woman.

"Ms. Jacobs, my name is Ivan Monk. I'd like to ask you a few questions about the time you worked at Hi-Life Liquors." He produced his license. Maybe, he absently reflected, he ought to have the thing stenciled to his shirt he was showing it so much.

"Okay. Come on in." The screen door swung outward revealing an African American woman in her mid-twenties. Her hair was dreadlocked and pulled back from a handsome face. She was dressed in jeans, a loose top and sandals. Her head was oblong shaped and the eyes in it were alive, observant.

"I didn't think any of us were Mike Hammer types." Her smile was genuine.

"I'm not, that's for the Hollywood tough guys." Monk passed through the door jamb into a neatly appointed apartment. Karen Jacobs closed and locked the screen door, leaving the inner door open.

"Have a seat." She sat in an overstuffed chair where two text books and a pad of yellow paper rested on one of its arms. Block printing covered the pad's surface.

He sat on the couch. "I got your name from David Chung. He says you'd been there asking about Mr. Kim."

"Yeah, that was terrible. He was really a nice man. But I don't know what I can tell you. I only worked in the store part-time up until the beginning of last year. I'm going to school at UCLA, you know."

"What are you studying?"

"Economics."

"Gonna start a business?"

"No, not how you mean. I plan to do economic planning and fundraising for community groups and nonprofits."

"Bet. We don't need more profiteers in the 'hood."

"You go to some kind of socialist private eye school?"

Straight-faced, Monk said, "I can't even spell the word. Did Kim Bong-Suh owe you money? Is that why you asked about him?"

"Nothing that mercenary. I'd heard that he wasn't around and was just curious is all."

"He was that nice a boss."

"Yes."

Monk said, "Really."

"Yes," she insisted.

"Okay, if you say so."

There was a gap of time that elapsed while Monk stared at her. "You sure this didn't have something to do with Conrad James?"

She looked at the ceiling and then at Monk. "Well, I guess you know Conrad James also worked there. I was kind'a curious as to what had happened to Conrad."

"When did Conrad go missing?"

"Around October of last year."

"He and Kim hung out?"

"The two of them got on well."

"Did you and Conrad get on well?"

"We went out a couple'a times. He was nice, and not like a lot of other guys. He could keep his hands in his own lap."

There was a smart comeback there, but Monk wasn't going for it. "What kind of guy was Kim?"

Her eyebrows went up a notch. "I don't know, really. Except I think he was kind'a aware, you know?"

"What lead you to say that?"

"Mr. Kim was a pretty bright cat. I saw him once reading a copy of Frantz Fanon's *The Wretched of the Earth*. And another time he came up to me to ask me about some words he'd read in John Steinbeck's *In Dubious Battle*."

Monk wrote in his notepad. "Did he talk about politics, or the local scene? Black, Korean stuff in Los Angeles."

She digested the question and pondered it for a few moments. "Actually Conrad would be the one to ask about that."

"Yeah?"

"Yes. He and Conrad got along, as I said. Conrad even took Mr. Kim to a Raider game since he hadn't seen American football in person."

"So he and Conrad saw each other socially?"

"They weren't ace boon coon, but yeah, you could say they socialized to an extent. I remember after the Du thing they'd get into discussions about the incident at work."

"Arguing?"

She paused, searching for the right words. "They didn't shout at one another, but it was more like two peers who had different points of view on the same subject."

"Interesting. Kim ever talk about his life in South Korea?"

"Mr. Kim mentioned he'd been married once."

"And."

"All he said was his wife had died back in South Korea." Her brows knitted. "It was a sad thing for him to bring up and he didn't again."

"You remember anything else he said about his life then?"

The handsome head moved from side to side then stopped. "I remember something about Yushi, no, Yushin, I think he said. Mr. Kim was on the phone talking to someone and they got into an argument in Korean.

"I remember the word because he said his wife's name, Jai Choo I believe, and then some more words, then Yushin repeated several times." She spread her hands before her. "He slammed the receiver down, then covered his face and cried." Her face clouded at the memory of another person's pain. "He was a nice man," she said in elegy for Kim.

Monk asked some more questions and got three other names of people who had worked at various times at the Hi-Life liquor store.

"Did you think Kim read or talked about Black folks just for show, you know, have his employees think he was down and all?"

"No, no. I think he was quite sincere about that. I mean I think he had a real interest in learning about his environment. He didn't ask a lot of goofy questions but he was always observing and reading the local news, you know. Not just the *Times*, but *The Sentinel* too."

Monk continued to write in his little notepad. *The Sentinel* was the weekly Black newspaper of Los Angeles. "What about his private life?"

She leaned forward. "Are you saying did he ask me out?"

"I didn't mean it like that. Did he ever say anything about what he did away from work?"

She spread her hands in the air. "I wouldn't know."

"But you and Conrad were still going out after Kim stopped running the liquor store in April?"

Warily, she said, "A couple of times, yeah."

"Until when? What month?"

"Sometime around September."

"And he'd seen Kim since he'd left the store?" He said it nonchalantly, slipping it into the conversation as if it were an afterthought.

A tick twitched the left side of Karen Jacobs's face. "Not that I know of."

"Why'd you and James stop seeing each other?"

"That's personal."

"Did the two of you talk about why you thought Kim quit the store?"

She was on guard and wouldn't play the game any more. "Look, Mr. Monk, I've got plenty of studying to do. Okay?"

"Sure, I don't want to wear out my welcome." He rose. "If you don't know where Conrad is now, could you tell me where he used to live?" She couldn't duck that one.

Jacobs hesitated, then went to a cabinet built into the wall and took out her address book. Monk drifted near her. She sat at a table and wrote down the former address and telephone number for the missing Conrad James. She tore off the corner of the yellow pad, almost an exact duplicate in size to the note she'd left at the Hi-Life, and handed it to Monk.

"Thanks." He put one of his cards on the table. "Let me know if you think of anything else." It occurred to Monk he was giving out more cards than an ambulance-chasing lawyer.

"I will," she said unconvincingly.

He drove away from the duplex, west up Washington toward his office. The Black woman with the ostentatious hair was still there next to the motel. She was talking to the men in the gray Blazer with the Weld-style rims. The vehicle was turned into a driveway, sideways to the boulevard so Monk couldn't get a look at the plates. He checked his mirror, but the Blazer wasn't following him.

At the address Jacobs gave him for James, Monk found an apartment whose current occupant never heard of the young man, didn't want one of his cards, and wouldn't tell him who the manager was. The private eye quit the place and grabbed a beer in a bar.

SIX

Father Divine, the Depression-era conman/preacher of Harlem, was giving him a lecture on the best method of preparing catfish stew and mustard greens. This he didn't mind. But they were having an argument on how many cardamom seeds to put in the Turkish coffee. Matter of fact, as the both of them sat in Tiger Flowers's sauna drinking Cuba Libres, the others in the room asked them to take their senseless discussion elsewhere.

Monk was about to say something to Paul Robeson, he being the most vociferous about his and Father Divine's departure, when the goddamn bell went off again.

"Shit, answer that motherfuckah," Monk mumbled, climbing out of sleep. He groped, found the handset, and pulled it to the pillow somewhere in the vicinity of his head.

"Sorry to wake you, my friend."

What?

"Mr. Monk, are you there?"

"Yes."

"As I'd said, I apologize for the earliness of the hour. But having raised five children of varying ages, my body clock is eternally attuned to getting up at five-thirty each A.M."

Jovial son-of-a-bitch. And then the voice made its way past the skull into the brain. "Mr. O'Day."

"Ah, yes indeed, sir. You are a detective."

"What can I do for you at"—he glanced at his clock radio—"five-forty in the morning?"

"I was wondering if you'd be my guest for breakfast."

Why not? "Where?"

"The Odin Club."

"I didn't know they let Black people in there."

"Mr. Monk, Mr. Monk, what a splendid man you are. Let's say a decent hour, shall we. Eight-thirty."

"Sure. I'll wear my tie rakishly askew."

"Of that I'm sure."

The call ended and Monk rolled onto his back, staring at the names in the case revolving around the inside of his head. He added O'Day's, unsure at the moment of how much prominence to give it. But time would tell. He got out of bed and trudged into the bathroom. Monk took an invigorating bath, all the while examining the facets of the case. Toweling off, Monk put on his charcoal gray sharkskin suit and a round collar carmine colored shirt which he buttoned all the way up.

He got a shot of Nicaraguan coffee from the espresso joint on the corner. With time to spare, he tooled his car west on Sunset, past UCLA, the Bel Air Estates (where the Great Communicator and Mommy lived), Brentwood, and on into the sphere of affluence which was Pacific Palisades. Drawing closer to the Coast Highway, Monk put the Ford onto a road winding into the Santa Monica Mountains. On a street called Apollo, he arrived at the gated driveway that led to the Odin Club.

On either side of the wide roadway was a guard booth, for the entrance and exit. Each was done in the shape of a five-headed plaster-and-lathe dog with a mane of writhing snakes sitting on its haunches. Cerberus at the port of Hades. In the belly one of the dogs was the two-sectioned door that allowed the guards to look out. Each was blonde, with pecs the size of Nebraska straining the black shirts of their uniforms. One was crew cut, the other splendidly Californian in a ponytail.

A column separated the dogs. At the top of it was a statue of someone Monk presumed to be Atlas. The muscular figure squatted and strained while holding up not a globe, but an oil well. They really mixed their metaphors and mythology around here, Monk concluded.

Ponytail, on Monk's side, leaned his large head toward him as he stopped at the closed gate. "Can I help you, my man?" He said it like he was used to turning away the unwanted and unwhite several times a day.

"Ivan Monk to see Maxfield O'Day."

Ponytail looked at Crewcut, a smirk stretching his thin lips. "Sure," he said. He arched back into the booth on the stool he sat on and punched something up on a monitor. He looked at it for a few beats, then turned back. "Go on in, Mr. Monk." He turned a knob on a console and the gate swung upward. Monk drove on up.

The asphalt drive, lined on either side by a low strip of flagstone, had large palm trees running parallel to it beyond the wall. At the end of the winding path, seemingly in another time zone—or was that another time?—was the Odin Club.

It was a multitiered structure, with several of its levels jutting into a mountain side. All white, sun-washed walls, pillars, tile roofs, maplewood shutters, chrome railing and cut glass panes in a mix-mash of Greco-Roman, Beaux Arts and Streamline zip. The total of it overwhelming and harkening back to the Roaring '20s when it was built with robber baron money. An ostentatious den for high society parties and some dirty, low-down sex with well-endowed chorus girls.

Monk went up the slab of steps to the entrance of dual oak doors embedded with wrought iron rings. He yanked on one of the doors, and was surprised to find it opened effortlessly. It was guided by pneumatic cylinders on the top and bottom. He stepped into the foyer with its stone composition floor. Instantly, a smooth-haired maitre d' appeared beside him.

"This way, Mr. Monk."

Monk followed the spry gent into a dining room of forest green carpeting, oak-paneled walls, and indirect lighting. Old and middle-aged white men, some in suits and some in designer work out togs, inhabited the eating ground of the powerbrokers. These were not the men seen eating in the Polo Lounge or Spago, talking on their cellulars while sending the water back because it didn't have enough sparkle.

No, these men ate bacon and eggs or cereal and half a grapefruit for a light breakfast. They drank their coffee black and strong and wouldn't know cafe au lait if you spilled it on them. Their names rarely surfaced in the pages of *People* or *Los Angeles* magazine, and their faces never graced the cover of *Time*. For they were the scions of Mulholland and Otis, Griffith and O'Melvany. Heirs not to gaudy, transient fortunes of celluloid or software, but the eternal stuff men and women fought and died for the world over. Land and water.

Monk made it to a table by a window where Maxfield O'Day stood to greet him. No one in the room had stopped talking to gape at him or drop food from their mouths. Monk imagined O'Day must have warned them that one of the inner city denizens would be in their midst this morning.

"Glad you could come, Mr. Monk."

"My pleasure," Monk replied.

The two shook hands. As he'd expected, O'Day's grip was firm and he looked you in the eye when he spoke. The attorney was natty in a tan gabardine suit, light blue single-stitched shirt with buttoned-down collar offset by a patterned aquamarine tie. They sat down. The Pacific, silent and purple in the morning light, rolled beyond the large thick-paned window bordered in etched filigree.

A waiter, another older, white-haired, white guy saddled up beside the table. "Coffee?" He stared down the middle of the table, neither at Monk or O'Day.

"Absolutely, Graham. And the breakfast menus, please," O'Day said.

The waiter drifted off. O'Day placed his elbows on the table. "I won't waste your or my time with a lot of useless small talk, Mr. Monk."

"Fine."

O'Day reached into this pocket and withdrew a sealed number-ten envelope. In the corner was the four-color logo of SOMA. He pushed the envelope toward Monk. "There's a check and some information in there."

Monk made no move for the envelope. "What's the job?"

"Finding the killer of Kim Bong-Suh."

The coffee arrived and the waiter left the menus.

Monk mixed in half and half and sugar. He sipped. "I'm sure you know that I already have a client in that matter."

"Nothing precludes you from having another client whose interests converge on a matter. Or, from working more than one case at a time." O'Day examined the menu. "The blueberry pancakes are quite good."

"Just eggs and toast, for me," Monk said to the waiter who'd reappeared.

"The pancakes and a side of bacon," O'Day said.

The waiter went away again, leaving a faint trail of moth-balls.

"Why is SOMA interested in Kim's murder?"

"Business, Mr. Monk. It's important that Save Our Material Assets demonstrate it is a responsible member of the community. And frankly"—the wattage came on in his smile—"we can't get that site going where his body was found."

"The police are holding it up?"

"The FBI. The bastards have managed to slap a federal injunction around the site and my law firm's been going around in circles trying to get it lifted."

"So they and you won't be satisfied until the Kim matter is resolved."

"Yes." O'Day drank his coffee. On his ring finger was a class ring inscribed with something in Latin Monk couldn't make out. He saw Monk staring at it and said, pointing at it. "*Lux Et Veritas.*"

"Light and Truth. Harvard."

"Class of '64. You were probably still on training wheels."

"I still am."

Their food arrived and they ate in silence. Midway through, Monk paused and opened the envelope. Inside was a check for five thousand pretty little green ones and some folded sheets. He unfolded the sheets. A 3x5 photo dropped out. Monk turned it over. On the back, typed on a label, was the name of Conrad James. He turned it over.

Its contrast was terrible and looked to have been shot from another photograph. The photo revealed a vital young Black man in his mid-twenties. James was standing in a park, a beer in one hand, the other around the waist of an unidentified girl. Dressed in jeans and a sweat-stained T-shirt, Conrad

James and his wiry frame and open face was a modern-day Neal Cassidy come to South Central. Monk could see why Karen Jacobs had asked around about him.

On the first page of the typed information the name of Conrad James was listed along with a physical description of the man. There was also his last known address, his social security and driver's license number, and known associates. Among them was an Antoine "Crosshairs" Sawyer, a cousin and reputed leader in the Hauser Avenue Rolling Daltons.

On the second sheet was a description, address and remarks about Sawyer. The last sheet contained information on two others who had worked in Kim's store, James Robinson and Ruben Ursua. Names Monk had received from Karen Jacobs.

"What do you think?" O'Day asked.

Monk refolded the sheets and placed them and the check back into the envelope. "Why isn't there anything in here about Kim?"

"Why should there be? James is the one missing and one of the others who worked in the store, Ursua, has a criminal record. He too seems to be scarce these days as well." Light came through the window and cast half of O'Day's face in an angelic glow.

"Meaning you think both he and James had something to do with Kim's murder?"

"I'm not suggesting any such thing. I'm merely relating the facts as I understand them."

Monk said, "And what do you think is the motive for Kim's murder?"

O'Day wiped a finger across his uncreased brow. "I don't know. He left no will nor seemingly had any assets." O'Day looked away to the ocean then looked back. "Somehow it always seems that money, real or the hint of it, is at the bottom of these things."

"I find it interesting you're willing to pay me for work I'm already doing."

O'Day lifted his cup of coffee. "Let's look at it as a good faith investment on the part of SOMA. It's my opinion as its president that there may be further"—he made circles in the air with his free hand—"bumps in the road to rebuilding. It wouldn't hurt to have someone like you around who may be available as our troubleshooter in these coming months." He lit up his sign of a smile.

"Then this isn't a decision of your board."

"There is a certain amount of discretionary funds I have control over. And of course I will send a memo around to them about this development."

"I'll send over a contract," Monk said, pocketing the envelope. "It'll spell out that if I discover anything that puts me in conflict with my primary client, our deal, and your money, will be returned."

"Fair enough."

They finished their meals and walked to the parking lot together. O'Day stopped at a shiny Lincoln Mark VII. The license plate read NEW DAY. The silver-haired wheeler-dealer stuck out his hand again, and Monk took it.

"I look forward to us keeping in touch. And please let me know if there's anything I can do for you in the course of this investigation," O'Day said.

"There is." Monk took out his notepad and wrote down the name of Jiang Holdings in Stanton, California. He handed the paper to O'Day. "This name has come up a couple of times. The only thing I've turned up on it so far is that it's a mail drop in Orange County. I'm sure your hot shot law clerks can do a more efficient and thorough legal search than I can."

O'Day got into his car. "I'll see what I can find out."

Monk said, "Thank you," and got into his Galaxie. Both vehicles made their way down the expanse of the drive. At the bottom, the exit gate lifted, and the Lincoln pulled off. Quite suddenly the gate descended again. Monk slammed on the brakes, glaring at Crewcut in Cerberus's belly. Nonchalantly, the kid sucked loudly on a lollipop.

Monk put the car in neutral, opened his door, stood up, placing his arm on the hood of the 500. "Is there some problem?"

"Problem?"

Monk engaged the emergency brake and stepped around to the guard booth. "Yes, is there some problem?" He reached into the booth, aiming his hand for the switch to lift the gate. The kid's hand snaked forward and latched onto Monk's wrist. Monk lurched back, taking Crewcut off his stool, breaking the grip on his wrist.

"That's your ass, nigger." The door to the booth came open and he stepped out. He was two inches taller than Monk and looked to be at least ten years younger.

"Your momma's a nigger," Monk growled, moving his body forward. He caught the other one around the waist with his arms, his weight driving the both of them back against the booth.

Crewcut brought a fist down between Monk's shoulder blades. Stars exploded in the corner of his right eye. He grunted in pain but held on. He wrenched to the left, upsetting their balance. They tumbled to the asphalt.

"That's enough," Ponytail said, running over to the two.

Monk's teeth came together sharply as Crewcut socked him hard in the side. He went over on his side and the younger man clambered on top of him.

"Cut it out, Stacy," Ponytail yelled, grabbing at the other's arm.

"Get the fuck off," Stacy hollered back, turning his head slightly. Just then, Monk jabbed upward, into the blonde farmboy's Adam's apple. Stacy's eyes bulged. Involuntarily, his hands clutched at his throat. Monk kneed him in the stomach and he went over.

Monk regained his footing, glaring at the crewcut Stacy. "Get up, so I can put you on the ground again."

Ponytail came between them. "Look mister," he said to Monk. "He's always bullshittin'. He didn't mean anything."

Stacy was on one knee, gaping at the other two. Monk pointed a finger at Crewcut and addressed Ponytail. "I bet Maxfield O'Day would like to know how his guests get treated around here."

"You ain't nothing to Maxfield O'Day except hired back-door help," Crewcut said, rising up.

Monk stepped closer to him. "What's it to you?"

Stacy looked at Monk, then Ponytail. "Sorry Bart," he said to Ponytail. "I didn't mean nothin'."

He started to walk off. Monk got in his way.

"Look man, it was just a joke that got out of hand." He said the words, but Monk heard no sincerity behind them.

Bart put a hand on Monk's shoulder. "Hey, bro, can't we let this slide. You know how it is." He turned his natural blonde head. An emerald Jaguar was stopped behind Monk's car. A heavy set man leaned his jowled face out the window, observing the scene.

Monk glared at Stacy, who glared back. "Yes. I know how it is." He shoved him, waiting for the comeback. None was to be had. Monk got in his car and drove off. It was past the morning rush hour and Monk burned off excess adrenaline by speeding back to Continental Donuts.

The middle knuckles on his right hand were skinned and had started to throb. The second joint on his left index was split open and was swelling. He swabbed Mercurachrome on his abrasions and taped a Band-Aid over the joint. Monk called his office.

"What's shaking?" he said to Delilah after pleasantries.

"Tina Chalmers called."

An electric charge pulsed along Monk's spine. "What did she say?"

"Wouldn't tell me. You're supposed to call her back at two. She'll be out till then."

"Okay. Talk to you later." Two was his appointed time with the task force, something he was desperate to avoid. He locked up his office and went out front. The only customers in the place were two of the regulars playing chess in one of the booths.

"What it is, Lenny?" He patted the man on the shoulder and nodded at the other one. "Hilton."

Lenny Levine was a retired union organizer who, with a fellow Black organizer, led the fight to integrate the docks of San Pedro and Long Beach in the fifties. Branded a communist—he was a "card-carrying," bona fide, hair-shirt-wearing member of the Communist Party-USA in those days—he was driven out of the union under the Tenney Committee, a California version of the federal House Un-American Activities Committee.

"Fine, brother Monk." Levine moved the rook, intently watching the board.

His chess partner sat back, contemplating his next move. Hilton was a mulatto in his late forties. The rumor was that early in life he'd passed for white and had risen to some prominence in a large petrochemical company. That was the most anyone had ever gotten out of him about his past.

"Hawkshaw." Hilton deployed one of his bishops.

Monk went behind the counter where Elrod sat, reading

the latest issue of a rap magazine. The private eye poured himself a cup of coffee and went back around the counter, facing the big man. "How many Rolling Daltons do you know?"

Elrod said, "Been sometime since I hung with that kind'a crowd, chief. Them young bucks a little too fast for my blood."

"Who?"

Big sigh. Moments into molasses. Eventually Elrod put the magazine down and leaned close to Monk. "Why you want'a go fuckin' with them hard-headed rascals?"

Monk told Elrod what he was working on.

"And you aim to find this James?"

"I want to find him before the FBI does. 'Cause when that happens, I'll never get to him."

"Some of them are all right. I've never met the other one you mentioned, Crosshairs, but I heard he's straight enough. A real OG, you know, a serious gangsta' in his day. But I hear he's on with the peace thing now."

"Can you put me in touch with him?"

Elrod puffed his cheeks and blew air out of them. "I suppose so. But you better come strapped. Some of them boys he hangs with ain't wrapped too tight. Truce or no truce."

"So Crosshairs is part of it?"

"Him and a few others are said to be the originators. He grew up in the Imperial Courts housing project, and all of his best boys come from around there."

"Solid." Monk put aside his still full cup. He got off the stool and made for the door. "But don't put yourself in a bind, Elrod. Nice and easy, you know?"

What might have been a smile creased the giant's face. "Always safety first."

Monk waved goodby and got in his car. He drove east on

Vernon until he reached Main then swung south along the boulevard. He arrived at 55th Place, then turned east on it and came to a clapboard house, the last known address for Ruben Ursua. The information O'Day had given him had jibed with what he'd learned from Karen Jacobs.

She'd told him that Ursua had done time in prison, hot car beef, and had worked at the Hi-Life while on parole. According to her, he was moody, distant. He didn't laugh and joke with the others the way employees do. Yesterday, Monk had called around and produced this address, the same one O'Day provided him this morning. He sat parked in front of the house.

It was a modest single-family job with peeling brown paint adorned with steel mesh on the windows and a metal screen on the door. Twin anemic columns sprouted from either side of the porch ending in a dilapidated canopy. A beat-to-hell lounge chair decorated the left side of the cracked porch. Angled across the lawn of dirt, dead grass and the walkway, was a gray-primed '77 Monte Carlo. It was up on floor jacks and the rear wheels and the brake drums were off.

Monk knocked on the door. Presently, he heard it swing inward. A soft rectangle of light shone through the screen. Whoever stood there didn't say a word.

"Is Ruben in?" Monk didn't offer his license.

"No," a woman's tired voice said.

"You expect him later?"

"Shit, I don't know." There was another gap, then, "Nice ride."

"Thanks."

"You a friend of his?" The voice got more animated.

"Friend of a friend."

"Sure you are."

"You betchum Red Rider."

There was a short burst of either contempt or joy. "What you want me to tell him, man?"

"Tell him his friends from the Hi-Life say hi." Monk began to walk away. The screen door opened to reveal a handsome Latina with hard eyes. She couldn't be more than twenty or twenty-one, Monk reasoned.

"You didn't work with him there."

Monk stopped on the steps, looking back. "How do you know that?"

"The car, how you dress." She thrust her head forward as if listening to an invisible voice. "You ain't the heat and you ain't no ex-con. That's the only kind of people Ruben knows."

"I'll keep you guessing for now." Monk got in his car, the woman still looking at him as he drove away along 55th Place. The Galaxie wound north then west, eventually gliding to a stop at the Oki's-Dog fast food stand on Pico and Sycamore.

Pico Boulevard was a sort of Maginot line of the Mid-City area, a buffer of the better-offs against the deprived hordes. South of it, along this stretch, there were the homes and apartments of mostly Black working-class folks. The populace included quite a few young people, and, as fall-out from the Federal cutbacks in social spending during the '80s, several were members of the Rolling Daltons. Not that Monk laid the entire blame for gangsterism at the feet of men like Reagan and Bush. Still, he had to admit that they had set a fine example as the biggest gangbangers of all with their violent escapades in Grenada, Libya, Panama and Iraq—all while the cities went to hell and the young folk emulated their elders.

North of Pico the homes and lawns got a little neater, a bit bigger. The demographics shifted from solely Black to mixtures including whites and Asians. Some green lawns had signs staked into them announcing this or that armed-response security service. Judiciously placed in the corner of some windows were stickers declaring that the house participated in the Police Watch Program or was a member of a particular block club. Which didn't mean these neighborhoods didn't have forays from the residents south of Pico, it just meant they were easier to spot.

East of the Oki's-Dog stand, on the northwest corner of Pico and LaBrea, was the Mexican fast food joint, Lucy's. Every day—and he could see them out there now—brown, Black and white men milled about on the curbs in front of the establishment. They whistled and gestured to the drivers of cars and trucks as they sped by on either thoroughfare. But these fellows were no sellers of crack, or aging chicken-hawks. Their product was indeed their body, but the market they sought was work as day laborers, or handymen, or movers, or painters, or whatever physical task, whatever payment in cash they could scrounge.

Men younger and older than Monk who once upon a time in post-'50s America worked in auto plants, attaching bumpers to Chevys, or steel mills, pouring molten rivers of metal. Maybe they worked the swing shift in the old Goodyear plant on Central turning out mountain-high piles of tires, or ran a drill press in a factory in South Gate. But the '90s and the deindustrialized core had little use for semi-skilled workers, displaced now because the factory relocated to a foreign country to take advantage of a homegrown, exploitable labor force. And even the service sector jobs at McDonald's or the frozen yogurt stand were out of their reach because they just couldn't take orders from guys too young to date their daughters.

Monk sat in the enclosed dining area of Oki's-Dog eating his pastrami sandwich, heavy on the onions and light on the mustard. The stand itself was neutral territory. Gang members, low riders, hip-hoppers and metal heads—there was a recording studio across the street—and beat cops all came to Oki's-Dog for at least a weekly repast. Customers often referred to the stand simply as Oki-Dog. Wilshire Division, where Monk was to be in about an hour, was less than two miles away on Venice.

The customers came to indulge in such fare as the establishment's wondrous heaping plate of fries, the spuds cut into long strips with the skins partially left on and served on a paper plate with a few green chili peppers on the side. Or a triple chili cheeseburger and a giant root beer. Maybe even the signature food item, the cholesterol-laden Oki Dog: two hot dogs swarmed in the secret chili, onions and cheese, and garnished with bacon wrapped in a flour burrito.

Monk ate, ruminating on the case. Two young men in their late teens entered the enclosed area. They were dressed in double-breasted suits of some shiny material and each wore bowlers. Scalp Hunters. They were a minor set as far as gangs like the Daltons, the Swans and the Del Nines were concerned. But they weren't partners to the truce and therefore considered loose cannons by all concerned.

Each one looked warily from side to side. The taller, beefier one's gaze settled on Monk for several seconds. Monk returned it with a baleful expression. Eventually he shifted his attention to the one Monk had noticed sitting in the rear booth. He wore the purple colors of a Dalton and had been intent on the three tacos before him. At least when Monk had last looked at him he had. But Monk was sitting with his back to the Dalton, the Scalp Hunters in front of him, standing near the order counter.

Monk stopped chewing and started calculating. He hadn't brought his gun and the only way out of the dining area, save a stupid stunt like trying to dive through the picture window, was out the open doorway.

"Say homey," the lanky Scalp Hunter began, talking to the other. "You got any money."

The other one, working a toothpick back and forth on the side of his mouth, had his eyes riveted on the back booth. "Naw, sure don't."

The first one patted himself down dramatically. Suddenly he stopped, dove a hand into a pocket, and produced a wad of twenties. "Oh yeah, I forgot about my ho' change." He flashed a twisted smile and turned to place his order with one of the cooks. Toothpick kept looking past Monk.

The Dalton strolled past the Scalp Hunters, holding his plate of tacos in one hand. The other was down at his side. Toothpick stepped into the doorway, blocking the Dalton.

"Why you in such a hurry?" Toothpick said in an unfriendly tone.

"It ain't none of your worry," the Dalton replied.

"Well, we just wanted you all to know the Scalp Hunters is ready to sign up on this truce thang."

"Is that right?" the young Dalton replied skeptically.

Monk continued to chew, listening, rather than heed his good sense and leave.

"That's right," the lanky one said dryly. "But first the Daltons gotta agree to split up they shit."

The Dalton put his plate of food on the table where Monk sat. He folded his arms across his chest and glared at the two. "Just how you mean that, my brother?"

"Well if we gonna be all for one and one for all, then y'all should divide that big money of yours up between all the ones that agree to this truce." He looked at his huskier companion. "That's only fair, right?"

The husky one nodded in agreement. He disposed of his

first toothpick and inserted another one, which he began to suck on with interest.

"And just what big money you talking about?" the Rolling Dalton responded. "A lot of them motherfuckahs still slangin' product ain't down with this truce. The ones that is been puttin' what little money they got toward legitimate shit for their families."

The lanky one grinned and raised his arms skyward in a pantomine of supplication. "Aw, home, we ain't stupid."

"This ain't no scam, fool. We about tryin' to do something for our community. About trying to get jobs for these brothers and sisters out here so they don't have to go knock somebody upside the head. This is a Black thing," he said, his voice rising. "You just about trying to get over," the Dalton said contemptuously to the two. He picked up his plate and started for the door again.

Toothpick feinted with a right and delivered a quick left, sinking it into the solar plexus of the Dalton. He must have been expecting they'd try something because he went with the force of the blow, his tacos spilling bright shards of cheese, tomatoes, and ground beef in a cascade of fast food minutiae. The Dalton's back slammed against the doorjamb and he came up with a foot into the husky one's groin.

The big one wasn't expecting that. He doubled over, holding his crotch. The lanky one's hand jerked into the space between his head and the Dalton's. A seventeen-shot Glock filled his fist and the void.

"Gat him, gat him, cuz," the husky one screamed, fighting for his breath.

A clipped reel, loose on its sprockets, runs in Monk's mind, pictures his eyes see and his mind interprets in a rapid-fire herky-jerky fashion. His brain tells his hand to launch his plate of fries and half-finished root beer toward the Scalp Hunter with the gun. The food explodes around him, but it doesn't knock the pistol from of his grip. Instead, he turns his attention, and the barrel of the gun, on Monk.

Monk hurtles forward on aging legs. Too old, too slow. The sick conclusion he'd be dead by the time he reached the Scalp Hunter. Goddamn. The Dalton tackles the lanky one and they go down. An eternity later, Monk covers that precious distance and plows a straight right into the bridge of the nose on the husky one's face.

"Fuck." Blood gushes from his nose like water from a busted hydrant. The younger man grabs Monk in a bear hug, and they rock back against the shell of the booth. Scuffling with him, Monk hears the stand's owners yelling something about cops and insurance.

The lanky one is on the ground, a welt swelling under his right eye. He gropes for his lost gun. The Dalton scoops it up where it lies under the table. At the same moment, Monk and his opponent tumble over the bench seat, hit the table and fall to the floor, a tangle of arms and flailing legs.

"Who's gonna gat who, motherfuckah?" the Rolling Dalton says, pointing the weapon at his lanky opponent's head.

Monk is aware of this in the background. A jab lands on his jaw and he grunts in pain. The two latch onto each other, then struggle to their feet. Monk spins around, his back to the Dalton and the other Scalp Hunter. The Dalton extends the Glock to the prone figure before him.

The kid he's fighting has raw strength and youth, but his technique is all charge, little deliberation. Monk drops his shoulder, shifts his weight to the balls of his feet and plows his fist into the kid's side, then follows with a flush clip to the side of his face. He goes down and stays there.

"No," Monk shouts, turning his body, breathing heavily through his mouth.

The Dalton laughs harshly and the gun erupts once. Monk watches the shell jacking from the chamber, falling to the floor into the pile of cheese, lettuce and tomato. The inner city salad. The larger Scalp Hunter, spent but looking up, shifts wide-eyed orbs in that direction.

The disjointed film in Monk's mind's eye catches and clicks into place, and the scene holds still before him.

On the floor, the other Scalp Hunter has curled up in the fetal position, a 3D cutout superimposed on a worn tile floor representing a universe of the lost hope of young Black men just like him. Monk looked at the body then looked up. The Dalton stood, hands akimbo, a wicked smile showing off his uneven teeth.

"Pussy." He snarled and kicked at the Scalp Hunter who drew himself up on the ground. A murmur issued from the inert form.

"Where did you shoot him?" Monk said, trying to decipher the Dalton's fierce countenance. Monk noticed the Dalton had two tears tattooed in the corner of his right eye, green and luminous against his dusky skin.

The Rolling Dalton pointed at the floor. A neat hole, singed black around its edges, bore into an area near the top of the young man's bowler which, oddly, had stayed on his head.

"You think I'm gonna ride a beef upstate for a chump like this," the Rolling Dalton spat. Not too far away, the approach of sirens punctuated the air. "I got bigger things to accomplish than dealin' with this bullshit." He wiped the gun clean with his T-shirt and tossed it to Monk. "There you go, hero." He ran out of the dining area and hopped into a '68 lowered Cougar. The twin carbs spat fuel into the engine, and the car flew east on Pico.

Presently, two patrol cars arrived. Two sets of LAPD's

finest tumbled onto the cracked sidewalk at the ready, shot-guns and 9mm automatics bristling. Monk, the gun on the table of the booth, the clip in his pocket, stood with his hands up in plain sight. The lanky Scalp Hunter sat on the floor, his back against the counter. A look of embarrassment and self-contempt contorted his features. The larger one sat in the booth, his ringing head held in his hands.

The cops cuffed everyone and told them they'd sort the story out at Wilshire Station. There they threw them together in a holding cell smelling of stale body odors and old fried chicken. Monk told the uniforms he was supposed to meet with Keys and Seguin. One of the cops went away and came back after a few minutes. They took Monk out of the cell and hustled him into an interrogation room he'd been in before. Only the last time it was to watch his friend the lieutenant go to town on a suspected arsonist and mur-derer.

Monk sat and yawned and watched his hands swell—he'd managed to add to his bruises with another split knuckle on the left hand—for forty-five minutes before the door to the room opened again. A uniformed policewoman stuck her head through the sliver. "You can go home after we get your statement about what happened at Oki-Dog."

"What about Keys?"

"They're busy."

"So am I supposed to come back or what?" he said, irri-tation surfacing in his voice.

She lifted a shoulder. "Give your statement to the desk sergeant." She went away, leaving the door ajar.

Monk did so and went home, tired, pissed and wrung-out. He and Jill were supposed to go out but he convinced her to come over to watch a rented video instead. Before she arrived, Monk soaked in the tub, then plunged his hands into a pail of hot water and Epsom salts. His entire upper body was one big ache.

"What the hell happened to you?" Kodama asked, taking off her jacket and heels after entering the apartment.

Monk sat in his wing chair, staring at nothing, thinking of everything, the plastic bucket of Epsom salts by his feet. Toweling his hands dry, he related his day, blow by literal blow. Afterward he said, "And what's happening in the world of adjudication, baby?"

"Compared to kicking the ass of half of LA's population, nothing, dear." They sat side by side on the batik-covered couch. "Just the usual sentencing of some poor kid for holding up some other poor working stiff in a 7-Eleven parking lot."

Monk rubbed her knee. "Did you bury him under the jail, baby?"

"Shit. The governor's cutting the hell out of the budget. These kids who should be going to youth camps where they can at least get some counseling, wind up being sent into prisons with hardcore bastards who only abuse and maim their minds and bodies until they can't help but be a stone gangster."

"Oh you card-carrying, ACLU-supportin', family-value-destroying, faggot-loving liberal." Monk shook his head in mock disapproval. "What happened to the kid?"

Jill took a sip of the tea he'd brewed for them. "I remaindered him to Chino over the objections of the prosecutor, a stiff prick asshole who wants to be the next DA."

"What about you?"

"Don't start that."

"Look Jill, you're high profile. A reasonably young—"

She glared at him.

"Asian woman jurist who's been on the cover of national

magazines and written articles for *The Nation* and *Newsweek* magazine."

Jill clasped her hands together and looked heavenward. "Born in a log cabin, studied her law books by candlelight."

"Who fights the good fight from the bench. The same bench that sent her parents to the concentration camps."

"Yeah, yeah." Jill got up and turned on the TV. She got the tape Monk had rented, a comedy about a white CEO who wakes one morning to discover he has become a Black welfare mother of four children. It grossed over one hundred and fifty million at the box office. Jill assessed the dubious fare in her hands. "At least it's not *Point Blank, The Glass Key*—

"The second version," Monk amended.

"*The Naked Kiss, Kiss Me Deadly*, or those god awful Matt Helm films with Dean Martin. Or any of the other countless crime films you and Dexter have seen at least ten times."

Monk drank his tea in silence. Jill crouched down in front of the set, slipping the tape into the VCR on the shelf below it. She was about to click the unit on when a burst of white light exploded in an aura around her head. She moved out of the way and Monk leaned forward.

Kelly Drier, the idiot-savant of yellow journalism emerged from the glare into the blare playing on the screen. He looked properly haggard. His collar hung loose, and a day's growth of stubble dotted his chin. Monk was willing to bet he'd had the makeup department add that touch.

The bright light receded as the camera pulled back. In reality a series of flares burned on a bare patch of ground. And Monk could make out men clad in black overalls dashing about, carrying semi-automatic rifles, while the intense beams from helicopters stabbed the ground in crisscross patterns.

"We are at an apartment complex in southeast Los Angeles," Drier intoned in his best imitation of a newsman. "The police and FBI, operating on a tip, are here to capture one Antoine 'Crosshairs' Sawyer. A known gang leader, and a man said to have information on the death of Kim Bong-Suh."

Jill sat next to Monk and they watched the cops and feds—on the backs of the overalls in big block white letters it either read LAPD or FBI—scramble around on the courtyard and upper deck of the apartment house, the camera a jittery recorder of their mission of search and seizure. Black men, women and children stood frozen next to the baked stucco walls of the complex, Edward Hopper renditions writ large in the grim fresco of urban drama.

"I believe," Drier whispered, as if somehow by talking in a normal voice he'd disrupt the organized confusion, "if you point your camera that way, José, we'll see the cops make an arrest."

The invisible camera operator did so and the lens zoomed in on an apartment door in the corner on the second level. The door was caved in and in the dark maw of its interior, lights flickered and anxiety-laced growls of men were heard on live TV. Presently, several men in black overalls emerged. An overhead beam swung into place, affording the camera an illuminated shot of a Black man in his twenties being marched down the stairs in their midst. He was muscular and clad solely in 501 jeans. His hair was done in long corn-rows and a small hoop earring pierced his left lobe.

Drier rushed forward to the bottom of the stairs. "Are you Crosshairs?" he breathed.

Somebody shoved Drier out of the way and the procession moved on. From somewhere else, another figure emerged in front of the camera, blocking the shot. He was a youngish white man of medium build. He wore tortoise-shell glasses, and his hair was slicked back. He adjusted something at one of his wrists, and Monk could see the guy was wearing gold triangular cufflinks.

"Hi," the man said affably into the camera. Then the picture went black.

SEVEN

It was as if he were strapped to a gurney and the tapokata-tapokata machine ran steadily and noisily in a corner. The shadow of the mighty device, backlit against the snowy muslin of a room screen, droned on like a pneumatic race horse, pumping precious body fluids through his failing body. His life-force slipping away like a dirigible yanking free from its tether to sail aloft over a football field where the combatants wore armor the color of fear and the ground was damp from the tears of crushed desires. Monk's eyes snapped open at dawn and didn't close again.

At eight-thirty that morning, Monk and Jill lay propped up in his bed. She read the front page of the morning *Times* and he the Metro section. Neither section made mention of the incident they'd witnessed the night before, happening as it did sometime after the early edition was put to bed.

Nine-twenty arrived, and Monk turned on the radio to one of the local all-news stations. Luis Santillion and Linton Perry were in the middle of a heated discussion on the merits of Perry's continuing campaign of shutting down rebuilding job sites that didn't include African Americans.

"This is where you're in error, Mr. Perry," Santillion said in a forced civility. "You're talking of a South Central that existed twenty years ago. If you were serious about making sure residents in South Central were hired at these sites, you'd be insuring that it was Latino residents too. We are, after all, more than fifty percent of the population now in sections of what had once been an all-Black part of town."

"I've got nothing against Latinos getting their fair share, Mr. Santillion," Perry responded in his modulated tone. "But I am concerned about a potential work force that is suffering unemployment somewhere in the double digits and climbing."

"So am I," Santillion responded testily.

Monk twisted the dial and found Tina Chalmers on another show being interviewed. "Do you think that Antoine Sawyer will be able to get a fair trial in Los Angeles, Councilwoman Chalmers?"

"Your old squeeze, huh?" Kodama said, punching him lightly in the side.

"Jealousy becomes you, dear."

Chalmers was talking. "That's hard to say when it comes to our young Black men entering what passes for the criminal justice system in America."

"Does that mean you advocate amnesty for Crosshairs as some radical elements are calling for?" the anonymous questioner asked.

"No, I don't. Any wrong must be accounted for."

"Tell him, honey," Kodama said.

"But I want to emphasize that like the four cops in Simi Valley, I want Sawyer to have a trial of his peers. I want it proven beyond a reasonable doubt that he did indeed kill Mr. Kim."

Kodama pulled Monk out of the bed, shutting the radio off. She put the Coleman Hawkins LP *The Hawk Flies* on Monk's battered stereo. The wizard of the tenor sax belted out tunes such as "Cocktails for Two" and "Sih-Sah." The classic driving, monster sound that only Hawkins could command shot from Monk's aged speakers true and straight to that part of the brain that dug the sound on the subterranean level where the cool came from.

Hawkins was a jazzman who could consume massive quantities of scotch, fried chicken and chops, and listened at home not to his contemporaries but to wigged-out straights like Verdi and Debussy. But the whiskey did him in as any vice—Monk reflected while holding onto Jill as warm water pelted them as they took a shower together—would get you if you were human and you wished to experience the world. Just as he knew one day he'd catch that bullet in the temple or feel the knife tickle deeper than the third rib.

Leisurely, they toweled one another off and padded, naked, into his living room. They sprawled onto the couch and started reading the paper. Monk read the comics to her, but soon forgot about Charlie Brown's troubles as Kodama's hand fondled his erect penis.

Later, they both dressed. For breakfast, Kodama drove them in her Saab 900 CS to a chichi joint in East Hollywood called the Flaming Parrot. It was where the boys and the girls wore eyeliner and, if you asked nicely, you could get your nipples pierced instead of a second cup of coffee.

It was Kodama's turn to pay after breakfast, and as she did, Monk stepped outside to the sidewalk. He leaned against the building, working his mouth with a toothpick, casually taking in the sights.

A little sensation touched his nerves, and something whispered in a corner of his cerebellum.

Monk jerked his head around, expecting some mugger's attack. But no one made any hostile move toward him. He glared down the block in both directions, and across the street. Only the heady mix of a bright day in the lower end of Hollywood assailed his senses.

Funky secondhand stores abutted hardware and electronic outlets as gay men walked hand in hand along the thorough-fare past heavy-thighed Central American women carrying laundry baskets on their heads. Vato Locos prowled in lowered four-door Chevys, and a woman on a Harley with a diamondback sissy bar rolled by.

"Ready," Kodama said, coming up beside him. "What are you looking for?"

"Wha . . . nothing, I guess. Just daydreaming I suppose."

"Why don't we go over to the newsstand on Melrose?"

"Sure, honey."

They got in the Saab and began driving toward Highland along Santa Monica Boulevard. Monk suddenly stopped feeling as if he were watching events from afar and jolted back into the normal space/time continuum.

"That wasn't Crosshairs they captured last night," he announced quietly. "That's what's been in the back of my mind all morning."

"How do you know?" she said in that controlled, yet prob-ing manner of a judge.

Monk stared at her. Kodama slipped on her sunglasses, looking like a spy on holiday. She kept her hidden eyes pointed to the front. Monk said, "Remember I told you that O'Day gave me a description of James and his infamous cousin?"

"Uh-huh."

"Well, it don't match up, baby. The brother they vamped on last night was too buffed to be Crosshairs."

"He could have been working out since the data was gathered."

"Yes, that's so. But Crosshairs Sawyer was shot on the side of his face in '89. A copy of the police report was in the envelope O'Day gave me. His left earlobe was blown clean away."

"And," Kodama added, "the young man on TV last night had an earring in his fully intact left lobe." She adjusted her glasses, then said, "A prosthesis?"

"Nah." Monk looked back through the rear window.

"What is it?"

"Pull over to that pay phone at the Chevron station over there."

"All right."

She pulled the car into the station and parked near the phones. Monk got out and walked over to Kodama's side of the car. The electric window sunk into the body of the thing, and Monk leaned close to her handsome face. He said something to her, and she pulled off the lot, again heading west in the direction of Highland.

Monk watched the broad expanse of Santa Monica east of the station. All sorts of cars went past with all sorts of people at their wheels. He heard the screech of tires and the blaring of horns as Kodama, per their plan, suddenly cut across the pair of double yellow lines of the street and aimed her powerful sports car back toward the station.

"Hey, big boy, want to get lucky?" Kodama said, zooming onto the lot, the passenger door thrown open.

"Punch it, baby." Monk dove in, and the Saab roared east on Santa Monica.

Kodama ducked and dodged around cars until she came to a red light. She grinned widely and said, "Yeah." The Saab kicked out and darted across the intersection as drivers, flowing in the north-south lanes, bleated their horns and stood on their breaks as the judge's car rammed ahead against the red.

Monk looked back through the rear window. A pale blue Le Baron emerged from the cars behind them still waiting for the green. It too made its way across the intersection and began to gain ground on the Saab. Just as suddenly, it slowed up and flowed back into the rest of the traffic. Monk settled into his seat.

"You can slow up, Jill. The experiment is a success. The patient is fucked."

"We were being followed."

"That's why Keys wanted to make sure he'd know where I'd be yesterday at two." Glumly, Monk looked out at the city passing by.

Kodama parked the car at the curb. They exited and walked several feet from it. Kodama looked up into his face, her brows in a deep V. "So what's going on here, Ivan?"

"Keys wanted me in one spot because I'm sure he's had my place bugged, and maybe your pad, and," he pointed at the Saab, "maybe yours and my car, too."

"I'll have the cocksucker's badge."

"This isn't something he's looking to use in court."

Jill removed her glasses. "The Bureau wants to make points since they've come under so much criticism for their involvement in anti-gang operations."

"And they want Conrad James so they can deliver the goods."

Jill sighed. "So what are we going to do?"

Monk stuck his hands in his back pockets and started to walk further away from the car, his nerves screaming to separate themselves from his skin. He looked at people strolling past, and wondered which pair of eyes was a window to a G-man or G-woman's gray soul. He looked up at the facades of buildings, envisioning which one hid the directional mike and the night binoculars.

"They've got so much fancy equipment, it doesn't actually have to be a transmitter inside the house, what with devices that pick up vibrations off of windows and all that kind of shit," Monk muttered.

"Let's not get more paranoid than we have to." Kodama put her arm in the crook of Monk's elbow as they walked. "I think your best move is to act like you know they've been tailing you, but don't suspect that maybe they've got you wired, too."

"You're right. But how in the hell am I going to conduct my business?"

"We better get ahold of Dexter." Kodama guided him to a phone booth. "He's the one with experience in this stuff."

Monk dialed Grant's number to his house in Lake Elsinore. Morricone's score from *The Good, the Bad, and the Ugly* greeted his ears. It quit and Monk said. "Dex, if you're there, pick up." A pause; nothing. "Call me tonight at the Cork." He replaced the receiver very carefully, as if jarring it might set off Pandemonium. He stared at the instrument.

"Hey, you still there?" Kodama placed a hand on his shoulder.

"Take me to my office, will you?"

"That's only going to escalate matters," she said, a disappointed tone to her voice.

Monk smiled weakly. "I think we could safely conclude matters have already escalated. Anyway, Charlton Heston, Ice-T and I think alike on this subject."

Kodama didn't move.

"Jill, we don't have time to argue the issue about the proliferation of guns right now. I've got the feds jumping on my ass and pretty soon probably some Rolling Daltons," he said, remembering the Blazer outside Hi-Life liquors. "And I'm a little too far into this to turn back and go home, telling all the fellas I don't want to play anymore."

She looked away, then looked back. "All right, I guess I can't have you running around unprotected."

He gave her a hug around the shoulders. "Sure you're right."

Kodama drove Monk to his office and waited in the car, as he went up. Presently he returned, carrying a gym bag which he put behind the seat.

"Is ol' Betsy in there?" she said, thumbing at the bag. Kodama pulled away from his office.

"The only name for my gun, is gun," Monk responded, absorbed in working out strategies for the coming days.

"Well, it did belong to your father in the Korean War."

"So I'm attached to it, okay?"

"Okay," Kodama replied tersely.

They drove in silence for awhile until Kodama spoke again. "Where am I going?"

"Let's just do what we were going to do." Monk rubbed her upper thigh as a sign of conciliation.

They went to the newsstand, took a walk along Melrose and got lunch at a barbecue place they both liked in the Crenshaw District. From a pay phone in the restaurant, the two called their answering machines. On Monk's was a message from Tina Chalmers.

"Ivan, I need to talk to you as soon as possible, call me."

He did, but only got her machine at her home. "Tina, it's Monk, I'll be at the Cork later tonight."

"Oh, a little rendezvous with Ms. Chalmers," Jill said.

"Business, baby, business."

"Make sure it ain't monkey business, sport."

They left the eatery and walked toward the car. A silver van with gold rims drove by with the SOMA logo emblazoned on its side.

"Creepy," Jill remarked, eyeing the cruising van. "Like there's been a silent coup, and tomorrow morning we'll have to wear our uniforms to work in the SOMA plant making soma."

"I'm hip. Hey, look at this."

They had stopped in front of a building undergoing some rehab work. There were the ubiquitous plywood boards thrown up around it as a barrier, and posters announcing upcoming movies and record albums had been slavered across the wood. Monk pointed to one about a meeting to take place at an auditorium of a Black-owned insurance company on Western Avenue. It was billed as a meeting of the minds between Linton Perry of Harvesters Unlimited and Luis Santillion of El Major. The event was to happen tonight.

"Meeting of the titanic egos is more like it," Kodama enthused, reading the announcement.

Monk smiled at her and they walked on, holding hands. Monk retrieved his car from home, and they took two cars back to Kodama's house. But they found intimacy impossible to initiate given the possibility of being recorded for the lecherous pleasures of the FBI. Instead, Kodama, an accomplished amateur painter, worked on a piece she was doing in oils.

It depicted two women, one Asian, the other Black, sitting at a diner's counter drinking coffee and rolling dice. The counterman, garbed in a forties-style white apron and three-corner hat, was a dead ringer for the late African liberation leader, Patrice Lumumba. Seen through the diner's window was a street scene of burning oil rigs. Monk always waited until after the paintings were done before he asked her what they meant.

The aroma of drying oil paint, like the smell of fresh

apricots, embraced the study. Monk read more from the book he'd started, *The Closest of Strangers*, the title gaining a new meaning for him. Dusk burgeoned and Monk prepared them a supper of broiled bass, southern dirty rice and sautéed carrots. A pall hung over them as they ate in near silence, looking at their food more than at one another, picking at it and moving it around on their plates.

Afterward, Monk rose and opened the gym bag he'd brought with him. He took out his well-worn shoulder holster and the Springfield Armory issue .45 automatic. Jill watched him in stony silence. He sat at the dining room table, the pistol before him on a sheet of yesterday's newspaper. Next to that he placed the gun kit he'd also brought along.

"Happiness is a warm gun," she said.

Monk didn't respond but disassembled the weapon which had originally belonged to his father, Master Sergeant Josiah Monk. Over the years, the younger Monk had replaced several of the original parts with aftermarket ones to insure continued proper functioning of the 1911-based model. He checked the slide, and the remanufactured stop which made for positive release of the slide and ejection of the magazine. He made sure the Wilson full-length guide with the Dwyer Group Gripper was the one he'd put on, as well as checking the neoprene washer he'd installed to reduce frame battering during firing.

Meticulously he wiped parts and oiled some others. He reassembled the weapon and put on his harness. "Just want to make sure it hadn't been tampered with." The .45 went home into the holster, and Monk shrugged into his loose camel hair sport coat hanging in Kodama's closet. "See you later?"

"You betchum, Red Rider."

He came over to her and they kissed passionately.

Monk drove the Galaxie into the heart of LA, heading for the Cork. Arriving on Western, not too far from the auditorium where the meeting between Perry and Santillion was to take place, he decided to stop there and see what was going on. The parking lot was jammed, and he had to put the car two blocks away and walk back.

Inside the auditorium, the joint was jumping. On the stage was a long folding table with chairs and two microphones. Linton Perry, casually hip in slacks and a muted sport coat sat on one end of the table. On the other was Luis Santillon in a three-piece suit, black shirt and blood-red tie. In between the two sat the moderator, Tina Chalmers.

The theater-style seating of the place was filled to capacity. Men and women, mostly brown and Black with a smattering of Asians, occupied all available seating. Most, Monk judged from their manner of clothing, were blue collar but a few he surmised to be professional types. Interspersed along the sides of the aisles and down into the front were African American and Chicano men who, it appeared, were the security for the event.

Several electronic and print journalists were also present, including Monk's pal, Kelly Drier.

A middle-aged Latino man in a plaid shirt was standing and pointing at the stage, his voice raised several notches above normal. "You say you're for jobs in the community, Mr. Perry. Well, I live in this community twenty years and pay my taxes and my kids go to school with Black kids. They come to our house for dinner some time, and mine go to theirs. So how come you only fight for jobs for Black people when it's brown people living here too?"

Applause and hooting erupted from some of the Latinos

in attendance. The Black security personnel flexed as one. Tina Chalmers's mouth twisted slightly into a wry smile.

Perry pulled one of the microphones close to him.

"Mr. Santillion has told me that when it comes to the concerns of Latinos, El Major is the organization that will take care of that." Perry waited then added, "And that Black people need to step aside since it's the Chicanos who have the numbers in this city." He pushed the microphone back.

Boos and catcalls emanated loudly from many of the Black people in the audience. The Latino sergeants at arms looked at one another and pulled back a step or two from the audience. Santillion, his face a mask of controlled anger, spoke into a mike. "What I've said is that if Black leaders like Mr. Perry insist on treating us as if we are invisible, then we will treat him and the ones associated with him with equal disdain."

"Rather than letting fly with accusations back and forth," Chalmers began, "why don't we try exploring those areas where we have commonality? Surely there's something to be gained in a joint project that involves hiring all unemployed or underemployed residents of a community, be they Black or brown, on some of these SOMA projects."

"And who gets priority?" Santillion demanded.

"We break it down by numbers, Mr. Santillion," Chalmers said, cooly. "There are some areas of this city where it's fifty-fifty, so that would be the hiring ratio."

"And what about Pico-Union which is heavily Latino?" Perry asked.

Chalmers glanced at him sideways. "I think the answer is obvious, Mr. Perry."

Monk was leaning against the back wall and turned his head at the sound of the rear double doors opening. Chung Ju Li, president of the Korean American Merchants Group,

Kenny Yu, and several other Korean Americans strode into the room. They looked around for seats, and finding none available, they too lined up against the back wall. Monk gave Yu a high sign, and he moved near the private eye.

"Mr. Monk, how goes the work?" The young lawyer extended his hand and Monk shook it.

"Progress, Mr. Yu, progress. Would you have time to see me on Monday morning? Say early, around breakfast time?"

"Your office."

"No. How about Maria's Kitchen on La Brea at eight-thirty A.M.?"

"Yes, I know it." Yu focused on Monk. "Why do you want to meet with just me and not Li and some of the others."

Plain-faced, Monk said, "Because I think you'll tell me the truth about Yushin and what it meant to Kim Bong-Suh."

Yu took a breath and was about to say something when shouting voices drew their attention to the front of the auditorium. Perry was standing and pointing toward the rear. He shouted, "Why don't you ask Mr. Li, Ms. Chalmers? Ask Mr. Li about the rumors of bought-up riot-damaged property on the sly and the cheap. That's about real economic displacement."

"The question was about the property you own around town. Like the commercial printing shop down in Compton, Mr. Perry. The shop where you fired two workers for trying to organize a union," Li said, moving down the center aisle. His hands held tight at his sides, his head thrust forward like an attack dog.

Perry shot out of his seat, upending it. "I think you've got a lot of nerve coming here and trying to lay that at my doorstep."

"I came here," Li began, "because I knew you'd use this forum to try and make the Merchants Group look like villains."

"If the shoe fits," Perry said. "Tell them I'm a liar about you funneling some of that seven million in relief money raised in South Korea for the Korean victims here and using it to buy property in South Central and Pico-Union through dummy fronts."

"You're a liar and, I think this is the right expression, a two-faced bastard."

Portions of the crowd reacted visibly.

"He just asked him to call him a liar, the bastard part he could have left out," Monk whispered to himself, pushing away from the wall.

Perry, standing behind the table, was rigid with fury. His voice a whisper of wind across an arctic landscape. "You should be wary of things you say, Mr. Li. Chickens always come home to roost."

Li advanced toward the stage. Several Black people in the crowd were on their feet.

Monk gently but firmly put his hand on his shoulder and spun him around. "My advice would be to consider that you've made your point, and now get the fuck out of here."

The head of the Korean American Merchants Group stared open-mouthed at the private eye. It took him several seconds to recognize Monk. Finally he said, "This is a free country. I can go up there if I want to." He shook loose from Monk's grasp.

Monk looked past him, at Perry up on the stage. Chalmers had her hand on Perry's arm, who now stood in front of the table. A look Monk could only interpret as expectation contoured his smooth face. Over to his left, Monk saw two Asian men stand up. Some of the members of the security duty inched closer to the rows the two men stood in.

"Give it a rest, Mr. Li," Monk said evenly.

"I think you forget who works for whom, Mr. Monk," Li said imperially.

"It hasn't slipped my mind. But I can't very well collect my fee if you wind up in a bed with a tube sticking out of your ass."

An odd grin shaped Li's features. "But it is you blacks who have taught me this lesson. That to get something out of this system, one must make noise and confront those who would deny you." With that bit of social observation, Li swung around and walked stiff-legged up to the stage.

Perry waved the guards aside and Li stepped close to the African American community leader. Chalmers too had come to her feet, standing roughly center and a foot back from the two. She spotted Monk and brightened as he approached. Luis Santillion remained seated, bemusedly gauging the antics of Li and Perry.

Past his shoulder, Monk heard a commotion. He pivoted at the noise. A young Latino man and two young Black men were standing up in their respective rows, yelling incoherently at one another. Some of the security, of both races, moved forward. They kept a cool head and managed to escort the three out of the auditorium. Monk started for the stage again.

Li was standing very close to the taller Perry, his finger wagging vigorously under the other's nose. "You don't know what you're talking about, my friend."

The guards stopped Monk, but withdrew at the urging of Chalmers. He climbed up.

"I'm damn sure not your friend, Mr. Li. And I'm damn sure of what I said."

"Silly rumors," Li responded contemptuously. In a fluid motion belying his age, Li turned, scooped up the mike, and held it close to his face. "What about those workers you fired,

Mr. Perry? You don't believe in fair pay for a fair day's work?" He was a minister exhorting his congregation, swaying his body to the emotional flow of the gathered.

Li turned his body in the direction of Santillion. Clearly enjoying the spotlight.

"And you, Mr. Santillion. What have you to smile about?"

"I don't own any property where I fire the workers," Santillion said.

"Ah," Li began theatrically, "but your organization does have payroll checkoff through the county employee system."

Santillion came alive behind his passive features. "What's your point?"

"I know that you're under investigation by the IRS for possible misuse of some of those funds."

Gasps went up from several people. Li was playing both men like a concertmaster. Monk was interested in where he got his information.

"How did you know that?"

Coyly, Li said, "I read a lot."

A large middle-aged Black woman rose from the assembled masses, adorned in a shapeless black dress of some dull, light-absorbing material. Cylindrical, muscular arms complemented her robust frame. She pointed one of the meathook appendages straight out. The index finger that extended from it was composed of misshapen knotted joints. This was a woman who had worked hard all her life, and only thankless toil would follow her to the grave. She had the attention of everyone.

"I can't speak to the business of the Korean gentleman or the Spanish fellow," she rumbled. "But I knows something about Mr. Perry. I been watching him since he came on the scene after the Watts riots in '65. Just a teenager then, but already a firebrand."

A couple of older Black women shook their heads in affirmation. Church was in session. Monk moved closer to Chalmers.

"What I'd like to know," the woman went on, "is since the Harvesters been goin' since the late seventies, how come since all that government money and charity money y'all get, you ain't never done no training in the community."

"We have several job programs that we administer, ma'am," Perry said.

"No. I meant training Black people to be a leader like you, Mr. Perry. Training some of these young mens and women we got to build their thing up, do for their neighborhood. Why you got to be the one always in front when the cameras go off? Why you got to be the one shaking the mayor's hand or O'Day's hand in the newspaper?"

Amens floated up to the ceiling. Li, recognizing the momentum was no longer his to control, graciously handed the microphone to Perry. Monk took Chalmers by the arm and guided her to the rear of the stage.

"Is this why you were trying to get ahold of me?"

"Not exactly," she said. "By the way, what was that about meeting you at the Cork? You know it changed names when the new owners bought it."

"I know."

She frowned at him but Monk didn't elaborate.

Forty minutes later, the meeting broke up and people filed out. The woman's comment and Perry's rejoinder to it had diffused much of the tension building between the three principals, the focus having shifted onto Perry and his justifying his life as a community activist. Li had quietly slipped out, and Santillion had contented himself with a mini-meeting of his own on the side of the auditorium with several of his constituents.

On his way out with Chalmers, the head of El Major pulled alongside Monk.

"I have some information you might find useful," he said in a conspiratorial tone.

"This is the first case I've ever had where people are tripping over themselves to help me."

"Well if you don't want it."

"No, no. I do."

"Good. Call me Monday." He drifted back to his crowd.

Monk and Chalmers drove over to the Satellite bar on Adams in separate cars. Years ago, when Monk had been a two-fisted bounty hunter, full of himself and playing out some character from a blaxploitation flick starring Fred Williamson, the Cork had been his hangout.

And it was a dive right out of a Chester Himes novel. Miller beer and Crown Royal scotch offered in front, a crap game on Tuesday and a three-dollar-raise poker game on Fridays in the back. Prostitutes with trowled-on eyeliner and teeth so brown they looked wooden prowled the bar while a couple of LAPD vice cops were paid to hassle other establishments unwilling or unable to pay the Cork's freight. Even freebasing made the scene in the back room of the Cork at its nadir.

Monk got his messages there, once in a while drank his breakfast there, and on more than one occasion after closing time, did the do with a good-looking young lady on the smooth felt of the bar's pool table. And if hazy memory served, Tina Chalmers was one such participant. Oh yes, in those days Ivan Monk was going to score some long green by tracking down America's most vicious and retire before thirty to Martinique.

But that was before Monk began thinking about what made a fifteen-year-old stab his father and run away from home, or a forty-year-old wife shoot her husband in the groin.

Actions and motivations, the past, and the things one did to
determine their future began to gnaw at his conscience.

Sometimes you had to peer behind the words on paper,
you had to listen to the chased and not a grinding bureaucracy plodding away on entropy. But that revelation was late
in coming to him, before he dropped the business end of a
hogleg on a seventeen-year-old who'd just stuck a shiv in
him. Before those young eyes opened wide knowing the
crush of fate was about to close them forever. Or maybe that
is when it occurred to him.

Monk escaped to the sea to unravel the Sphinx his own
life had become to him. Yet the haunt of those young eyes,
forever sealed against the light, would always revisit him.

They arrived at the Satellite, the renamed Cork. The
previous proprietor, one Samuel "Juke" Nunn, had been
found with a Macintosh knife buried to its hilt in the back
of his neck, his body laid out across the cracked and missing
tiles of the women's restroom. The new owners stopped the
graft to the vice squad boys and sent the hoes packing.
The crap game floated to other environs, and so too the
practitioners. The bar wasn't exactly a family place, but its
iniquity was mostly confined to the pedestrian these days.

"Incredible," Chalmers said upon hearing Monk's suspi-
cions about the FBI crawling into bed with him.

"So that's why I was cryptic in my call." They stood at the
bar and Monk said hello to Channa, the co-owner/bartender
with the masters degree in engineering.

"Hi, Monk, Tina," she said amiably. "I thought you might
be in tonight." She reached below the bar and produced an
index card. She handed it to Monk.

On it, printed in uniform capital letters was a note from
Grant. It read ON THE YUSHIN TRAIL, CAN'T MAKE IT
TONIGHT, DEX. "When did he call, Channa?"

"It was on the answering machine when I opened up this afternoon. But the call had to have come in sometime between two this morning and then." She handed them their order, and Chalmers and Monk took a seat in a booth. Monk placed the index card on the table between them.

Chalmers tapped the card. "Do you know what Yushin means?"

"Jill told me it's from a Chinese word meaning restoration. And apparently in the context of Japanese history, the Yushin period signaled the beginning of their military and industrial expansion in the eighteen hundreds."

"And Pak Chung Hee, who bought his third term as President of the Republic of Korea in '71 with money from Gulf Oil and Japanese industrial giants, used it to describe his suspension of democracy and cracking down on political and labor organizations."

"How the hell do you know all that?" Monk said.

"My district is changing, Ivan. More influx of Korean businesses, and I don't mean just mom-and-pop stuff. Things like shopping plazas and large supermarkets that only cater to a Korean clientele. Where there's money and influence, there's bound to be some right-wing politicos manipulating it. Shit I need to be aware of."

"Does this have something to do with why you called me."

"Could be. I called you because I heard from Ray."

"What made him surface?"

Tina Chalmers tilted her head back, flaring her dreadlocks. Monk took it all in.

"He wanted some money."

"That's not new with him."

"He wanted reward money from the City Council. He says he knows where to find Crosshairs Sawyer."

EIGHT

Kenny Yu was five minutes early for their breakfast meeting at Maria's Kitchen on Monday morning. He was dressed in a somber Perry Ellis suit, a button-down oxford cloth shirt and a paisley tie. He carried an attache case with a scuffed finish and placed it at the foot of his chair when he sat down at the table.

"Are you familiar with what Yushin means, Mr. Monk?" Yu said, after they had ordered their breakfast.

Monk told him what he knew and added, "I'm much more interested in what it meant to Kim Bong-Suh. Was he involved in a political organization in South Korea?"

Yu arched an eyebrow. "I don't know. My involvement with the Merchants Group is not what you'd call"—he rotated a hand in the air, conjuring up the word—"deep."

"Why are you a part of it?"

"Because it makes sense politically. As you may know, my organization, the Korean Urban Council, has taken public stands against some of the more reactionary positions of the KAMG."

"You think you can change the Merchants Group's perspective?"

"Provide an alternative viewpoint at times. As Rodney

King said in the wake of 4/29, 'We're all stuck here for a while.' So we either try to build it up as one, or LA might make Sarajevo look like a rehearsal."

Their food and coffee came. "Why wasn't Kim a member of the Merchants Group?" Monk asked.

"The way I understand it," Kenny Yu said over a mouthful of eggs, "is that early on he was, but gradually he came to fewer meetings, until finally they expelled him."

"Any reasons given for why Kim didn't come around."

"Like I said, it was before my time. Contrary to popular belief, Koreans can have sharp differences of opinions like anyone else. And there's plenty of chances of that in the Merchants Group"

"Yet you're a member."

"It's only when I and some of my comrades from college and law school started the KUC that the elders took attention of us."

"Particularly since you began to get better press than them."

"Uh-huh."

"Who are the big players in the Merchants Group?"

Kenny Yu swallowed a dollop of coffee and wiped his mouth with a napkin. "Li you know."

"Aside from being the president of the Merchants Group, what does he do?"

"Business ventures, import, export, has a little money in property and a couple of car dealerships."

"Where'd the money come from?"

"You'd have to ask brother Li about that," he said wryly. "Though I have heard his family had it back in the old country. Heavy industry or something like that."

"Okay. Who else?"

"Park Hangyoung owns property big-time. The office

building where the Merchants Group is, for instance. He was one of the developers of the Western Gardens Plaza, and has some land out in Orange County."

"In the name of Jiang Holdings."

Yu looked at the ceiling then at Monk. "It sounds familiar, but honestly, I'm not sure."

"Are either of these two on the board of Ginwah Bank?"

"Both of them are as well as John Hong."

"And he's in the Merchants Group?"

"Yes, he'd taught math on the university level in South Korea and does some consulting work here and some teaching in junior colleges."

"I see."

"Possibly you don't. It's not some grand conspiracy for three middle-aged, connected men, men who know how to work the American system, to be on boards where those abilities can come in handy."

"Capitalists are capitalists after all."

Yu lifted his coffee cup and tipped it in Monk's direction.

The meal ended, Monk paid the tab, thanked Kenny Yu for his time, and went to his office.

"Hey, you look tired." Delilah stood at the coffee machine pouring herself a cup. She wore acid-washed denims so tight Monk swore they were tattooed on.

"You ain't never lied. Dexter didn't call, did he?" Involuntarily, Monk found himself twitching his head, as if the FBI's listening device would suddenly appear at the sound of the secret word.

"Somebody called the machine around three-thirty this morning. There was some beep, beeps, you know like punching the star button repeatedly, then—"

"Give it to me," Monk shouted, cutting her off.

"Sure." Delilah removed the standard cassette from the

answering machine and Monk ran down to his car. For the better part of Sunday, he and Jill had inspected the Galaxie searching for a bug. They found nothing, which didn't totally relieve Monk's anxiety, but it was as safe a haven as he could manage under the circumstances.

Monk turned on the car's ignition and placed the tape into the radio's cassette player. He heard the phone coming online and then a series of long and short beeps. It wasn't Morse Code, which he'd learned in the Merchant Marines, but they were deliberate bursts. Therefore, he knew it was from Grant. His message about the Cork had put Grant on guard. That, and probably what he'd learned about the past of Kim Bong-Suh.

Monk replayed the beeps. Again, and again. Whatever it meant, it wasn't coming to him. He was thinking too hard about it, wanting to solve it right then and there. He played the tape once again. But this time to put it in his brain, let it gestate there and hopefully the answer would sprout in the relaxed soil of his mind.

He turned off the power and got out of the car and returned to his office, the tape in his jacket pocket.

He called O'Day's office but was told he was out of town. He then dialed Luis Santillion, but he was out and not expected back until the afternoon. He got Elrod on the phone.

"Any luck on what we talked about?"

"A little something. Matter of fact—"

Monk stopped him. "Right on. I'll be over there around two. We'll talk about it then."

"Sure, boss." The big man severed the line.

Monk went out into the rotunda. He got another tape from a desk drawer and inserted it into the answering machine. He could feel Delilah's curiosity burning into him. "I'm sorry about yelling at you, D."

She cocked her head. "It goes with the job."

"I've got some stuff to do away from the office, and I'll probably be in after three if anyone calls."

"All right," she said, still waiting for an answer.

Monk only gave her an enigmatic look and turned at the sound of the door to the reception area opening. Marasco Seguin and another cop, a large brother he didn't know, entered.

Seguin said hi to Delilah, then to Monk. "They want to see you over at the station, right away, home."

Monk looked at his friend. "I'm kind'a busy right now, Marasco. You're the ones that stood up our last date."

The other cop slid his hooded eyes over Monk, lingered on Delilah, then swept the room. Effortlessly, he dipped a large hand into an inside pocket and produced a summons. He put it on the desk, stood back, and winked at Monk. He clasped his hands in front of his body. A copper Golem in a business suit.

Seguin looked at Monk. "This isn't just about what the Bureau wants, Ivan. The captain wants you brought in to answer some questions about the death of Stacy Grimes."

"Who?" Monk said sincerely.

"Crew cut blonde gentleman who worked as a security guard at the Odin Club. A young fella you had an altercation with last week," the other cop said quietly.

Monk felt the air rush into his open mouth.

HE SAT at the table in the room he'd waited vainly in last Friday. Seguin and the Black cop, Roberts, sat opposite him. FBI agents Keys, who Monk recognized as the one who'd blacked out the camera at the televised bust, and Diaz leaned against the wall on either side of the door. Each had their hands buried in their pockets and impassively assessed

Monk. White-shirted bookends looking to put the squeeze on him, he reasoned pragmatically.

"What was the fight about?" Roberts asked casually. Those sleepy eyes of his and easy-going manner didn't sand-bag Monk. He knew it was all an act, that underneath it lay a taut intelligence waiting to crush you in its coils.

"As I've already told you several times, Detective Roberts, after my meeting with Maxfield O'Day, I went to raise the gate which Mr. Grimes deliberately brought down in front of me, and subsequently, he and I got into a fight."

"But you're the one that tackled him," Diaz contributed.

Who the fuck was in charge here? Monk wanted to know. "He called me the big N, Agent Diaz. And from his hostile body language, it was apparent Grimes intended bodily harm against me."

"You don't know that for a fact," Keys declared.

"I know that from experience, Agent Keys."

"Bart Samuels says the gate was up and you stopped your car, rushed out of it, then pulled Grimes out of his booth, attacking him for no reason," Roberts said.

"Samuels is lying. You know what size Grimes was, does it look like I could just pull him out of the booth? And if it did happen like that, why didn't Grimes press charges?"

"Maybe he was scared you'd kill him," Roberts offered.

"Why? What's my motivation for killing a perfect stranger?"

"In addition to his duties at the Odin Club, Grimes did freelance strong arm stuff. Could be you two crossed paths and you had an old score to settle," Keys emphasized.

"Could be my sister's got wheels, you know what I'm saying."

They all gave him the universal I've-heard-it-all-before bored-cop look.

"For whom did Grimes do some of his work?" Monk asked.

"You're here to answer our questions, Mr. Monk," Keys retorted, straightening up from the wall and folding his arms across his lean body.

"Can you establish your whereabouts for last night?" Roberts said, shifting his powerful frame uncomfortably on the plastic chair.

"For what hours, and where was he killed?"

A perturbed look made a fleeting impression on Roberts's face. Legally, he had to tell Monk. "Around eleven-thirty last night. Grimes was killed in his apartment in Hermosa Beach."

"Yes."

"Judge Kodama," Keys said.

"That's right," Monk replied. It galled him that his life was a file on this bastard's desk, but what were the lives of others he too had compiled information on? Fuck it. Monk wished he had a file on Keys.

"She'll swear to that?" Diaz said skeptically.

"What do you think?"

"You tell me, champ," Diaz replied, coming off the wall and walking half the distance to the table.

Monk sat and said nothing.

The phone rang in the corner. Roberts ambled over to it and picked up the receiver. He listened for a moment, said something, then hung up. "That was Monk's lawyer, Judge Kodama. There's an electronic writ on the way releasing Monk." Roberts came back to his seat. "Solid chick to have around, bro." He winked at Monk again.

Monk realized that everyone in the room knew that sitting judges could not, ethically speaking, represent clients. He also figured they wouldn't push it, not at this stage, anyway.

"The writ only applies to the subject of the murder investigation," Keys began. "The task force still has questions concerning what you know or don't know about the whereabouts of Crosshairs Sawyer."

"I have another game we can play, Agent Keys." Monk sat up straight in his chair. "Why don't you tell me why it was the task force that arrested me on what would appear to be an unrelated murder charge? No, wait, I'll tell you. I'm betting because the expired Mr. Grimes is another piece in the puzzle."

"You're in no position to be flip," Keys said irritably.

"I'll tell you what I'm in a position to do, Agent Keys. I'm in a position to tell you that Grimes was probably found with at least one, if not more, .32-caliber screw-turn brass bullets pumped into the back of his skull."

Keys tugged on a cufflink. His eyes, clear and narrow behind the thin lenses of his glasses, transfixed themselves on Monk. Roberts nodded slightly and Seguin smiled. Diaz looked beside himself.

Diaz leaned on the table, pushing his face toward Monk. "And just how would you have knowledge of that?"

"It's called deduction, Agent Diaz. That's how Kim Bong-Suh was murdered. 'Course maybe you overslept the day when they had that lesson at the Academy."

Roberts snorted. Diaz fumed. Monk sat back in the chair and crossed his legs. Keys again leaned against the wall. Diaz returned to his position midway between the table and the wall. He took out a stick of gum and eased it into his mouth. A puff adder devouring its prey.

"What do you know about the whereabouts of Sawyer?" Keys said.

Unwaveringly, Monk said, "Nothing."

"It's a federal offense to lie to a member of the Bureau,"

Diaz offered, meticulously chewing his gum. "Not to mention the possibility of an obstruction of justice charge." He turned sideways, chewing, and staring at the wall.

"If you can prove different, oh excuse me, if you can prove legally that you know different," Monk emphasized, "do it." He stood up and started for the door. Keys opened it for him.

"This isn't our last visit, slick," the bespectacled agent said. He tilted his head in mock deference to Monk.

"I'm counting the hours until our next encounter." Monk stepped out into the hall. The door closed at his back. And the chill that fluttered along his neck wasn't from its wind.

NINE

Monk got over to his donut shop after three. Entering the place, he saw Abe Carson perched at the counter. The tall carpenter methodically stirred a cup of coffee, lost in his thoughts. He turned at the approach of Monk.

"What's going on?" he said.

"The usual, Abe. Elrod around?"

"He wasn't here when I got here." Carson pointed a lengthy digit toward the back. "That kid, Lonny, is here though."

Lonny was a member of a rap group called The Exiles, and they played rave scenes and underground clubs around town waiting to be discovered. To make ends meet, he worked at the donut shop part-time. "Okay." Monk disappeared into his office and called Elrod's home, an apartment over on Denker. There was no answer. Monk returned to the front.

Lonny was waiting on a customer and Abe now sipped the coffee in his slow, precise way.

"What up, chief?" Lonny drawled, handing two jelly donuts to the customer. He was dressed in baggy print shorts, a Cross Colours oversize T, and a Raiders cap backwards on his shaved scalp. A club-worn pair of Doc Marten boots rounded out his attire.

They shook the soul handshake and Monk said, "Do you know where Elrod went?"

"He told me it had something to do with what you'd asked him to check on. He said he'd call you tonight."

The last thing Monk wanted was Elrod calling to tell him where to find Crosshairs with Keys listening in. Monk hurried toward the rear. "If he comes back, tell him I'll call him."

"Solid, Ted, see you later, Fred."

Monk went by Elrod's place and left a note explaining that if he called him later, make it seem as if he'd rung up about something else. Realizing it was past four, Monk drove to the address he'd been given for James Robinson, another ex-employee of the Hi-Life liquor store. The information O'Day had supplied stated that Robinson got off work at three-fifteen in the afternoon and got home around four. Unlike Karen Jacobs and Conrad James who were in their twenties, or even Ursua who was in his thirties, Robinson was listed as fifty-two. And he lived with his mother.

The house was a neat and trim Spanish-Mediterranean located close to Manchester and 10th Avenue. The lawn had been cut within the last week, and the hedges that surrounded the home were shaped into organic green rectangles. Monk walked up to a road-weary '73 Olds Cutlass with mismatched tires in the driveway. He felt the hood, it was still warm. He walked to the door and knocked. There was no answer, and he knocked again.

A surly "yeah" leapt from the other side.

"Mr. Robinson?"

The same "Yeah" repeated.

Monk said who he was and what he wanted.

"What the fuck do I care about that dead Korean?" came the reply through the door.

"Look man," Monk said to the door. "I'm not going to take much of your time, I just want to ask a few questions."

"Ain't nothin' I can tell you 'bout that Korean mess."

"You talk to me or you talk to the cops," Monk bluffed.

"Shit." A beat, then the door swung inward. The man on the other side of it was over six feet tall, about Monk's color, and carried a pot belly topped with a sunken chest. He wore faded Levi's and an athletic shirt with a purplish stain over his right breast. His feet were encased in dirty white socks, and his left hand, the right was still on the knob, held a red plastic tumbler that clinked with ice.

"Goddamn," Robinson said. "They make Black private motherfuckin' dicks like Shaft an' shit?"

Monk showed him the proof and entered uninvited. The door led directly into the living room. The rug was of the industrial variety and needed a shampooing. The furniture did not match Robinson's personality. Bright flower-print fabric exploded on all the pieces, and everything was preserved in plastic. Robinson took a seat in a low-slung upholstered chair, his leg draped over one of the arms. The front door stood open.

Monk stood in front of the other man. "I've talked with Karen Jacobs about the time she used to work at the Hi-Life."

"That uptight bitch." Robinson took a swig of his drink, which Monk could tell was booze from its odor.

"You ask her out, is that it, Mr. Robinson?"

A baleful eye peered at Monk over the rim of the cup. "You here to ask about Kim, or my love life?" he said, lowering the tumbler.

Monk swallowed a witty comeback. "I'm sorry, that's none of my business."

"Fuckin' right it ain't."

Monk sat on the couch. Plastic crinkled like dry cereal

giving in to the weight of his body. "Is there anything you can tell me about Kim that might be of interest?"

Robinson farted and didn't try to hide it. "Now what the fuck do you think, home stump? I worked there, I went home. Me and Kim didn't get all buddy-buddy like James and him. Shit, he's the one you should be askin.'"

"Do you know where he might be?"

"Fuck no." He took another pull on his drink.

"Son?"

Monk and Robinson turned at the new sound. An elderly woman, wrapped in a thick shawl, rolled into the dining room. An archway separated it from the front room. She was in a wheelchair, and her hands, younger looking than the rest of her, gripped the rubber rimmed wheels. "Son," she repeated, "are you going to get that gate fixed tonight? Those dogs are getting into my carnations, you know." She jabbed a finger at Monk. "I don't have time for your no account friends dropping by when you got work to do."

Robinson pushed the air in front of him with a palm. "I'll get to it, Mom."

"Tonight," she intoned.

"Tonight," he sighed.

Robinson's mother wheeled away. He rubbed his face and stared into his cup.

Monk said, "My mom gets on my nerves too sometimes."

"Is that right?" He emptied the tumbler.

"Sorry to take up your time." Monk rose.

"Say man, how much you makin' on this? I know from the papers that them Korean grocers are paying you plenty, huh?"

"They're paying just fine."

"Well," he said, rubbing his jaw. "I might have something you can use if you make it worth my while."

Monk had lost interest in anything Mr. Robinson or his

sad neighborhood of a disposition had to offer. "Write me a letter."

"This is for real, man. This is something I saw about a month after the riots."

Doubtful, Monk shot back, "What did you see?"

Robinson snaked a palm toward Monk. He put down the tumbler, and tapped it with his other hand.

Monk's eyes narrowed, but he produced a twenty. He handed it across.

The palm stayed open. Another twenty was laid down with its cousin. They traveled into the back pocket of the Levi's. "'Bout a month after the niggas and the Mexicans tore up everything, me and my partner O.T. was riding around on Washington, cruising for hoes, stray TVs, and what not." He giggled at the brilliancy of the plan.

"Yes."

"Yeah, so we gets to goin' down Hauser toward Wilshire where there's this club, you know where the old theater used to be."

Impatiently, Monk nodded.

"We passin' by the Hi-Life, and I'm all surprised it's still standing and shit and you know how the parking area is behind it? Well, I see one of them small Caddies parked on the lot."

Monk waited.

"And there's a light on in the rear, where the stock room is. Security screen door to the back cracked wide open."

"And that's all you saw?"

He giggled again, driving a hot spike into Monk's scalp. "I tell O.T. to stop, 'cause I'm thinking it must be Kim Bong-Suh, see?"

"He didn't have a Cadillac."

Robinson gave Monk a look as if he were a simpleton.

"Man, all them Koreans got long green. Kim Bong-Suh driving that poor-assed Jap car like all them motherfuckahs do in the 'hood trying to hide they money and shit. You know they got two, three cars waiting at the crib. Benzs and BMWs." He waved an indignant hand in Monk's direction.

Monk didn't put up an argument to Robinson's racist-tinged logic. He was on a roll, and it would only side-track things.

The other man went on. "I knock on the back door." Robinson pantomimed the action. "I hear scuffling inside. Then this dude peeks out."

"I gather it wasn't Kim Bong-Suh."

"Hell no," Robinson said emphatically. "He's a Oriental though. Ugly motherfuckah, kind'a hunched over too."

"You ain't makin' this up, are you?"

"Square business, bro. The cat's got something wrong with one side of his face, I think. It was dark and only the light behind him was on, so I'm not too sure."

"You said he was hunched over. Was he carrying something?"

"No. But he walked with a stoop, his head sorta' forward like a turkey's or something. And there was at least one other in there, because I heard some movement inside."

"What did he say to you?"

"Son," pealed through the air.

Robinson stood up. "He didn't say shit. He gave me a cold-blooded stare and closed the door and I heard the lock click. Me and O.T. split after that." Robinson walked away, no goodby, not even a burp.

Monk left, closing the door quietly. As he stood on the porch, a black van with darkened windows cruised past. On the side of its sliding door was a large imprint of the SOMA logo. It passed slowly in front of Monk, reached the corner, and drove away.

TEN

The phone rang and Monk picked it up the second time it went off.

"Yo, Chief," Elrod's bass voice said, "my battery went out on me."

"Damn. Where are you?"

"Near the Coliseum, on Menlo and King."

"Hold on, I'm coming." He replaced the handset and went down to his car. Monk fired the Galaxie to life and took the 110 freeway east. Tailing someone was harder on the freeway. Monk got off, took a circuitous route through several neighborhoods, watching for a tail and headed for Elrod's mother's house in the West Adams district.

The note he'd left Elrod earlier in the day had said to say when he called that he'd broken down at the Coliseum, home to college and professional football games. If Keys was listening in, then he'd dispatch someone on a false errand to Exposition Park where the facility built for the '32 Olympics resided. And after more than forty minutes of driving around, Monk was sure he wasn't being followed.

Once upon a time, the big Tudors, Craftsmen and Queen Annes along the palm-tree-rich streets of Harvard Boulevard, Hobart and other byways in the West Adams District had been the homes of Black entertainers. Hattie McDaniel, Ethel Waters and Louise Beavers—so many times denied roles of dignity in make-believe Hollywood, except as wise-cracking maids or swaying in their rocking chairs on the porch waitin' for de Lawd to take them to Heaven—had bought homes here. In the '40s and '50s, West Adams was an enclave of what could then be termed, in revisionist history, a Black pop cultural elite.

Part of the area was known as Sugar Hill, and Saturday night fish fries would bring out the neighborhood. Block parties where the tangy smell of hot sauce dashed liberally on fried catfish seared your taste buds and the night air. Where laughter along with the music of Louie Jordan and Roy Aldridge tickled your ears. And at one such event, before the coming west of the 110 freeway and the leveling of portions of the district, a returned Korean War vet, busting his knuckles in a garage over on Avalon, met a sharp chick named Nona Riles.

Monk remembered his father and his war buddies sitting around the kitchen table over a game of dominoes, taking sips of whiskey and gin, bullshitting about some cracker officer in the war and the times they had over on Sugar Hill.

He pulled to the curb in front of the two-story Queen Anne on LaSalle. Tucking the images in his mind safely away again. He eased out of the Ford and walked along the driveway toward the rear of the house. The backyard was gated by a wrought iron barrier done in a style of twisted bars, the sculpted metal a symbol to Monk of how this case had him feeling. Bruno, the German shepherd watchdog, came to the gate, tail wagging. Monk bent down and petted the muscular flank of the dog through the bars.

"Glad you remembered me, big fella."

"You ain't never lied." Elrod thundered from the dark. His

light-swallowing hand enveloped the padlock on the gate, gave it a pull, and it sprang open.

Monk's eyebrows went up.

"It was already unlocked," the giant said.

Monk stepped through, and Elrod closed the gate. Bruno lapped at their heels as the private eye followed the big man to the garage, where he could see a thin line of light bisecting the middle of the building. They stepped through the open door into the warm glow offered inside. Monk closed the door behind them.

Elrod opened a cooler and pitched a can of Beck's to Monk underhanded. He caught it and sat in one of the broken-down easy chairs. Elrod sank into his. Bruno laid down at his feet. A partially rebuilt flathead Indian motorcycle, circa 1950, occupied a section of the cement floor as well. A roll-away tool box rested near the bike.

"What ya got, home skillet?" Monk took a refreshing pull on the brew.

"I met with a brother I knew from the old days. An OG who's been goin' straight."

"He knows Conrad James?"

Elrod shook his large head slowly in the negative. "He used to run with Crosshairs."

"So what did he say?"

"He called me the day after and told me to get you here tonight. This time."

Monk looked at the garage door. "He's comin' here?"

Both large hands spread themselves in the space between them. "He said he'd send someone."

"Who?"

"Wouldn't tell me."

They were into their second beer, and fiddling with the magneto of the motorcycle when Bruno leapt to his feet, on point. Elrod stepped to the door and opened it. At the gate was the outline of a man of average height and weight. Bruno started to bark and Elrod shushed him. Monk walked over to the still figure.

"I'm the one Elrod was told to expect."

Elrod turned on a floodlight over the garage door.

The man was no kid. Monk judged him to be in his late twenties. He wore a full-length leather coat and a gray homburg with a feather in the band. His face was a stretched oblong turned on its axis, the eyes little yellow oblongs turned the other way. The orbs that floated in them were expressionless, and it seemed to Monk they existed in a world of voided hope.

"Open the gate, please." The voice was reserved, like a preacher at a funeral.

Monk unlocked it with the key Elrod had given him. The man stepped inside the yard, waiting, his hands clasped before him in a solicitous manner. Monk indicated the garage.

"After you," the man said.

Monk grunted and went back inside. Silently, he felt the presence of the other man behind him. The kind of quiet walk a man developed in the joint. Once inside, the man stood with his back to the open doorway, his legs spread apart. Elrod sat down in his chair. Bruno was curled up in the one Monk had been sitting in earlier.

"I'd like you to set up a meeting for me with Crosshairs."

"Why?" the man breathed. He took in the garage without moving his head, allowing his eyes to drift side to side.

He knew why, goddamnit. Monk said, "Because the FBI and the LAPD are kicking in doors and throwing mother-fuckahs down stairs. They've set up their big guns to bring him in. They think he, or with his cousin Conrad James, murdered Kim Bong-Suh."

"Nobody goes to all that trouble when it's a blood who gets it." The visitor's body remained immobile in the doorway, the lips barely parting.

"It's a headline case where you can make a name for yourself." The dour visage of Special Agent Keys popped into his head. "You, me and Elrod, hell even Bruno here"—the dog looked at Monk—"know that ain't right. But that's the way it be, brother. We gotta keep our hand in and hope it don't get chopped off."

"You workin' for them Koreans, though. How I know you see Crosshairs you don't drop a dime on him with them? Or your friend the cop."

Monk reacted with a start.

"Oh yeah, I do my homework."

"Then you know I play it straight."

"What if Crosshairs did it? What if he and Conrad cooled the Korean?" the man in the homburg said.

Monk didn't hesitate. "Then I'll at least know why." He didn't need to add that if they had murdered the shopkeeper, then no doubt he wouldn't be returning from their meeting.

There was no change on the other's face. He stared at Monk for several seconds, then said, "Let's say they didn't do it. What can your sorry Black ass do for the brothers against the cops and the FBI?"

"Look, man, these brothers can't stay underground long enough and run far enough away. They're too hot and the authorities are too eager. If they're innocent, you got my word I won't leave them hanging."

The other man considered it. His old eyes didn't blink. Bruno yawned, and Elrod popped the tab on a third beer. Finally he said, "Maybe you'll hear from me, maybe you won't." He turned to leave.

"Do you know Ray Smith?" Monk said to his back.

What might have been a laugh escaped from the other man. "Sure do." He didn't bother to elaborate as he departed.

Monk shooed Bruno out of the chair and he sat heavily in it.

"What do you think?" he asked Elrod.

"You said all the right shit. I hope you meant it."

"I meant it, I just hope I can deliver if it becomes necessary. Otherwise, losing my license will be the least of my worries." He finished his beer and said goodnight to Elrod. He got home and called Jill.

"Hi."

"Hey, baby, you coming over tonight?" she said.

"I'm too beat."

Silence.

"If we moved in together then we wouldn't always have to go through this," Monk said.

"It's an idea we've talked about." She was using her goddamn judicial tone.

"I'm not trying to box you in, Jill. But I think we've arrived at the stage in our relationship where we need to move off of center."

"I don't know, Ivan."

He felt like pushing it tonight. Working a case like this one, he felt the forward motion, the desire to resolve it, and the mindset carried over to other portions of his life. "Why don't you know? We love each other. People in love have a tendency to want to be together at the end of the day and the beginning of the morning."

"We do, honey."

"I know, but you're the one that's always evasive when we discuss this matter. You know I'm not a possessive man, you can't be worried about not having your independence. It ain't like you're a shrinking violet."

"Ivan, you always want to confront everything immediately, deal with it, and move on to your next problem. Well, our lives aren't like that."

"Is it my income? I know you make more than me even when I have a good year. But I don't care. We can have separate bank accounts."

"See? I'm not going to let you do that. You want to break it down to category A, category B and so on. That way you argue each point like a lawyer rather than address the broader issue."

"And what is the broader issue?" he heard his voice ratcheting up a notch. "You're the one's that's a lawyer."

"Don't yell at me."

"Okay," he said reluctantly. "But will you answer my question?"

"It's not one simple answer. Get some sleep, and we'll talk about this later. I don't want to go into this over the phone."

"Fine."

"Goodnight. I love you."

"So you say."

Monk tossed the handset onto its cradle. He stalked into the kitchen and poured himself a shot of black and red label rum. He drank it down swiftly and instantly regretted it. Intent on his discussion with Jill, he hadn't paid attention to the dull throb working its way into a corner of his brain, a product of the two Beck's he'd had at Elrod's. Now with the potent mixture of the rum hitting his system, the ache was metamorphosing into a laser beam slicing his head into sections.

Monk got undressed to his boxers, brushed his teeth and slipped into bed.

"Women," he grumbled, feeling sorry for himself. He turned off the light on the nightstand and laid awake for the next hour.

ELEVEN

In the morning Monk received a message from one of the
attorneys in Maxfield O'Day's office. O'Day would be in
touch with him on Thursday when he got back to town. No,
they hadn't as yet been able to pierce the paper veil as to
who were the true owners of Jiang Holdings.

He called Luis Santillion, but he was out again. Yes, they'd
told him he'd called the other day, and yes, they'd tell him
he'd called again.

Down at the library, Monk spent some time poring over
phone books covering the cities that made up the greater
Los Angeles area. He found a Bart Samuels in Redondo
Beach, one in Santa Monica and one out in Diamond Bar.
Monk wanted to find out from him if he really did tell the
cops he hadn't seen Grimes bring the gate down on his car.
There was no listing of a residence for Stacy Grimes.

Monk drove out to the address in Santa Monica. It was
on a street south of Pico and east of Lincoln, the more
working-class section of the trendy city by the sea. The
apartment was a rambling two-story complex fenced in by
a water-damaged wooden fence. Monk read the mail boxes
and, in blue-and-white Dynamo lettering, found the listing
for Samuels.

He walked to the apartment and knocked. No response. If it was the right Samuels, he'd be sitting in Cerberus's belly this fine sunny day, working on his tan. Would he come straight home after work? Stop for a drink? Go by the gym and pump some iron? Maybe swing by the old lady's pad and spend the evening with her? Too many variables. Maybe any one or two of those things in combination. And it meant one thing. The number-one pain-in-the-ass part of detective work Monk abided. Stake the fucking place out.

Problem number one was the apartments had a carport off the alley in the rear. But the alley was too conspicuous a spot for Monk to park his Galaxie. Which meant parking in front. Problem number two was Samuels knew his car. Which meant parking far enough away to not be spotted and yet be able to keep an eye on the complex.

Monk left and bought two sandwiches at a stand and returned. He repositioned the car down the block and waited. Early on when he was bounty hunting, he'd ignored advice from Grant and used to bring a large thermos of coffee on stakeouts. So, of course, after downing half of the contents of the container, he'd have to relieve himself.

It was on one such occasion, watching for a bail jumper at his mother's house, that Monk had to leave his car and find a secluded spot to pee. When he got back to his car, he knew the jumper had been and gone because the mother's car was then absent from the driveway.

Monk eased down into the Galaxie's seat. He emptied his mind, concentrating on being at one with his environment. Zen and the art of surveillance. Bullshit. Listening to one of the Governor's speeches was more exciting.

The shadows on the lawns got longer. Teenagers on their way home from school passed by. The loud banter of the young men and women, fueled by raging hormones and the seemingly biological urge to be hip, made Monk wistful for a moment. A sure sign of his advancing years, he realized.

He finished one of the sandwiches, absently considering if he'd developed a flat spot on his butt by sitting on it for so long. The late afternoon came on and the working stiffs began to arrive. A middle-aged woman with a beehive hairdo drove her Ford Escort twice around the spot Monk was parked in. It was obvious that she parked there every day at this hour. The woman glared daggers at Monk, and he smiled at her like an imbecile. She snarled and found another place.

Monk watched several people enter the apartment complex, none of them Bart Samuels. He stretched and checked his watch. Six-forty-five. Waiting until seven, as the light of day started to fail, Monk got out of his car and walked back to the apartment.

He knocked on the apartment door.

"Yes." The man who opened it was slight of build and had a receding hairline.

"Are you Bart Samuels?" Monk said.

"I am. What can I do for you?"

Monk gave him a lame story about investigating an auto accident and looking for the witnesses. He parted with another business card and left. Angry with himself that he'd wasted a day, he drove to the Norm's on Lincoln. Sitting at the counter and waiting for his order, it flashed on Monk how he was going to get something on Stacy Grimes, as well as the correct residence for Bart Samuels.

And it was as easy as going to a baseball game.

THE DODGERS beat the Astros four to two. There were ejections for fighting, and some guy spilled his beer over a woman in a Teamster Local 417 jacket.

Monk wasn't overly fond of baseball—football and

roundball were his favorites—but his nephew, his sister Odessa's son Coleman, loved it to death. There was a shelf in his room lined up with the plastic encased baseball cards of Maury Wills, Hank Aaron, Nolan Ryan, and other stars.

Trophies attesting to Coleman's own prowess in the sport were stacked along another shelf. Atop that shelf was another one that was testament to the teenager's other passion.

Computers. On it were technical manuals, magazines about new and powerful software, books about cyberspace and virtual reality, and other publications intended for the practicing hacker. Which his nephew was, to a degree.

"Did you see that hit Robinson got, Uncle Monk?" Coleman said, his fourteen-year-old voice edging into the baritone it would soon become.

"Yeah." Monk finished his Dodger Dog. "He hasn't lost much since his back surgery."

"Yeah," his nephew agreed.

The crowd started to leave and Monk and his nephew exited the stands to his car. Since it was a weekday, traffic wasn't too bad leaving Dodger Stadium, and Monk took Scott Avenue down to Glendale Boulevard. There he went south and wound his way to 3rd Street and headed west, into the haze of the setting sun.

"What's happening in school?" Monk asked nonchalantly.

Coleman pulled his X cap low on his forehead. "Same ol', same ol'."

"How about a little more elaboration?"

Coleman smiled. "I ain't one of your suspects, you know."

"Every teenager is a suspect."

"That's what the coach says."

"Speaking of which, how does the season look for you guys?"

His nephew proceeded to tell him how his team was

coming together if only the starting pitcher, Martinez, could get his fastball under better control. They traveled south along Western toward Continental Donuts.

They arrived as evening darkened the contours of the city. The plaster donut on the roof of the building looked like the lost wheel of Paul Bunyan's buckboard. Monk cut the motor, and he let them in through the back door.

"What kind of information do you want me to bring up?" Coleman said, sitting down in front of the computer as it warmed up in Monk's room at the donut shop.

"I want whatever I can get on Stacy Grimes and Bart Samuels. Addresses, credit reports, et cetera." He elected not to tell his nephew that Grimes had been murdered. Not that the kid was fragile, he did go to public school in Los Angeles. And certainly he had classmates who had friends that had died by violence, by drugs, or by their own hands.

If anything, Monk was sure Coleman, like his peers, had an almost nihilistic attitude to their coming of age in this town on the edge of the abyss. How else could you psychologically balance dealing with zits on your face and what route to walk to school to avoid a crossfire?

But it was a mixture of family love and a certainty in his being that whatever he could provide in the way of a father figure to the young man—albeit a flawed one, but one that at least was consistent—provided one more rung for one more young Black man in the ladder out of self-destruction.

Coleman's fingers depressed several keys then hit the return bar. "The online service I had you subscribe to has a sub-service called PhoneBank."

"It provides phone numbers?"

"And addresses and something about them sometimes." Coleman got his prompt and typed in Grimes's name, backslash, then the name of Hermosa Beach.

"How does PhoneBank gather its information?" Monk asked, pulling up a chair next to his nephew, worried that his sister would kick his ass if he got the boy in trouble. The screen went black momentarily.

"Don't sweat it, Unk. They get it from phone directories, birth certificates, real estate and stuff like that. Everything we're gonna get tonight is legal."

"If not exactly ethical," Monk remarked. "Good thing it's for a good cause, huh? Maybe I should feel guilty that I'm corrupting you?"

"Naw. This is what they call situational ethics, right?"

"It is the way the world works."

"Mr. Rationalization."

Monk rapped a playful shot on his shoulder. "Where you learning them big words?" Yes, quite a father figure. Maybe his sister could remarry a priest.

Grimes's name reappeared along with his birthdate, place of birth, address and a phone number. Below that was a record of a '89 Ford Bronco he'd bought on credit from a used car lot in the Valley.

"What about criminal records? He was supposed to have been busted for assault."

"I have to exit PhoneBank and try Recon."

Monk queried, "They're the ones that offer one of the databankers who do pre-employment criminal checks of public courthouse records?"

"Yeah."

Monk's nephew punched the code and soon had a service called Recon on the screen. An 800 number flashed below the logo.

"You need to call them and give them your detective's license number."

Monk dialed the number and got a service rep. He gave

the required information, along with his bond number, and charged the information retrieval to his credit card. Numbers into data, data into information, information available to those who know how to work the circuits.

Was Keys sitting at his computer calling up Monk's record, reviewing it, changing it? Maybe that natty, cuff-linked son-of-a-bitch was looking at Jill's data. Maybe he and his boyfriend, Diaz, were drooling over the fiber optic lensed video of Jill and him making love in their bed. Jesus. Monk felt like Winston Smith falling down the rabbit hole. He replaced the phone's handset and sat down again.

On the screen was a listing of three arrests and one conviction for Stacy Grimes. All the charges revolved around assaults of one kind or another. In 1987, Grimes had been arrested for allegedly putting a man's head into the side of a car. Coleman did a cross reference, which showed that Grimes had been a bouncer in a bar in that incident, released on his own recognizance.

In 1989, Grimes was convicted of armed assault in an incident involving a former girlfriend. In 1992, he was again arrested for assault. This time against a man named Roy Park. Cross-indexing brought up an address in South Central where the incident took place. Grimes was bailed out and had been currently awaiting trial on the charges.

"It should be on record who posted bail," Monk said.

Coleman drew down a selection from the on screen menu. "Nothing."

"Interesting, must mean they paid cash. Let's see what we can find on brother Samuels."

His nephew repeated the inquiry for the other man who guarded the Odin Club. No arrests came up. "How about an address," Monk said.

After several moments three Bart Samuels and their

respective addresses tumbled onto the ether of the computer's field. The one in Santa Monica, and the other two in Redondo Beach and Diamond Bar. Monk stared at the Redondo Beach address. He wrote it down, and opened a drawer in the desk, taking out a Thomas Brothers Map Guide.

"Now go back for Grimes and see if you can punch out the address for that night club he worked at."

"Okay." Some blips and taps later, Coleman brought up a club called Frothy and an address in Redondo Beach.

"Now how about Samuels's employment record?"

"Can't do it. At least not with this service. That's one you've got to fill out a form for and they come out and interview you." Coleman took a sip of hot chocolate and a healthy bite of the raisin square his uncle had brought him.

"Let's do this," Monk began, "let's look up Mr. Park. Try the PhoneBank again." On the map page for the section of Redondo Beach he was looking for, Monk found the approximate area where Frothy is, or still was. Not far from it was the street where one of the Samuels lived.

Monk looked up. Several Parks phosphorized onto the screen along with their numerous addresses.

"Damn," Monk said. "Hey," Monk looked at the notes he'd been taking. "Try this address where the assault happened with Grimes and Park.

"Try it how? I need to know what field you want to be in."

"Roy Park's name, then the address in South Central."

"Okey-dokey." Coleman's fingers worked the keyboard as he watched the screen, its yellow glow casting his face in pale saffron. In seconds, more information appeared along with the name of Roy Park and the address on Vermont Avenue.

"Well, well," Monk said. He recognized the address as some small stores on Vermont near Jefferson.

Puzzled, Coleman said, "What is this?"

"It's land Mr. Park owns, Cole. Rental property that he holds the deed to." And the words of Linton Perry from the other night flooded Monk's memory. Absentmindedly, he tapped the plasticine cover of the map book.

"You did good work, youngster. But I better get you home 'fore your mother skins me."

The young man rose, and Monk was startled to see he came to his shoulders. "When the hell did you start growing?"

"Always," he said, gobbling down the remains of his raisin square. "Anyway, it's a proven fact, as you get older, you get shorter."

"Come on, slob head."

Monk took his nephew home, and walked with him inside the modest house on 4th Avenue. His sister was sitting at the dining room table, getting her lesson plans together for tomorrow. Odessa taught sixth grade in the massive, and massively underfunded, Los Angeles public school system.

"Hi, Mom." Coleman leaned down and kissed her on the forehead.

"Hi, sweetie." She patted him on the cheek.

Coleman waved at his uncle. "I got some homework to finish. Thanks for the ballgame, Unk."

"Sure, man. See you soon."

The nephew entered a door with a poster of Michael Jordan taped on it. Over that it read in blue letters on a white field FEMALES ONLY NEED ENTER. Monk sat at the table where his sister worked and massaged the back of his neck.

Odessa looked at him over the rim of her half-glasses. "This case getting to you?"

"A bit."

She put down her pencil. "How are things with you and Jill?"

"What makes you ask that?"

Odessa did a thing with her lips. "Just wondering."

"I don't know," Monk answered honestly. He got up, uneasy with the prospect of exploring where his relationship with Kodama was going, unsure of the territory he was in. More willing to see what would happen rather than intervene and try to alter the course of fate.

"I asked," his sister said, "because someone I know saw you and Tina being all cozy at the Satellite last Saturday night." She leaned back in her chair, waiting.

Monk said, "That was just about this case. Tina had heard from Ray who said, for a fee naturally, that he'd tell the City Council where to find Crosshairs." Inwardly, a stab of guilt assailed his psyche. He had been mesmerized by the image of Tina throwing back her head and her dreads haloing around her strong features. There was a strong pull in him to those times in the past when each of their bodies was attuned to the sexual rhythm of the other.

"Ray, Ray Smith?" Odessa asked incredulously.

"Uh-huh."

"Do you believe him? Did Tina know where he was?"

"No and no. I told her he was full of shit like all the times before."

"He wasn't always," Odessa said, who knew, as Monk and Tina knew, a once-kind and charming Ray Smith. The one that still existed for them in their collective past.

"I'll let you get back to work." He gave her a kiss on the cheek and started for the door.

"You talk things out with Jill, Ivan."

He halted.

"I used to be against you and her going around, as you know. Being a Black woman, I thought you should only be with another Black woman."

Monk turned from the door.

"I'm not saying that all of a sudden everything's the rainbow and all that shit," his sister went on. "If anything, things have gotten worse as far as race relations go. God knows I see it enough even in elementary school. But the world is too small and our time too limited to live by rules the heart can't keep."

He smiled at her and left.

The next day Monk had the unshakable perception he was being watched again. He searched the Ford but couldn't find anything. Still, driven by the palpable feeling knotting his stomach, he switched cars with his sister at her school. Just as well, since later he planned to keep an eye on Samuels's place in Redondo Beach. And he knew the Galaxie by sight.

Monk got a call from Luis Santillion's office shortly before noon. Delilah put it through.

"Mr. Monk?" the woman on the other end of the line said.

"Yes."

"Mr. Santillion would like to know if you can meet him at the Taquito Factory in the Grand Central Market at one tomorrow?"

"Sure. Exactly what does Mr. Santillion have in mind?"

"Tomorrow at one," she said.

"All right," and he rung off.

His inside line rang, and he picked it up.

"Yes."

A series of beeps, long and short greeted his ears. Monk listened as it repeated again, then the line went dead.

He replaced the receiver, thinking. Somewhere in a pocket of neural synapses, Monk got a tickle, like a savory taste long absent from the palate. He concentrated not on the sound, but on the things that he and Dexter Grant had done. Their history together of places they'd been and people they knew.

But only the hint, amorphous as morning fog, ebbed around his thoughts. The fog wouldn't part, wouldn't allow the answer to emerge. Monk swore and got up from his desk. He went down to the Cafe 77 for a lunch of teriyaki chicken and rice and a bottle of Bud. He then drove over to Ruben Ursua's house on East 55th. The Monte Carlo was no longer anywhere in sight. Monk knocked but got no response. He went around back.

The rear yard was overgrown crab grass bordered on two sides by a wooden fence missing several slats. There was a clapboard garage that the fence connected to, and two trash cans leaned against the garage. Monk took the lids off the cans. In one were two empty pints of Jim Beam, and several white plastic garbage bags. In the other were more sealed trash bags. Monk went back to his car and drove to a hardware store over on Main. He returned twenty minutes later with a pair of leather work gloves and proceeded to open the plastic bags. Carefully, so as to seal them back when he was done.

After many minutes of combing through the personal debris of the inhabitants of the house, Monk found something of interest. A crumpled-up napkin with a women's name and phone number written on the back. On the front was the imprint of a bar called El Scorpion. It depicted the black arachnid, gleaming as if its body were sheathed in ebony chrome. The deadly stinger of the insect was curled in the air and poised to strike a shot glass filled with booze beneath it.

Monk pocketed the napkin and kept searching. He unearthed, among other items, a fragment of a Lotto ticket, an empty Colonel Sanders cardboard bucket, beer bottles, wrappers from McDonald's, and so on. Then Monk heard a car pull into the driveway in front. Quickly, he set the lid back on the can and went around to the rear of the garage. He wedged himself between it and the rickety fence. Feeling like one of those sleezy reporters for a supermarket tabloid, Monk strained to listen. He remained still for ten minutes.

Then he eased around the corner of the garage and made for the front, glad he was driving his sister's straight car rather than the Galaxie which Ursua's girlfriend knew by sight. Maybe he ought to start driving a more nondescript car on cases other than his bad-ass '64. That shit that TV private eyes did, like Magnum PI tailing guys in a bright red Ferrari, was dangerous if you really believed you could get away with it.

Sitting in the driveway was a big-barreled 1974 metal-flake-blue Cadillac Eldorado with gangster-white sidewalls and polished crushed red leather seats. Ursua had taste, if somewhat on the ostentatious side. Stealing away from the house, Monk could hear raised voices originating from inside. He paused, then went on as the loud talk continued. Maybe, he somberly opined to himself, men and women were meant to always be at war with one another, forever bound in a social/sexual/psychic dynamic old as the universe and just as mysterious. Monk got in the car and drove away.

He made a stop at a coffee shop and called Delilah for his messages.

"Nothing important except Tina Chalmers called and said for you to call her when you had a chance," she said.

"Okay, thanks." He hung up and dialed his machine at home.

"Monk, it's Marasco, call me tonight."

That was a surprise. Monk called Kodama's house and got her machine. "Just seeing if you were in, Jill, I'll call you later." He had a cup of coffee and a bagel and headed out to Redondo Beach.

Some years back, while chasing down a bail-jumper who'd been arrested for a series of burglaries and rapes, Monk had waltzed into a bar in the south bay town for a drink after a day of futile effort.

A man wearing a banner marking him as a plague carrier would have been more welcome. Couples, huddled close and intoxicated with the smell of one another, stopped talking to gape at him. Men, standing at the bar belting back beers, turned as their fellow drinkers pointed or nudged one another. Every eye was on him as he entered the all-white watering hole. But he'd be damned if he was going to back out. He walked up to the bar and leaned on it, acutely aware of the stares locked onto him. The bartender, a pleasant-enough-looking middle-aged gent with a trim silver mustache, wiped down the bartop in front of Monk. He then said, in an even tone without rancor, "We don't serve niggers here."

Monk considered his options, all of them ending with him either in prison or the infirmary. He about-faced and marched out of the bar, mad, scared and humiliated. That wasn't the last time he'd come to Redondo Beach, and he knew some Black folks lived here now, but it was the last time he'd considered buying a drink in the town known for turning out volleyball and surfing champions.

He arrived as the early evening traffic of the 405 dis-gorged power-suited men and women in their BMWs, Infinitis and even the occasional Volvo, into the belly of the upmarket community. Killing time, Monk meandered through the fashionable King Harbor section with its upscale shops and one-hour fanny tuck salons. Eventually he took Prospect north and found the street he was looking for, a palm-infested lane close to the Torrance side of the geography. On it were single family houses and a turquoise-stuccoed apartment complex with one of those sunken car ports, on one end of the street. Monk passed by Bart Samuels's place, a recently painted duplex. The address for Samuels was the second floor unit off a landing and stairs covered in gamma-ray-green astro turf.

Monk parked diagonally across the street and hunkered down in his seat. An hour later, Bart Samuels, ponytail and all, drove right by Monk in a 1976 Pontiac Le Mans whose out-of-adjustment valves he could hear tapping through his half-open window. The car swung into a driveway and went into the back of the building.

Momentarily, Samuels appeared, walking back into the front by way of the driveway, a lone grocery shopping bag grasped in one meaty arm. He ascended to his apartment and entered. Monk waited. He wanted to confront him, but he also wanted to do it to his advantage. He was strapped, the .45 snuggled beneath his herringbone sport coat, but he wasn't about to go up there, bust in the door and shove the gun under his nose.

One, that could cost him his permit, and two, Samuels was bound to shove the gun up Monk's ass sideways. No, in a situation like this, where obtaining information from a potentially hostile source was the goal, the psychological approach was the best method.

He'd give it another twenty minutes or so, let Samuels sit down to his dinner, maybe quaff a glass of beer or wine. Relaxed, unwary. A knock on the door, who might it be? Surely only a friend would come calling at the dinner hour. The time passed, Monk readying himself for his approach, his opening line. Casually, like a man delivering a pizza, he went up the livid green stairs. Reaching the top of the landing, Monk raised a brass knocker, a large ring through the nose of a lion's head impaled on the slate-blue door.

Before the thing left his hand, the door swung inward. A stooped figure—Monk instinctively knew it wasn't Samuels—stood in the doorway, backlit from within. At the same moment, something loomed on the periphery of his right eye, and Monk turned to it, reaching for the automatic. Orange flares blossomed around his corneas, and a purple ball rose from the astro turf. Monk was keenly aware his head was down and his body tipped forward. The lavender sphere enveloped his head, blackening out the light.

He felt a hand grasp his, which held onto the .45. As the well of unconsciousness vised his head, Monk dully registered a loud noise. Pain lanced his knees, and he descended into the well and its soothing purple water.

TWELVE

Monk came to, rolled onto his side and vomited.

The head was not meant to be socked. It upset your thinking after a while, as Muhammad Ali and countless fighters of lesser stature could attest to.

When you were unconscious you didn't cough, and your breathing slowed. The light stage, as it was euphemistically referred to, was a temporary concussion, with the more pernicious state being a coma. And even if you should awake—and Monk was painfully aware that he was conscious—there might be disorientation, dizziness, loss of memory and continued vomiting.

The sudden rush of night air into his lungs caused Monk's chest to ache and the food he'd had earlier to collect in his throat. Fighting down the bile, it suddenly came to Monk where to find Dexter Grant. It's funny how your brain works after being slapped upside the head unconscious. What the beeps meant had come to him as he drifted somewhere between the purple sleep and the harsh awakening. Maybe there was some kind of drop-off point. Get hit in the head every now and then, and it cleared up the tangled morass. But get knocked once too often, and your thought processes became mush.

Sure.

Monk got to one knee, braced by his elbow on the raised wall that bordered the landing. He looked out onto the street and instantly went down behind the wall. A Manhattan Beach patrol car was parked in the street. Two muscular cops, standing under a street lamp, were talking with a woman in a designer sweat suit in front of a house trimmed in green.

Sitting with his back against the wall, Monk stared at the closed door to Samuels's apartment. He looked up and was thankful that the porch light wasn't on. He felt a second grip of nausea, and it made him act. There would be way too much explaining to do if the cops caught him dazed and armed on a porch in the middle of the night. And just where was his gun?

Monk looked to his left onto the enclosed end of the porch. There was a pile of old newspapers, a lawn chair with several busted plastic straps, a squat hibachi and two potted plants. Monk crawled over to the area. Searching between the plants, hidden in deep shadow, was his automatic. He sniffed it and could tell it'd been fired recently. He didn't remember pulling the trigger, but otherwise why had the woman called the cops?

Monk crawled back toward the front end of the porch. He peered around the corner of the wall and watched the two cops walking along the sidewalk, coming toward the apartment complex.

One of them was using a flashlight, but neither seemed to be in any hurry. That meant the woman must have heard the gunshots but had not seen the tussle up on the porch, and wasn't sure where the shot had originated. But Monk couldn't rely on luck to keep him safe.

He twisted his body in the direction of the door and pushed on it with his outstretched hand. Nothing. He looked up at the latch, and it seemed as if he were a Lilliputian trying to get into the giant's castle. If he reached up to tug on it—and there was no guarantee it was unlocked—would his arm be seen? He hesitated. The footsteps of the two cops got closer.

Fuck it.

Monk reached up, got his hand around the thing and tugged downward on the cold metal with his thumb. The latch didn't give. His heart stopped beating. Then it released, and the door moved inward on hinges Monk was sure could be heard in Bolivia. He scrambled inside and shut it, quietly as possible. The room was dimly lit by a table lamp. Moments dragged into minutes with Monk, sitting on the floor with his back against the door, imagining the cops stationing themselves outside on the landing, their 9mms ready to blast him to Kingdom Come. If there was one, as his mother believed.

After some time, his queasiness subsided, and he got off the floor. He went to a window that overlooked the street below. Monk pulled back the shade and saw one of the cops, the one with the flashlight, meandering around in front of the apartment complex. Damn. They must have heard the hinges. But, he rationalized, they thought it was only a nosy neighbor sticking his head out to see what was going on.

The other cop knocked on the door.

Monk got his anxiety under control and pulled off his sport coat, tossed his holster and gun into a chair out of sight of the doorway, and unbuttoned his shirt. He went to the door and opened it.

"Excuse me, Mr. . . ."

The member of Manhattan Beach's finest couldn't have been more than twenty-three. There were still pimples along the base of his lantern jaw. He was blonde, blue-eyed, and could have been the iron-lifting buddy of Samuels.

"Monk," he said. He thought he remembered there was no name on the mailbox at the foot of the stairs. But the cop just stared at him. Goddamnit, was there a name? Did he smell the vomit on the porch?

Finally, the puffed-up kid said, "Did you happen to hear anything about forty minutes ago?"

He was looking past Monk, into the room behind him. Monk said, "No, I'm sorry I didn't, officer. But I was in the tub and had the radio going. I looked out because I saw you and your partner out there in the street through the window. Something happen?"

"Mind if I come in and talk with you?"

"Well, yes I do, officer." He gave it the right pause. "I wasn't alone in the tub, you see."

A corner of the young cop's lip lifted and he said, "Some other time, eh, Mr. Monk?"

"Absolutely."

He shut the door as the cop started down the stairs. Monk exhaled, and locked it. He turned on another light in the living room, a lamp whose shade was screened with an Erte design, and began a search of Bart Samuels's quarters.

And what was it James Robinson had told him about that time he'd stopped at the Hi-Life after the uprising? There was a man in there who was a hunchback. And Monk had the impression that the man he'd seen, the one who'd opened Samuels's door as he was about to knock, was different. The body slightly off-kilter.

What he had dismissed as bullshit from Robinson— something to tell him for the forty he'd weaseled out of him—was starting to sound like it had legs.

Surprisingly, the living room was furnished in pieces that displayed a certain sense of style and taste. The chair he'd thrown his gun on was one he'd seen with Jill at Civilization, a hip furniture store on Venice Boulevard in LA. And the other stuff was not particularly expensive, but smart and functional. Monk finished in the living room and went into the other parts of the house.

The kitchen had been done in amber and sea-green colors. The counter was of polished stainless steel and there was an overhead rack of stainless steel pots and pans. Monk went to the back door and opened in onto a set of wooden stairs leading down to the small backyard and the dual garage. Evidently that was how the other man had entered. But Monk had a memory of turning to his right on the porch and someone grabbing at his gun. A third person. Or Samuels, after having gone out the back door. Worry about that later.

Monk closed the door and went about the search. Samuels kept a goodly supply of natural food products, pasta and vitamins in his cupboards, and fresh fish and chicken in the refrigerator. Along with several canisters of muscle bulking powders of the kind Monk used in his twenties on a free-standing butcher block table.

In a drawer of a glass-fronted cabinet built into the wall, which contained wine and highball glasses, Monk found an unused smoke detector and a file folder. He removed the folder and spread it open on the kitchen table. There were insurance papers, some credit card bills marked with check numbers, and a few auto repair bills.

Monk returned the folder to the drawer and noticed some business cards that had been underneath it. He picked them up. One was from a garage, another from a health food store, and the last one from Maxfield O'Day's office. Monk looked at it and considered what it meant.

Samuels and the late Stacy Grimes had worked at the Odin Club where O'Day was a member. Did Samuels need legal help? But he couldn't afford what O'Day spent on his tie allowance, so why the card? Maybe O'Day was being generous to the natives, giving the kid a thrill. Monk tossed it back in the drawer, and it landed upside down. In a compact, masculine hand, a phone number had been written on the back. Monk retrieved the card and wrote the number in his memo book.

In the bedroom, there were several items of clothes, clean and folded, on the made bed. The sliding door of the closet was pulled back and the lineup of shoes on the floor had been disturbed. Obviously, Samuels had packed.

On a shelf in the closet, in a cardboard box, were some fascinating items. Monk found two crocheted socks done in the shape of a penis and testicles, a pink eight-inch dildo which he didn't touch, a ceramic set of vaginal stimulation balls, one day-glo vibrator and a black one, an assortment of flavored edible body oils, and some leather straps. He closed the lid and returned the box to the shelf.

Monk sat on the bed next to the nightstand where a framed photo of a muscular young woman in a bikini resided. She was on one knee with both of her arms extended in the classic pose of flexing her biceps. They were quite impressive. Her sculpted body was set against a backdrop of the kind of gray wrinkled cloth used in photo studios. She'd written on the photo "From one big hunk to another." It was signed Myra.

Monk slipped the photo out and turned it over. The name of the photographer and a phone number were on the back. From now on, Monk grinned to himself, he could just go around turning over pieces of paper all over town and get clues. Stray bits of information, a name here, a phrase, the title of a song, a partial phone number there, and so on. Then he'd get his nephew to construct a computer file with all the stuff he'd gathered, waiting for a client whose case would connect him to his vast array of seemingly useless data. But of course, he'd have to memorize all the information, and that meant taking some kind of memory course, and this was a sure sign he was going crazy.

He made a note of the name and number and put the photo back. Another hour of searching yielded nothing further. Besides, the blow had produced a sizeable headache, and Monk had to sit down more than once as he got a spell of dizziness. He realized he was running on the rush produced by his encounter with the cops. It was wearing off and he was wearing down. Monk made a call in the living room. After the familiar strains of *The Good, the Bad, and the Ugly*, he said, "We're on. Tomorrow, you know the time."

He quit Bart Samuels's home. The cops were gone and Monk walked to his car, trying to look casual but deliberate just in case the woman in the sweat suit was watching. He got in and drove home on automatic pilot. He swallowed three Excedrins and two glasses of orange juice and dropped into a deep sleep. He didn't even bother to play the messages on his answering machine, though its light blinked incessantly, like a one-eyed oracle awaiting its acolyte.

THIRTEEN

"Ivan, Key seems to be nosing around, trying to dig up dirt on you to put the squeeze to you through official channels." Marasco Seguin's voice paused on the tape. "You know if it comes down to it, I'm in your corner. I have a meeting with the chief in a day or two, stay in touch."

A thin smile crossed Monk's unshaven face. The next message from last night played. "It's me, baby. I miss you when I don't see you."

The third and last came on after Jill's. "Long time no see, bro. I hear we might be of some aid to one another. I'll try you again."

Monk played the third message again to make sure it was who he thought it was. Ray Smith. He was glad it wasn't a long message and Smith didn't leave a number. What with the shadow of the FBI falling all over this case. It was already past ten so he left a message for Jill on her private line in her chambers.

A long shower, shave, including trimming his goatee, and a breakfast of turkey sausage, three eggs—scrambled hard—two pieces of wheat toast and two glasses of orange juice shored up his energy and chased the vestiges of bleariness from his head's encounter with whatever it was that sapped him. A bruise behind and to the left of his right ear was tender, but Monk felt good, confident despite what Keys was doing. He was gathering the intricate fragments of the meaning of the riddle. And it was the solution that beckoned him forward.

But every answer has to obey the laws that govern the known world. Every answer has a reaction, a consequence. And what would be the repercussions of finding the killer of Kim Bong-Suh? Another fire? Another outburst of rage and frustration? Would Monk feel compelled to bury the truth for the greater good if he found out that Crosshairs Sawyer did indeed murder the Korean shopkeeper? Monk had to admit that he was no purist solely in the pursuit of the eternal truth. It was actually the working of the problem, all the permutations on achieving the desired results that really charged him, made him feel useful, alive.

Buttoning his shirt, he wondered if it came to it, would he make a decision to suppress evidence because it was politically expedient?

Monk was born in a hospital, Queen of Angels, that had been shut down due to county budget cuts. He could remember from his childhood when the first Black City Council member got elected in this town. And the Helms Bakery truck would cruise along his street and sell those goddamn, sugary sweet, heavy-as-a-lead-weight donuts. Or when Watts exploded, or the first time he got jacked-up by two of then-Chief Davis's Boys in Blue.

LA might very well be lurching toward a Balkanized future, each ethnic group carving out its larger or smaller fiefdom. It might make a lie of the theory of multiculturalism, American history having long since made a lie of the great melting pot. The city might indeed become a low-rent *Blade Runner*, too beat and too broke to pay for the special effects.

But it could also be the example, the last possible chance for sanity in a world where the law of the pack—led by the rapaciousness of the big-money boys who fed at the trough that Reagan and Bush slopped for them from the pickings of the poor, the working and middle class—had to be halted.

Men like Maxfield O'Day believed the salvation of Los Angeles lay in the will of the corporate patrician. Possibly that was part of the equation. But Monk was also convinced it resided with her everyday people, those folk like his sister working day to day, under the onus of budget cuts and top-heavy bureaucracy, trying to do their job because they believed it made a difference. It had to.

Monk's Galaxie took him to his office and a worried Delilah.

"A Ms. Scarn from the Bureau of Consumer Affairs has already called twice for you this morning, Ivan."

"What did she say?"

"She heard some news that concerned her in regards to you. She'd like you to call her as soon as possible."

One of the architects who did some work for Ross and Hendricks came out of a suite at the opposite end of the rotunda where Monk and Delilah stood talking. He strolled over and handed the administrative assistant some papers, and they briefly talked about what he wanted done with them. He left.

"Call her back and tell her she better put whatever the hell it is she wants in writing and that I will pass it along to my attorney," Monk said, checking his watch for the time. "I'm going over to meet with Luis Santillion. After that, I'll call in to see what's happening."

Delilah put a hand on his arm. "Ivan, she didn't sound like she was playing."

"Neither am I, baby." He started to exit, then said, "Call

Maxfield O'Day's office and tell them I need to meet with him, soon."

Designed by part-time architect George H. Wyman for a mining magnate in the late 1800s, the Bradbury Building on lower Broadway in downtown Los Angeles was best known as a movie prop. With its wrought-iron railings, old-fashioned elevator, and general noir ambiance, it had been the office of many a movie detective, from Boston Blackie, to Miles C. Banyon, to Marlowe, to Deckard in *Blade Runner*. It was even in an *Outer Limits* show with aliens crawling all over it, battling an android who thought he was human. Seeing that episode had kept him up half the night when he was a kid.

Monk turned from gazing up at the wonderfully restored Bradbury and walked across the street and entered the exquisite chaos of the Grand Central Market, a sprawling indoor facility of stalls of fresh poultry, fish, fruits and vegetables. And vendors selling every imaginable chachka from Elvis dash ornaments to Navajo throw rugs made in China. People eddied back and forth through the maze-like setup of the place, haggling and bargaining over quantity and quality while mariachi music blared from one section, and Chicano rap from another. There were a lot of Mexican food places in the giant mercado, but there was only one called the Taquito Factory.

It was ten to one, and as Monk approached the stand, he didn't see Santillion or anybody who looked like they worked for him. He took a seat at the counter and ordered the especial numero dos and a glass of iced tea. At precisely one, while Monk was slathering guacamole on his chicken burrito, the head of El Major rounded a corner near the stand. Two other men, in severe suits of charcoal gray, trailed four paces behind him. He strolled over to Monk.

"Glad to see you're on time, Mr. Monk," Santillion said, extending his hand.

Monk had half-turned in his seat to face the other man and rose to shake his hand. As he did so, a flashbulb went off and Monk stared at the two in the dark suits. One of them was working a camera with the flash, and the other one seemed to be there to keep other people from entering the picture. Monk turned to look at Santillion.

"What's all this?"

"Something for our next newsletter. Just showing that I'm not opposed to Black and brown unity." Santillion sat down beside Monk. The two ciphers faded from view.

"Do you have something to tell me?" Monk had also sat down again and was intent on finishing his lunch. He felt too used to it now to be pissed for being suckered into another publicity angle one of these jokers who think they represent the people seemed hell-bent to use him for. Everybody's favorite Black private eye pinup.

The waitress brought Santillion a Corona and an empty glass with a wedge of lemon perched on it. He poured some of the pale brew into the glass and took a liberal sip of it. "About six or seven months ago, I got a call from a man who is not in our organization. He's a small businessman, he and his wife own a launderette and corner market over on Atlantic Boulevard near Compton. They had suffered some damage in the riots, and were still trying to get through all the red tape to get an SBA loan so they can expand."

"If he's not in your group, then why did he call you?"

"I've known him a long time. He's one of those kind of people who've always believed that you only needed the sweat of your brow and a strong woman to make your way in the world."

Santillion's order came. Monk said, "And not the help of

some guy who wears eight-hundred-dollar suits and sits on the board of SOMA."

Santillion bit into his taco, grated cheese spilling onto the counter. He chewed and swallowed. He turned his head slightly to look at Monk. "My brother and I were born and raised in City Terrace, Mr. Monk. We both ran with the White Fence gang, and he was the one who got the good grades in school." A slight grin creased his weathered face. "But none the less, we're brothers, and I'm the one he felt compelled to call."

"So he swallowed his pride and asked you to help him get an SBA loan."

"Of course not. He'd cut out his tongue first. He'd been approached by two men who said they represented a company who'd buy his distressed property. Of course they offered below market value. Way fucking below."

"And what did your brother say?"

"In his own warm way, he told them no." He took another sip of his Corona. "But these two representatives seemed intent on not taking a no and they suggested he rethink his decision."

Monk had stopped eating and waited for the other man to continue.

"The roof of his car was caved in one morning, the side of his house was chopped with a fire ax, and his daughter had a rock thrown at her on her way to school. It took five stitches to close the wound in my niece's head." Santillion halted, reliving the image in his mind.

"So your brother was scared?"

"I said we were crime partners in White Fence, man. He called up some of our old homies, some of these carnales who've done time in Pelican Bay and Q, and had them do bodyguard duty. The trouble went away."

"Both of these gentlemen were white, buffed and one had a ponytail?"

Santillion nodded. "I never saw them, but I remember my brother mentioning the ponytail."

"And they said they represented Jiang Holdings?"

As an answer, Santillion took out a card and slid it across the countertop toward Monk. On it was the name of Jiang Holdings and a phone number in Orange County. Nothing else.

"He called me because he wanted to know if I'd heard anything about them. I hadn't up till then."

"And now?"

"I've heard from a few small landlords, some in Pico-Union and some in South Central, that they've been approached by this Jiang Holdings. But much more discreetly, much less harsh than with my brother. Some have sold and cut and run."

Monk tapped the card against his index finger. "So are we to believe there is some kind of conspiracy of Koreans buying up property all over town?"

Santillion raised his hands palm up into the air.

"That kind of talk could set off another goddamn conflagration."

Santillion eased off his stool. He laid a five on the counter. "Yes, I'm aware of that. But I felt you should know. And there's something else. Several of the properties that have been bought are in areas that the Administration in Washington are targeting as Revitalization Zones."

"But the federal money won't cover all costs."

"That's right. But if you were someone who had the land, and had the start-up capital that enabled you to get things going once the zones were established . . ." He patted him on the shoulder and walked away.

Monk left his meal unfinished and placed another five on the counter. He walked out of the bustling Grand Central Market into the hustle of Broadway with its discount electronic stores, cut-rate gold jewelers and knock-off designer jeans. He walked south until he came to Temple and then into the Municipal Court House at 210 West. He hadn't worn his gun and didn't have to go through a hassle at the metal detector at the entrance. He took the elevator to the floor where Jill Kodama's courtroom was.

"Are we to believe, sir, that when you pointed the AK-47 at Mr. Wade, you didn't think that would anger him?" The attorney who said that was a tall, portly man Monk had met at a dinner party once. He sat down in the area of the court reserved for observers and watched as the trial progressed. A little after three-thirty, Kodama recessed the trial until ten in the morning. The defendant was led away, and several people who had been in the gallery, including a young woman with an amazing amount of mascara over her eyes, exited the courtroom. Monk got up and walked over to the bailiff.

"Sherlock, how's it hangin'?"

His name was Jory. He was a white guy in his mid-fifties, and he'd been over to Grant's house for poker games off and on for the last fifteen years. "Same old sixes and sevens, you know," Monk said, leaning on the rail separating the jury section from the rest of the courtroom.

"I hear you're hip deep in it."

Monk lifted a shoulder.

"Yeah," the bailiff began, shaking a Pall Mall loose from a rumpled pack. "I never thought Los Angeles would wind up like New York, but damned if it hasn't." The smoke from his cigarette plumed from his straight line of a mouth. "I'm taking my early retirement in two years and blowing this hell hole."

The door to Kodama's chambers opened and she stepped through sans judicial robe. Smartly dressed in a double-breasted cream-colored linen suit and an electric-blue blouse, she smiled at Monk.

"And if you two are smart, you will too. Go someplace where you can have a lot of babies and fish all day," Jory said, emphasizing his statement with a tap of his back hand on Monk's stomach.

"There's a war on all over the world. There is no such place, Jory," Monk countered.

"Ain't it the truth."

The bailiff left. Monk stared up at the handsome woman standing beside the large swivel chair upholstered in black cracked leather. "How are you?"

"Fine," she said.

"Want to go for a walk?"

"That sounds good."

They wound up going through Pershing Square on Olive Street, stopping twice to give change to a homeless person in the one-block-square plot of greenery. There were numerous men and woman sitting on the stone benches erected by the city to deter the homeless from gathering. "So what were we arguing about?" Monk asked.

Kodama put her arm through the crook of his elbow. "Our future."

"Oh yeah, I knew it was something insignificant."

"He-yuk."

They went across the street and into the Beaux Arts–designed Biltmore Hotel, an old institution that had fallen into ruin, and was then restored during the brief laissez faire portion of the '80s. They got a quiet booth in the bar.

"I apologize for what I said the other night, honey," Monk said, holding onto her hand across the table.

"Well, I was a bit vague, wasn't I."

"What's bothering you?"

"Maybe I just want us to clean up all our business and get the hell out of here."

"Like Jory."

"Some days I feel like that. Like this whole thing, the very idea of the urban metropolis, was a mistake of the twentieth century." She paused, watching Monk.

"What does that have to do with us, baby?"

"You know exactly. I'm a judge and you're a private detective. We're two sides of the same dollar and nobody will give us change."

"That's a little too cryptic for me."

"It's what keeps us going, Ivan, it's our reason to live. And it will also be our undoing."

"Not if we try."

She leaned back, the stark gloom of the place temporarily swallowing her chiseled face. Momentarily, Monk had the irrational feeling that the monsters of the city had abducted her for daring to speak of their secrets. Her voice floated to him. "We aren't cops, Ivan. I try to be detached, objective. I'm not. That is to say, I do my best to render fair and impartially, but I carry the burden with me."

"You're a good person."

"Shit."

"You can't escape it."

"Speaking of which, how's the case coming?"

He filled her in on recent developments, including the threat against his license. "But it's starting to come together. It's starting to make sense."

"You should see your face. You're addicted to this way of life."

"It takes one to know one." He pointed a finger at her.

"See that's what's got you worried. You think our relationship is built on a vicarious thrill we each derive from one another."

She waved a hand in the air to dismiss the words. "You can stop with the cheap psychology, Dr. Freud."

"Remember, a cigar is just a cigar."

"Uh-huh, except when Ivan Monk waves his around, right?"

"Absolutely."

"Do you think that's our only attraction for one another, Ivan?"

"We can't divorce it from who we are, Jill. But that's not to say if tomorrow one or both of us were doing something else, we'd fall out of love."

She raised an eyebrow.

Monk sat back in his chair, studying the woman before him. "I'll always want you."

Kodama leaned across the table and kissed Monk. "You're such a romantic."

"We can't all be hard-boiled like you," he said. At length they arose from the table and went back to Kodama's house above the reservoir in Silver Lake. She made dinner, a rarity, and afterwards they snuggled near a fire Monk built in the study's fireplace. "I've got to see a man about a horse."

"What?"

"I've got to be down in Anaheim by eleven-thirty tonight."

"Why does that not surprise me," she said, sneering at him.

He opened up a magazine on the coffee table and wrote something on a page. He tore it out and handed it to her.

She read it, then threw the page into the fire. "Put on some music, honey. Put on some Diz, will you? His music is magic, and you'll please his ghost by invoking it," Kodama said. "You'll need his protection in the days ahead."

The phono played a scratchy album that was one of the

lord of be-bop's outings with him and Roy Eldridge on trumpet, Oscar Peterson on piano, Ray Brown on bass and Mickey Roker on drums. By the time the needle found the opening groove of "I Cried for You (Now It's Your Turn to Cry for Me)," Monk laid a blanket on the sleeping judge. She'd fallen asleep with her head in his lap and he'd managed to place it on one of the couch's pillows.

As John Burks "Dizzy" Gillespie plowed into the second chorus of "Indiana," Monk eased out the house into the chilly evening, the moon a broken quarter of bitter light. Faintly, he could hear the strains of Eldridge's solo as he got in his car and drove away. Monk took pains to make sure he wasn't being followed and he got out to San Pedro seventeen minutes past eleven.

It was a harbor town and its population included an interesting mix of Italians, Greeks, Serbs and Croats. They each had their own social clubs, expressed by their segregated soccer teams, and several community papers. Monk drove past a storefront whose Slavic lettering had several large flyers pasted up in the picture window. He couldn't read them, but could guess it pertained to the continuing bloody conflict in the Balkans.

He reached 4th Street and went along it till he got close to Beacon and the water. Once upon a time, Dexter Grant had informed him there was a hill here, and the radical union of the Industrial Workers of the World held their rallies then for the Maritime Union which was one of their locals. And, Grant had gone on to tell him, in 1925 there was a big rally here where Upton Sinclair, teetotaler, the author of *The Jungle*, and who ran for governor as a socialist in California in the '30s, came to speak. This was another facet of life Grant's Wobblie Uncle Logan had bestowed upon his nephew.

Liberty Hill was what they called it. Parked at the curb along Beacon Street was Grant's 1967 Buick Electra 225. Monk pulled in behind it and watched the older man get out of his car and into the passenger seat of the Galaxie.

"I was about to give up hope on my number-two protégé," he said.

"Who's number one?"

"Me, baby, me," he said, putting a file folder on the dash, and holding onto a Winchell's styrofoam cup of coffee.

"It was a good clue, Dex. Using beeps for the foghorns of the harbor here."

"Just like your first time in the sack. You don't forget where it was that someone first took a shot at you. Or the time."

"And people say you're a bad influence on me."

"Fuck 'em, and feed 'em fish. What's happening on the case?"

Monk filled him in, then asked, "What did you find out about brother Kim?"

"There's an all-night strip joint over on Gaffey. Let's go over there and talk."

Monk stared at Grant.

"The place is circular. We can sit at a table and one of us watches the front while the other keeps an eye on the back. The music's a good cover in case your girlfriend Keys is using a directional mike or some of that other sophisticated eavesdropping equipment. We're both good at shaking tails, but let's face it, the Bureau's been at this longer than both of us have been alive."

"Okay," Monk said, gunning the motor to life. "I think it's just an excuse for you to leer at naked young women more than half your age."

"Sure, there's that, too."

The Chain Puller's clientele was sparse, but diverse. A

couple of the typical middle-aged businessmen with their ties askew in their Hart Schaffner & Marx costumes, a trio of bikers—one of whom gave Monk an I-dare-you-to-fuck-with-me look—some collegiate types who looked underage, and a lone woman in a peasant dress who drank in a corner and scribbled on a pad of paper.

Grant and Monk took a table toward the middle of the rear. The stripper, a thin brunette with a protruding rib cage, did her act on stage as heavy metal music played. It was loud enough so that they both felt safe talking, but not so much that they had to shout.

It was a two-drink minimum in the place, all well drinks were five dollars, plus the cover charge. They both ordered beer from the topless waitress. Monk browsed through the contents of the folder.

"Kim Bong-Suh," Grant began, "was a labor leader in a large steel mill in Inchun."

The waitress returned with their order, and he waited until she put down the order to continue. Monk said, "I don't think there's anywhere on her to hide a bug, Dex."

The older man was staring at the departing woman's backside and didn't respond. He went on. "From 1945 to about 1965, the US supplied the sometimes less-than-democratic governments of South Korea over twelve billion big ones in military and economic grants. Not to mention some spare change they picked up from the World Bank, the International Monetary Fund and so on."

"All in the name of stopping the red hordes to the north."

"Something like that," Grant conceded. "Anyway, the South Koreans sniffed the then-subtle shifting of political winds, and knew they best be about developing some economic independence. They started what would be the first of several five-year plans."

Monk took a sip of his tepid beer and made a face. "That sounds kind of socialist to me."

"National Socialism, I guess. After all, the Nazis began Germany's nationwide healthcare system, and it's still used today."

"But we digress."

"The first five-year plan called for economic diversification. They normalized relations with their former colonizers, Japan, and received eight hundred million in government grants and loans, and private industry loans, too. With that, and the fact that US aid also continued, they achieved some degree of their goal."

"Which was?"

"Increase in electrical energy capacity, upping the production of food for internal use, and building up the industrial infrastructure."

"This leads us to the second five-year plan."

"Absolutely, weed hopper."

One of the bikers and a businessman had gotten into a shouting match but one of the frat boys had stumbled over to them. A drunk referee. After several moments of consultation with the young man, the bikers and the businessmen pushed some tables together, and all of them commenced to have a grand time of it.

Grant returned to his subject. "In the second phase, the economic wizards sought further food production, an increase in employment and retooling of industries such as textiles. As a matter of fact, GNP shot up damn near twelve percent during that period."

"The beginning of the rise of South Korea as an economic power in the East."

"Partly accomplished because most of the union officials were paid by the company."

"Handmaidens of the government," Monk elaborated.

Grant continued. "In the sixties the workers lived on industrial estates or towns near the factories they worked in. Bad pay, long hours, lousy housing and no playgrounds for your kids, quite a fucked-up deal. Most of the unions worked in concert with the big companies to fuel the economic miracle."

"The only place to go, as far as the workers were concerned, was up," Monk added, having given up on trying to drink the swill the Chain Puller passed off as beer.

"Right. And there began a new militancy on the part of some workers who put it on the line with their unions. But"—Grant held up a finger—"General Pak Chung Hee, who'd been in power since 1963, wasn't about to have any of that. And he wasn't about to step down, though two terms was the prescribed limit on holding the presidency."

"This is about in '71, right?" Monk said. "He declared martial law."

"Sort of. He finagled the National Assembly to allow him a third term. Everybody was screaming, the people, the business leaders and so forth. But he managed to squeak through in a very shady election. Chung Hee could see democracy was not for him, not if he wanted to stay in power, so he declared a national emergency and suspended the constitution. The Korean Central Intelligence Agency and the cops got a free hand. Chung Hee used the spectre of communism as his excuse to crack down on unions, political movements, university students, and whoever else pissed him off."

"Old story," Monk mused. "His version of Yushin."

"You've been doing your homework, youngster. Anyway, during this period, as you can imagine, there was a lot of opposition to this iron hand of government, particularly in

the ranks of labor. As I said—" Grant stopped because the
screeching music had suddenly stopped. It was now quiet in
the strip bar save for the carousing crew of bikers, businessmen and students. But all of them seemed too drunk to
notice that the stripper had left the stage as they continued
to laugh at one another's jokes. The woman in the corner
continued to write.

Grant went on. "Like I was saying, Kim Bong-Suh was a
worker in a steel mill and he was also a member of a group
that didn't express themselves as socialists, but they definitely
were left of center. He'd been through trainings for union
leaders at church-based organizations who, later, would be
influenced by the Liberation Theology movement. Kim was
bright, articulate and courageous. He became a shop steward
on a platform of more union independence and more militancy."

"I imagine he got his hand slapped once or twice."

"He made a visit to South Mountain, which was a nice
way of saying you got picked up by the KCIA and taken to
their headquarters. There they practiced a little bit of the ol'
ultra-vi to make you see the error of your ways."

"And did he?"

"He took it, and more. He and some others organized a
strike in the late seventies that resulted in the deaths of some
twenty workers."

"Anything about his wife?"

"That's a bit sketchy. But I concluded she was involved
in some union business, textiles. Seems there was a job slow-
down and the bosses hired some goons to teach the ladies
the true meaning of labor relations. She was killed sometime
in the mid-seventies."

"Damn. What else on Kim?"

"Well," Grant said, sipping his beer, "that's where I got

my hand slapped. The background stuff we've been talking about, most of the stuff that's in that file, can be obtained from books and magazines written about South Korea. My contacts at State were okay about supplying that."

"But when you started to ask about Kim?"

"I got as far as his labor background and the strike in the late seventies. Then all of a sudden, my contacts dried up."

"Like they got a memo to be cool," Monk offered.

"There's no doubt."

"Keys must know about you and me, so he must figure I have this info."

"But he must know the complete history of Kim."

"Which raises the question as to what it hides. What bearing does it have on his death in South Central Los Angeles?"

The waitress returned without being summoned. She placed two more beers on the table and said laconically, "That'll be ten dollars plus tip."

Monk's eyes assailed her, but he could not pierce the veil of distance he'd seen on the faces of women like her, those who mostly by factors they could never control found themselves trapped in the sex trade. He put a ten and five on her tray. "Okay."

She picked it up and looked at him. "Thanks, man." And off she went.

Grant hunched forward across the table. "How about this scenario? After the strike there came reprisals from the government, Kim flees and for the next several years bounces around and winds up here in '82, okay?"

"Yeah. But something makes him close up shop a week before the upheaval and then he starts keeping odd hours where he lives."

Grant's brow furrowed. "Like he was on to something.

That would explain closing the store. Harder to find a guy if he ain't where he's supposed to be."

"Yet his actions would seem to indicate he was working on something. And it has to be all tied in with Jiang Holdings."

"But you told me the phone number you got for them is now out of service."

"And the address is an empty lot. But Jiang holds the liquor certificate on the Hi-Life liquor store, the non-operation certificate for Kim's car was filed by the concern, and most importantly, it would appear that Bart Samuels and the late Stacy Grimes were employed by Jiang."

"For the purpose of buying up distressed properties."

"So I need to know who is behind Jiang," Monk said.

"Kim Bong-Suh probably found out and paid for the knowledge."

Monk nodded in the affirmative.

FOURTEEN

"Law office," the efficient female voice said.

"I'm a friend of Bart Samuels, he recommended this law office, but I can't remember the name of the lawyer."

Monk could hear the quiet buzz on the line, then, "Was he a client?" Some of the efficiency had worn off.

"Yes. He'd been arrested on assault charges."

"Oh, hold on."

He listened to the Muzak version of Tone Loc's "Funky Cold Medina," then another female voice, older than the first, came on the line.

"This is Sheila Evans, can I help you?"

"Miss Evans, I . . . I got involved in a little something helping out my buddy Bart Samuels." He let it hang in the air but no words were forthcoming from the other end. "Well, actually, it involved him and Stacy Grimes."

That got a compact intake of air. Sheila Evans said, "Where did you get my number?"

"From Bart, I told you."

"I don't know you."

Monk picked up an edginess in her voice that was more than annoyance. "But you know Bart and Stacy."

"Mr. Grimes is . . ."

"Dead."

"Who are you?"

"More importantly, Ms. Evans, how is it that you came to represent Grimes?"

She cradled the handset. Monk got up from his desk and stuck his head out into the rotunda. "Delilah, check with the bar association for a current business address for a lawyer named Sheila Evans."

"Okay. I've got some work to finish for Ross, and I'll get on it after lunch."

Monk closed the door and returned to his desk. Momentarily, his phone rang and he picked it up. "This is Monk."

"Mr. Monk."

"Mr. O'Day, I'm glad to hear from you."

"I'd been out of town on SOMA business. I understand you've been making progress."

"I have. As a matter of fact, I've just been talking with a lawyer named Sheila Evans. Do you know her?"

"Yes, yes I do. She's a lawyer at a firm whose senior partner is an old classmate of mine."

"Did you recommend her to Stacy Grimes?"

"I may have. I understood he was in some trouble with the LAPD and I might have told him or Bart Samuels about them. A professional courtesy, you know. Does this have something to do with the case?"

"It may. When can we get together?"

"I've got a meeting with the mayor this morning. Why don't I call you this afternoon and if not today, then on Monday."

"That's fine."

"Mr. Monk."

"Yes, Mr. O'Day."

"How close are you to finding Crosshairs Sawyer?"

"I'm not sure. I'm not sure it matters."

"I see."

"I'll talk to you later."

"Indeed we will."

Monk made further notes on the case on a tablet of yellow paper. Later, he would flesh them out in his report when he wrote it up on the computer at the donut shop. He finished, arose and stretched, then headed out.

"I'll be back by one-thirty, D," he said. "I'm expecting a call from O'Day this afternoon. If I miss him, ask him where I can find him. Oh, call Li at the Merchants Group and tell him I'll be dropping off my report to him over the weekend."

Monk took the 10 freeway east and got off at Vermont. He went south until he came to a low-slung two-story building of first-floor storefronts with apartments on the second level. An empty lot was next to the building. It was boxed in with cyclone fencing, another piece of archaeology from the spring of '92. Park's building still had scorch marks on it, and had unrented spaces in it, too. He parked and looked into the vacant spaces. Debris was strewn about the floor, and a portion of the wall that faced the lot was missing.

Monk entered the carniceria at the apex of the building. He walked up to a middle-aged, heavyset Latina behind the counter.

"Excuse me, ma'am, I'm interested in renting one of the storefronts in this building. Can you tell me how to get ahold of the landlord?"

"His name is Park," she said. "I've got the number to his office around here somewhere." She rummaged under the counter and produced a dogeared Rolodex. She flipped through it and came to the entry she was looking for and turned it for Monk to see. He wrote down the address, which was in Monterey Park, and the phone number in the 818 area code.

"Thanks a lot."

"Sure."

Monk then drove over to a pay phone and called Roy Park's office.

"Triple A Realty," the woman on the other end of the line said when it connected.

"Is Mr. Park in?" Monk asked.

"Not at the moment. How can I help you?"

"I'd like to rent out one of his storefronts on Vermont near Jefferson."

"If you leave your name and number, I'll have him get back to you."

Monk gave her a false name and the phone number that was the fourth line into the office space he shared with Ross and Hendricks. He rang off. Delilah had been briefed, and she would answer it accordingly. He wasn't sure how Park might take hearing his real name—maybe he was a member of the Merchants Group and it didn't matter, or maybe it did.

He grabbed some bland lunch over at the food court in the shopping center across the street from the University of Southern California on Hoover and Jefferson. Then he called into the office.

"No, Mr. Park didn't call, or Mr. O'Day," Delilah said. "But Ms. Scarn did."

"Who? Oh. What did she say this time?"

"She said be in her office at ten in the morning on Monday, or your license will be suspended for thirty days for failure to appear."

Monk exploded. "Give me that stiff-backed bureaucrat's number. I'll—"

"She faxed over a formal summons, Ivan."

"Fuck. What's her basis for the summons?"

He could hear the rustle of papers as Delilah retrieved the document. "It is alleged that you fired your weapon without filing a discharge report."

Frozen water collected along Monk's spine. Had Keys been able to follow him out to Bart Samuels's apartment? Had it been Keys that night on the stairs? The third person who slugged him. He shook himself. "All right, thanks Delilah. I'll be back in a while."

Monk left the shopping center and took the Galaxie over to Hi-Life Liquors. Pulling into the parking space behind the establishment, Monk recognized a gray Blazer, the color of dull gun metal with sport rims, parked there also. He got out and warily entered through the front.

One of the kids who had been in there the last time he was there was again playing a video game. Mrs. Chung was standing next to a rack of sugar-loaded snack cakes. Her nephew was behind the counter. He shifted his gaze from Monk to one of the others in the store, a medium-sized young Black man in a cheaply made double-breasted suit and a brown bowler. He was standing next to Mrs. Chung at the rack. It was very quiet in the Hi-Life save for the kid racking up points on the video game.

"Good day, Mrs. Chung," Monk began, scanning the remaining parts of the room for the other one. All he could see were the aisles containing such delicacies as Wonder Bread and canned Spam.

"What can I do for you today?" she said.

"I came back because I had some more questions I wanted to ask you." He moved forward and the one next to Mrs. Chung turned his body slightly, his shoulder out to Monk but he was looking straight at him.

"Why don't you come back later, cuz?" he said, smiling. "I've got an order to fill here."

It might be, Monk reasoned, that the other Scalp Hunter had a gun trained on him. That's why he wanted to be closer to the one he was talking to. "It can't wait that long." He stepped forward.

"Too motherfuckin' bad, then." The one next to Mrs. Chung brought his fist up and into Monk's stomach.

He gritted his teeth and, even as he clutched at his stomach, he let loose with his other hand. He caught the Scalp Hunter on the side of the jaw, sending him backwards into the rack. Ho Hos, Ding Dongs and Little Bettys sailed through the air. Mrs. Chung moved off, and Monk shouted at no one in particular, "Where's the other one?"

"In the backroom," the nephew shouted back.

The one closest to him was regaining his balance, and Monk lashed out with his feet, catching him in the ribs. There was a burst of air from him like a busted soda bottle. Monk propelled his body forward over the fallen rack. The other Scalp Hunter, similarly dressed, appeared in the doorway leading to the back.

He was small but the gun in his hand made up for it. There was too much ground to cover if the gang member had a mind to pull the trigger. Monk hadn't worn his gun. Not that it mattered, he wouldn't have been able to draw it in time anyway.

"You just won the wet T-shirt contest, homeboy," he said.

Monk could already feel the rounds penetrating his chest, cutting into his head. There was a loud retort behind the detective which caused the Scalp Hunter in front of him to momentarily look in that direction. Monk leaped and drove the other man back through the doorway. The two collided with some stacked boxes of beef jerky and a variety of canned nuts. They went over along with the boxed goods in the half-light of the stock room.

"Motherfuckah," the Scalp Hunter exclaimed. He was trying to free his gun hand which Monk had a serious lock on. He jabbed with his free hand into Monk's side but his small stature was no match for Monk's greater height and bulk. The private eye got to his feet, holding onto the other's wrist who was still on his back. He brought his foot down on the young man's torso for leverage and twisted and jerked the arm forcefully.

The other one hollered and let go of the gun. Monk grasped it and reached down for him on the floor.

"Hey."

Monk turned at the sound. The Scalp Hunter he'd kicked was standing in the doorway with a gun in his outstretched hand. "Jesus, does everybody have a gun in Los Angeles?" Monk said under his breath. Keeping the small one between them, Monk hauled him to his feet. He kept the gun leveled at his back.

"Put the gat down," the one at the doorway commanded.

"No," Monk said flatly. He was hoping that Mrs. Chung and the nephew had run out of the store. That had to be why he wasn't holding one of them hostage. "How long do you think it'll be before the cops get here?"

The one in the door allowed his head to turn in the direction of the window looking out onto Pico Boulevard. He looked back at Monk. "Let him go or I'm gonna have to cap you."

"Then he dies with me," Monk said, trying not to show whether he meant it or not. "And what would your homies think of that?"

The one in the doorway began stepping backwards.

"What's up with that, man? You just gonna leave me hangin'?" the other one squawked.

The first one kept backing up. Monk and the remaining Scalp Hunter, the gun pressed into his spine, remained motionless.

The gang member who'd been in the doorway disappeared from Monk's sight. He could hear the jingle of the bells over the front door.

"So now what, man?"

Monk cracked the barrel of the gun, a nickle-plated 10 mm Delta Elite, across the base of his neck. He started for the floor, dazed. Monk was already turning and heading for the rear door. He opened it a slit and could see the front end of the Blazer. But he couldn't see the driver's door and would have to open the door further to do so. He crouched down and shoved it open.

Two bullets sent pieces of the doorjamb flying. Monk flattened out behind some crates. He heard the motor of the utility vehicle come to life, and by the time he looked back out again, the truck was moving north, fast, along the alley. Monk considered giving chase in his Galaxie. And almost laughed out loud at the absurd thought.

He could just see himself tearing after the Blazer, upturning trash cans, causing cars to plow into one another, people diving onto the sidewalk as he and the kid—well, not exactly a kid, they both looked to be in their mid-twenties—tore up city and private property. Losing his license would be the least of his problems. He'd be buried so far under lawsuits he wouldn't see daylight for eight hundred years. Monk closed the door and reentered the room.

"You okay?" the nephew asked Monk. He was breathing hard, standing in the store room.

"I'm fine. David, isn't it?"

He indicated yes.

Monk moved over to the Scalp Hunter on the floor. He

bent down, rolled him over and felt his neck. The pulse was strong and regular. The eyelids fluttered. Monk rose. "You call the cops?"

"Yes, I did. I got my aunt in the store a couple of doors down," he said, jabbing a finger in that direction.

The two moved into the front room. "Where's the kid who was playing the video game?"

"He ran off too. He's okay."

"What the hell was that noise that distracted our friend?"

David walked to the counter and Monk followed him. Behind it on the floor was a tall gumball dispenser with the shattered remains of the plastic bubble which held the sticky treats. A multicolor assortment of gumballs littered the floor like psychedelic hail. "I backed up into it," the young man said sheepishly.

"You saved my life, man." Monk extended his hand and the young man pumped it. "Look, David, for a lot of different reasons, I don't want to be here when the cops get here."

Incredulously, he said. "What do you want me to tell them?"

"Tell them everything that happened, just the way it happened, except you don't know my name. And if you don't mind, be a little vague on my physical description."

"Okay. I figure you saved us a lot of hassle, if not our lives."

Sirens were now audible. "What did the Scalp Hunters want?"

"They said they wanted us to push some of their crack across the counter. Said it would make us all a lot of money. The short one said it would be like the old days with Kim and the Rolling Daltons."

Monk said. "I still need to ask your aunt about Jiang." But he knew time was against him. The sirens were almost on this block.

"She won't say anything now, Mr. Monk. She'll be too terrified."

Monk was back in the storeroom, heading for the door. "Okay, okay. How about your uncle, where is he today?"

"Merchants Group meeting."

Monk was getting into the Galaxie, David watching him from the doorway. "Does he know a Roy Park?"

"Sure. Mr. Park used to be president of the Merchants Group."

Monk tore away from the building, down the alley in the same direction that the Blazer had taken.

FIFTEEN

Monk got back to his office and there was a message waiting for him from Maxfield O'Day. The head of Save Our Material Assets stated his apologies that he had to go back out of town again and the two of them would get together by Wednesday of next week. Monk sat down at his desk and leaned back in his swivel. His inside line rang just as he was dozing off. He reached over and picked up the handset.

"Hello."

"Mr. Monk, glad I caught you. I'm on my way to the airport, but thought I'd chance a call from the car here."

It was O'Day. Monk said, "The mayor give you a new assignment?"

"Money and who has it is a very fluid thing in today's world, young man. We have to catch it where we can. Anyway, I know it's imperative that we get together. I'm anxious to review your progress on the case. Why don't you fax your report to my office and they'll get it to me this weekend and I'll be up to speed."

"Sure. I'd like to get your thoughts on a few things."

"By the way, one of the researchers in my firm informed me they found out a little something about this Jiang Holdings."

"Good. Like what?"

"Let me see," he said, his voice momentarily fading away from the mouthpiece. He then came back on the line. "Jiang is a wholly owned offshore company. It is registered in Hong Kong, yet as far as we can tell, it only does business in the States."

"Who are the partners?"

"That's been the stickler. Hong Kong, as you know, will be reverting back to the Mainland in less time than it took for Mao's Thousand-Mile March. Needless to say, a lot of the old running dogs are enacting various constructs, shall we say, to protect their precious shekels."

"And identities," Monk added.

"Exactly." The transmission started to break up. "I'll have my man keep on it, though. But we did get . . ."

The lawyer started to fade out again. Monk strained to listen.

". . . some kind of other office . . ."

"Say it again, will you?" Monk wrote down the address that O'Day recited on his yellow pad. Like a voice at the bottom of a canyon, Monk could hear Maxfield O'Day say goodby, followed by the white noise of electronic nothingness. He hung the phone up, looking at the address. He dialed Jill's chamber. Jory, the bailiff, answered.

"No, Monk, she left already. One of the attorneys got sick after lunch, so she recessed till Monday."

"Thanks." Monk picked up the slip of paper with the address, got on his coat, and left the office again.

JILL KODAMA parked her pearl-black Saab in the parking space the Camaro had just left. She got out, beeped the alarm on, and strolled into the Beverly Connection. There was a new attache case she'd had her eye on in the tony accessory shop on the second floor. She looked at it again, but decided against it. Though she made good money, she still felt self-conscious if she spent too much on herself. The product of a lower-middle-class upbringing, she didn't want to signal to her friends at Legal Aid and the ACLU that she had sold out.

Kodama bought herself a cup of cappuccino in the food court and berated herself for berating herself. Just because one became a judge, that didn't mean you'd stopped fighting for social justice. It had been as much a push from Asian Pacific groups who wanted her in the high profile position as it had been her own ambition. Who better to mete out justice than one who represented a group who had been on the receiving end of injustice so many times. But wasn't that the rationalization of every hungry politician?

She bared her even teeth and took another sip of her coffee. So you've revealed your true motivation, Kodama. In your heart of hearts you want to run for office. DA? Hell, no. County Supervisor, huh? The judgeship a mere stepping stone to further your insatiability for righting wrongs and punishing evildoers. And the fact that Supervisors oversaw huge kingdoms of the sprawling County of the angels. Jill Kodama, County fucking Supervisor. Bullshit. She threw away the empty paper cup and left the mammoth complex.

Kodama drove over to Betsey Johnson, the woman's clothing store on Melrose. She walked along the side street where she'd parked her car and was near the corner when someone screamed. It was a pair of young girls in ripped jeans and layered lace tops. The red-and-blue-haired one was yelling and pointing. A sick fear in the middle of her chest blossomed, and the judge couldn't help it. She half-turned, yet stumbled and ran all the same, knowing what was coming.

"Rolling Daltons, bitch."

The shotgun blast could be heard above the young girl's screams.

THE PLACE didn't look like money, it looked like hell. It was a squat affair off an alley/street near Riverside Drive on the border of Glendale. There was no sign on the building, only a tiny address over the roll-up door which matched the address Monk had received from O'Day. He tried the door, but it was locked. He walked around the building, but all the windows were up high near the parapet. In addition, they were barred and their panes composed of frosted glass.

A trash container was next to an inset door. That too was locked tight. And there was nothing—no paper, no cups, no plastic bag, zip—in the unlocked trash container. Monk got a roll of transparent tape out of his glove compartment and tore off a small piece. This he taped on the bottom edge of the door and across the door jamb. He repeated this with the roll-up door and the concrete slab beneath it. He quit the building and drove back into Los Angeles proper.

Monk got to his office as dusk began to settle. An unmarked police car he knew well was parked at the curb in front. Marasco sat at the wheel, smoking. The private eye walked up on the driver's side.

"The only time you smoke is when you got something on your mind, homeboy."

Seguin threw the cigarette to the ground. Quietly he said, without looking at Monk, "Better get in the car, Ivan."

"Why?"

"It's Jill, she's been—"

"What," Monk yelled, cutting his friend off. He grabbed his shoulder, squeezing hard.

THE TAPOKATA-TAPOKATA machine was surging in his head. He stared at the picture before him, people's voices buzzing all around him, but it was only the steady pump of the all-purpose, all-weather machine that he could hear. Slowly, as if his ears were unplugging as he descended a great height, Monk began to filter in the voices.

"She was lucky," one voice said.

"Luck, nothing," the other voice intoned. "It was a warning intended for Monk."

"They don't think that complicated," the first voice rasped.

Monk turned to the voices. "Marasco's right, Keys. How the hell do you miss with a double-barreled shotgun from less than twenty feet unless you really want to?"

"So why not just kill her?" Keys retorted, adjusting his glasses.

To stop himself from planting his fist in the upwardly mobile fed's mouth, Monk turned back to look at Jill.

"If they kill her, Monk's got nothing left, and goes after them," Seguin said. "This way, a close shave on purpose, he's got more to think about, more to consider."

The doctor who was bandaging Kodama's arm finished and wrote out a prescription for her. "In case there's any pain," she said, handing the slip of paper to her. The doctor left the room. Kodama sat on the examining table, incongruously dressed in her slacks and a paisley print paper gown.

"He's not the only one who's got something to consider, boys," Kodama said, getting off the table.

"Was it Crosshairs who did this, Judge Kodama?" Keys asked.

"I really don't know, Agent Keys. As I've told Marasco, they wore ski masks. They were both big, that I could tell."

Keys glared at Monk. "What do you have to say to that, Monk?"

"Look, man, if I knew where to find Sawyer, I wouldn't be standing here right now having you give me the blues."

Keys shook his finger at Monk. "You think you're slick, Monk. But the Bureau gets what it needs to see that crimes are solved."

Monk almost laughed. "Jesus, Keys, did you get that from the one hundred and one quotations of J. Edgar Hoover?"

"It's people like you, who subvert the law for their own ends, who are the danger."

"I'm not the one fast-tracking Black and brown youth for a bullshit few ounces of crack, Keys."

"Drug dealers shouldn't be punished, huh?"

"There shouldn't be two tiers of justice, Keys. Possession of powder cocaine, favored by middle-class whites, is not prosecuted under harsher federal sentencing like crack is. And anyway, you damn sure ain't throwing no real drug dealers in jail. What with the DEA, the Justice Department, and members of the Peruvian and Colombian armies on the pad to the drug lords."

"Let me tell you about the brave men and women who've died to—"

"And let me tell you about the brothers dying in the streets every day," Monk began, cutting the FBI man off.

They moved closer to one another, jaws tight, muscles tensed. Seguin got between them. "All right, that's enough." His attention went to Keys. "The judge said she couldn't identify her assailants, Keys. She didn't get a license number on the car, nothing. That's it."

"No it isn't," he said, boring his eyes into Monk.

A silence attached itself to the room. A shroud under which nothing happened for several long moments. Eventually, Keys said, "I want to see the report on my desk this evening, Lieutenant." He departed.

"Well, if you boys are through waving your dicks around, give a girl a lift, will you?" She put an arm around Monk's waist, and they hugged each other.

"What the hell is going on with this case, Monk?" Seguin said, thrusting his hands in his pockets.

"I know you mean well, Marasco. But you've got to believe me, I don't have all the answers yet."

"But you won't tell me what pieces you do have?"

"You'd have to tell Keys."

The left side of Seguin's face twitched. "I'm still my own man, Ivan. You know I don't give a shit about Keys."

"Everybody wants something different out of this." Monk bit down on his bottom lip. "You've got all the machinery, Marasco. All I've got is my next check and the client's signature on it."

"I'm sorry this had to come between us."

"It's the nature of our work."

Seguin's angular face arranged itself into hard lines. "I know." He walked out.

Monk kissed Jill on the forehead. He whispered, "I'm sorry, baby. I couldn't stand it if anything happened to you."

"It's all right. Just some glass from the car's windshield and a few buckshot pellets."

"Right. You could have been cut in half by the blast or your body lit up with 9-mm slugs from an Uzi."

"It could happen walking down the street, honey. Or more likely it'll happen because the crime partners of some guy I sentence to hard time will be just smart enough to find me and pop a cap on me." She looked up into his face. "I'm not saying I'm not scared. I am saying I can't let it paralyze me. I won't just curl up in a ball and wait for the end."

"Damn, you're tough."

"Shut up."

Kodama got dressed and they checked out of the Kaiser. They drove to El Coyote, a Mexican restaurant over on Beverly, and had a meal out on the patio. Afterwards, Kodama retrieved her car and they went back to Monk's apartment. They took a shower together and went back out to catch jazz bassist Charlie Hayden and his quintet at a club in Hollywood. It was past one-thirty in the morning when the two got back to Monk's place in Mar Vista.

The red light blinked on his answering machine. Monk rewound the device. "Ivan, Ray Smith again. I'll try you in the morning."

Monk and Kodama headed for the bedroom, taking off their clothes as they went. "What did he want? You haven't seen him in a long time," Kodama said.

Monk pulled her close and said in a low voice, "I think he's going to get me to Crosshairs, and hopefully, his cousin Conrad James."

"It could be a set-up."

"I realize that. But like you said, I've got to go forward on this thing."

"You make sure you be careful."

They went to bed and made love by the light from the light on his nightstand, casting ever-changing dark shapes across their taut muscles. Damning the watchers if, indeed, they were also under visual surveillance as well as sound by the FBI. The light of morning arrived too quickly, and Monk got out of bed and made them a breakfast of wheat toast, poached eggs and spicy beef sausage. They were just sitting down to it when the phone rang.

"Hello," Monk said, answering it on the third ring.

"Ivan, this is Ray, man."

"Long time no see, brother."

"Yeah, well, we ain't got time for traveling down memory lane."

Before he could proceed, Monk said. "We have to meet but I—"

Smith cut him off. "You be around on Sunday, about this time." The line disconnected.

DIAZ SAT ramrod straight in the plastic chair in front of the window with the slats. A pair of binoculars on a fixed tripod was to his left. To his right sat Agent-in-Charge Keys at a steel table. On the table was a telephone, a monitoring device which had a wire leading to a cassette recorder, and a pair of headphones. Keys leaned away from the desk and fiddled with one of his silver cufflinks.

"Ray Smith has made contact," Keys said.

"Time to drop the hammer," Diaz commented sardonically.

Keys picked up the phone's handset and punched out a number. After a moment, he spoke. "Bazeco, this is Keys. I need for you and Roberts, and Haller in another car, to be stationed around Monk's apartment by"—he looked at his watch—"six o'clock tomorrow morning." He listened, then said, "That's right, Lieutenant Seguin is known to Monk and might be spotted. Agent Diaz and I will be in another car. We'll all use channel three for all communications. See you then."

Diaz raised his hand in the air, made a closed fist and brought it down like he was pulling a weight. They both grinned.

THE PHONE'S bell jangled the dark of two A.M. Monk, positioning himself onto his back, picked it up on the fourth ring. "Monk." Kodama put a hand on his stomach and continued to sleep.

"It's time to get going."

Monk came fully awake. "What do you want me to do?"

"Be down in front in three minutes."

Monk rushed out of the bed, not bothering to hang up the phone. Kodama stirred in the bed but didn't rise. He got into a pair of loose fitting Dockers and a flannel shirt. He reached for his harness in the closet, thought better of it, and opened one of the drawers of his dresser. Down below a tangle of boxer shorts and socks, he found his ankle rig and the small .38—a Smith & Wesson Bodyguard revolver with a hidden hammer—and strapped that on. He got into his worn and comfortable Blacktop tennis shoes and a wind-breaker.

Furiously, he scratched out two lines in his notepad to Kodama which read: *I'm off to the races. Love you always.* He tore out the sheet and placed it on the nightstand. He slipped the notepad into his back pocket and went downstairs. At the curb, its motor running, was a four-door Chevy Caprice with fender skirts. At the wheel was an individual who had the hood of his sweat jacket pulled over his head. Rising out of the car on the passenger side was somebody Monk knew. Once.

"Yo, blood, get in," Ray Smith said to Monk as the latter hurtled into the car.

Monk got in behind the driver as the car pulled away from the curb. He looked back and saw a car round a corner. It was trying to look casual, but considering the lack of traffic this time of the morning, it couldn't help but stand out. Monk jerked his thumb along side of his face. "I think that's a FBI car back there."

"I know," the hooded driver replied.

The way he said it, so calm and self-assured, Monk felt a knot of apprehension twisting his stomach. He couldn't sit by and let them start shooting at the Feds. No matter how much he despised Keys.

The driver took the car another mile east and then pulled to the curb. The car that had been following discretely behind them also pulled to the curb. Monk looked toward the two men in the front seats, but they didn't turn around. He could imagine either Keys or Diaz—it had to be those two back there—on their car phone calling around to wake up the other members of the task force and try to get them in position. "Don't you two think we ought to get moving?"

"In a minute," the driver spat out, turning slightly in profile. His purple hood the mark of an inner city Druid.

A phone rang and it took Monk a moment to realize it was in the car he was sitting in.

The driver picked it up, listened, then said, "Okay, count ten, then go." He handed it to Smith and in ten seconds, left the curb at great velocity. Monk looked back and could see the other car following suit. The hooded driver took a hard right down a narrow street and as they passed a darkened alleyway, another car emerged behind them. Monk could see that it too was similar in shape to the Caprice. In the dark of the night, a duplicate of the one he was riding in. They took another turn and then zoomed along behind a row of industrial buildings.

Presently, the faux Caprice, which must have been traveling parallel to their course, shot out of a side street and rejoined them. The two cars did a sort of exaggerated figure-eight down the street, each car weaving in and out of the space the other occupied. By now they were in Culver City and the Caprice Monk was in took another sharp turn and plowed to a stop in a darkened parking lot near the Denny's close to the Fox Hills Mall.

"Move," the driver commanded and the three exited on a

run. Somebody emerged from the building's shadows, and they got in the Caprice and whipped off. Monk was herded between the building and a concrete wall. They all crouched down into the ebony recess afforded by the wall.

Minutes elapsed as Monk could hear the screech of tires and the pounding of V-8 engines swallowed up by the city. He felt a hand pulling on his upper arm, and he stood with the driver and Ray Smith by his side.

"Pretty smart, huh?" Ray Smith enthused.

Monk looked at Smith but couldn't see anything but indistinct features, a reflection of the distance between the two who had been through junior and senior high school together. "What's the game plan now?" Monk said.

The driver extended his arm and pointed. "Over there." He led the way through the gloom and the trio came to a late model Ford Bronco parked behind a series of industrial trash containers. They entered the vehicle and wound over to Slauson Avenue and headed east, Monk again riding in the rear.

Getting close to Western Avenue, Smith said to the driver. "I don't know about you, but I'm hungry. Let's get some grub over at the Golden Ox."

"Okay," the driver responded.

He turned right on Western and traveled several blocks until he got to Gage and pulled into the drive-through of the all-night burger stand. The Bronco came to rest alongside a yellow plastic silhouette of an ox. The menu of the establishment, which included such nouvelle junk cuisine as chili cheese fries with blue cheese, and a pastrami burger with spinach and dill, was delineated on the cutout in neat, precise script. The microphone was in the head of the ox.

"What do you want, Ivan?" Smith turned in his seat to look at him.

"Coffee, three creams and one sugar."

The driver gave their orders, and they pulled in behind a cab that was also waiting for its order at the front of the drive-through. Monk stared at the back of Smith's head. He'd been taken aback a moment ago. It was the first time he'd gotten a good look at him.

Smith's once-handsome face was now drawn and of a grayish pallor. The folds under his eyes were puffy, and the eyes themselves were cloudy, seemingly unfocused. He looked ten years older than Monk yet he was actually younger by almost a year. The cab moved off, and they slid to the window in the Bronco.

The driver turned slightly to look at Monk. It was the Rolling Dalton who had the skirmish with the two Scalp Hunters at the Oki's-Dog stand. Under the lighted carport, Monk could see the tattoos of the two tears in the corner of his right eye. Did it mean he was always sad, or that his sorrow was only a surface job?

"Heard you handled yourself with a couple of bums."

Bums was the belittling term the Daltons used when describing Scalp Hunters. "How'd you hear about that?" Monk said to the driver.

He smiled, his teeth yellow and wolfish in profile. "The young brother who plays the video games in the Hi-Life."

"One of your lookouts." Monk was aware of the sharp tone in his voice.

The driver turned back in his seat to look out the windshield. "Something like that."

Their food arrived, and the Bronco pulled over to the parking lot. The driver killed the engine. They ate and Monk sipped his coffee in silence. He didn't know how to play it. There was no way for him to think too far ahead, plot out his moves. It was reassuring that they had demonstrated such good planning in outwitting Keys. It meant clarity and organization. It meant people who could be reasoned with. But there was always a wild card.

"Look here, Monk," Ray Smith began while washing down the remains of his double cheeseburger with a root beer. "What can happen in the way of some ducats on this thing?"

"You mean how much money can you wrangle out of it, Ray?"

The driver's hood remained looking straight ahead, but Monk imagined his eyes taking in Smith in a sidelong glance.

Smith said, "You need to talk to Crosshairs, I'm the one that can get you there."

"What exactly are you to the Daltons, Ray? You're too old to be running with them."

Smith spun his head around. "I'm one of the ones who helped get the truce going, blood."

"You set the meeting 'tween us and the Swans, Ray. That ain't the same thing as makin' the truce," the driver corrected.

Smith dismissed the comment with a wave of his hand. "Whatever. Fact is Monk needs to talk to Crosshairs and I know where to find him."

"I bet a lot of people know where to find him," Monk said. "And you got it wrong, Ray. I want to talk to his cousin, Conrad James. If Crosshairs can get me to him, fine. Otherwise, if one of you knows where to find Conrad, that's cool, too."

The driver's hood moved slightly to the right. "Look man, Ray's got his thing, we got ours."

"Ours?" Monk said.

"The truce that me and some of the OGs from the Daltons help put together with the Swans and the Del Nines.

Brothers and sisters done had it with bangin', home. Your boy from SOMA and Perry and all them ain't got us in mind when they set they shit up."

Monk leaned forward. "So what do you want to do?"

The young man turned around to look full into Monk's face. "What I want to do is reach those brothers that still be bangin' and get them to stop. Black man on Black man and we all goin' down the sewer. I don't give a fuck 'bout Ray and you and all your old times together." He paused, swallowing some fries. "I do a favor for you, you do something for us. It's like that."

"What's the favor?"

"Get us a grant from SOMA. Or at least get us a meeting with somebody there who will listen to us. Somebody who won't chump us off. Get us something to get a leg up so we can start some small businesses and do some more reachin' out to others still in the life."

Monk essayed, "Don't you have enough drug money to do that?"

"Don't believe everything your cop buddies tell you. Every gangbanger ain't rollin' in dough. And some of them don't live long enough to be eligible to vote."

"I promise I'll do what I can. I'll get you a meeting." He hoped that was a promise he could keep.

"See that you do more than talk," Smith said.

"Excuse me, Ray?" Monk snarled. "For damn near ten years now you been nothing but one long disappointment to all your friends. You got nerve telling me to be responsible."

"Is it my fault I've had rough times?"

"Times you made."

"Say fellas, I'd love to sit here all night and hear this shit, but we gotta be steppin'," the driver said. He started the Bronco and they again headed east along Slauson. At

Budlong, the vehicle made a right and continued along the street until it reached 76th. They made a left and came to rest in front of a house with a peaked roof.

"Who are we meeting?"

"Nobody yet, Mr. Detective. I gotta set things up."

"Yeah, smart boy," Smith said. "Mad-T's gotta go back and meet with the others now that you said you gonna play square and all."

"Yeah, so?" Monk said, getting edgy.

Mad-T, the urban prophet in knitted gredelin, pointed at Smith. "He's your babysitter until I get back."

"He couldn't watch a dog pee," Monk said between gritted teeth. "What the hell you mean I've got to be watched?"

Mad-T shot back. "This ain't no play, private eye. Ray knows you, he spoke for you, he's gotta be responsible for you. I take back what we agreed on and we'll see."

Smith and the hooded Dalton got out of the car. Briefly, Monk considered telling them to fuck themselves and walk away from it. Waiting around in some gang crash pad with Ray Smith was not a must-do activity high on his list. But what choice did he really have? Conrad James may have part of the answer. But since he wasn't likely to get him on the phone, Monk got out of the car and followed the two up to the house.

Mad-T unlocked the door to the house. It looked like many other working-class homes that comprised the housing stock of South Central Los Angeles. The trio entered. Smith brought the lights on and Monk surveyed the room he stood in. Various pieces of furniture, encompassing the styles of the '40s through the '70s, made up the design of the living room. A widescreen TV dominated the room along with a scarred coffee table strewn with empty malt liquor cans and the refuse of fast food meals.

"Gee, guys, this the club house?"

"There's food in the fridge, and the roof don't leak." Mad-T moved back to the door. "Sit tight. You'll hear from me tomorrow." He left, closing the door behind him quietly.

Monk checked the time. It was three-thirty. He looked at Smith. "You don't mind if I take the couch, do you?"

"Always on guard, huh?"

"That's something you wouldn't know about."

"How come you got such a tight jaw for me, Ivan? We used to be down for each other."

"That was about three or four thousand dollars ago, Ray. Before you fucked up your life with cocaine and washed out all the bridges your friends tried to build for you."

Smith sat on the arm of the couch, "Hey, man, I admit I made some mistakes. Sure, I borrowed money I didn't mean to pay back. But that was then. I've been clean for more than a year now."

"But you're still hustling, Ray. Still working any angle you can to make a dollar."

Smith leaped up from the arm of the couch, shouting. "Like you so noble working for them Koreans."

"It's an honest buck," Monk said defensively.

Smith snorted loudly. "Shit, who you foolin'." He started to head toward another room, then turned around. "You asked me why I was hangin' with the Daltons. Well, I wasn't always fucked up on dope or running from the consequences of my last scam. I actually did some gang intervention work for the city for a while. Some of these kids got to really trust me." He stepped closer to Monk. "Until I fell back into the pipe and almost caused the death of a young brother by letting the wrong word slip. It was a Scalp Hunter so none of the other gangs cared. But I did. Deep down, I knew I couldn't go on in life looking for the next high."

"So this is your way of making up for lost time."

"Yeah."

"Yeah, but you called Tina looking for money."

Smith bowed and spread his hands. "It was a hustle, but for a good cause. You might say I was fundraising in the only way I knew how for the truce." He went into another room and closed the door.

Monk mapped out the remaining parts of the house. Past the living room was what had been the dining room. In it was a futon with quilts on it and a mattress with only a dirty sheet. Two end tables were in the room and on one of them sat a lamp minus its shade. On the other was an old-fashioned dial telephone.

The kitchen was spotless and the refrigerator was well-stocked, if lacking robustness in its fare. There were cold cuts, processed cheese slices, commercial half-pint tubs of potato and macaroni salads, candy bars, sodas and cans of beer and malt liquor. The cupboards held dishes and glasses and an assortment of canned goods. The windows were barred and the back door was of solid wood and triple locked.

Off of the kitchen was a back bedroom which had a mattress on the floor, a portable radio and various posters of rap artists taped to its wall. Connected to that room was a bathroom tiled in old-fashioned ceramic like the ones in his mother's house. The door leading out of there led to another room which seemed to be the study, for lack of a better term.

There were various chairs in various stages of disintegration about the room. It also had a large drafting table populated with writing pads and loose pieces of paper. There was a bookshelf which contained a stack of comic books, some shotgun shells, an ashtray with reefer butts, a couple of watch caps, a green-tinged braided gold chain, a fake skull with a candle stuck in it, a book about gangster

rap and *The Wretched of the Earth* by Frantz Fanon. Revo-
lution a la hip-hop.

Monk looked at the papers on the drafting table. It was
an outline showing the prominent gang members in favor
of the truce, those that were against it, and a lengthy dis-
course on the next phases of the truce.

The door from this room led into the room that Smith
was in. The detective retraced his steps and went back into
the front room, carrying the outline.

He removed the quilts from the futon and took off his
windbreaker, shirt and shoes. Monk lay on the sagging couch,
covering himself with the quilt. Fatigue overtook him while
he read the outline. It included a series of ideas for micro
enterprises and there were passages urging those members
who'd made their money illegally to take what they had left
and put it into legitimate concerns. There was even some
thought given to what kind of structure they envisioned to
run these businesses. Top down management versus more
worker-owned or something in-between. Monk's eyes closed.

In the still of the early morning, his mind reeled off
images of the people and incidents involved in the case.
Names and locations floated in Monk's brain. Some of
them were stacked in a small file on his colonial desk. The
others were kept in a mile-high chamber. It didn't worry him
that the structure was brimming with files. What worried
him was losing the one key he had to opening the massive
containment tank. And the key was in the base merit of the
SOMA offices.

"Monk," a voice said to him.

His eyes came open. For a moment, he was disoriented.
Where was Jill and where did this quilt come from? Then he
remembered. "What's up, Ray?" Pretending to scratch his leg,
Monk checked to make sure his gun was still there. It was.

Smith's head jerked toward the phone. "Mad-T just called, said he'll be here in about an hour."

"He say he's bringing anybody with him?" Monk swung his legs onto the floor.

"He said be ready to roll."

"Shit. What is this, a fuckin' Chinese puzzle box?" Monk picked up the truce document from the floor and placed it on the coffee table.

"It's the way it is, Ivan. The cops and the FBI are running around out there looking for Crosshairs and Conrad, and you, too, now. And quiet as it's kept, some of us have the opinion that there are some on the police department who don't want to see the truce succeed. 'Cause they know the next step for these young brothers and sisters is to become politicized. From there it might be the next Black Panther Party."

Monk got up and stretched. "As long as they learn from the past, Ray, as long as they learn from the past." He went into the bathroom to wash up. Afterwards, he and Ray each had a cup of instant coffee and Monk ate a couple of pieces of the beef salami cold cuts in the icebox. Presently, Mad-T arrived, and he and Monk departed the house. Ray Smith was left behind.

They traveled east in a military green 1973 Bonneville. Mad-T took them on a route that eventually headed south along Alameda until they reached Imperial Boulevard. The car made a right and Monk knew where they were going. Over to the Imperial Courts housing project in Watts.

It was a vast subsidized complex built in 1944, one of four public housing projects built in Watts during the war years. Watts, once called Mudtown, had been incorporated as a city in 1907. But the cigar boys downtown maneuvered to disenfranchise its growing Black population, and the city was annexed back to Los Angeles in 1926.

Mad-T entered the front gate into Imperial Courts and wound the car through the tracts of cinder-block abodes and trimmed lawns. A car marked security passed them and the driver nodded at Mad-T.

"He just know you, or is he something else?" Monk asked.

The young man stuck a toothpick in his mouth and said, "We got to be like the motherfuckin' CIA and have our ears everywhere if we want to know what's goin' down."

He parked the car in a stall of a block of units along the southeast end of the place. They got out and Monk followed the Dalton along an alleyway, then between two buildings. They arrived at another set of units and Mad-T knocked on an unmarked door. The door swung inward on quiet hinges.

"After you," Mad-T said.

Monk walked into the apartment, a two-level townhouse, followed by the young man. It was dark due to the fact that the drape was drawn against the large picture window. Two men sat on chairs at opposite ends of the front room. One was decked out in an oversize prison-style jean jacket, Dee-Cee khaki pants, Nike tennis shoes and a purple basball cap with the words South Central stenciled on the crown. The other one Monk recognized.

He wore coal black jeans, a smokey gray shirt with gold colored buttons and a rounded collar buttoned all the way up, black wingtips, and his apparently omnipresent gray homburg with the feather stuck in the band. As in their previous meeting, his eyes took in everything but betrayed nothing. Neither man moved or acknowledged the presence of Monk or Mad-T, save the one in the homburg who looked down at his hands then looked back up again.

"What it be?" the one in the purple cap said.

"It be like that," Mad-T responded.

Monk thought he was trapped in a hip-hop episode of
Get Smart.

Homburg rose and stepped close to Monk. "You gonna
do what you said."

The lack of inflection seemed to make it more of a command than a question. Monk said, "I'll get you a meeting
with SOMA. I don't promise that you'll get any money out
of it."

"You search him?" Homburg said.

"What for? So what if he's carrying a piece. Every moth-
erfucka' in this room's got a piece and then some. What he
gonna do?" Mad-T smirked.

"A wire, genius." Homburg stepped back, moving his head
slightly to glare past Monk at Mad-T. The light through the
open door illuminated the left side of his face. The ear was
missing its lobe. Something that Monk hadn't noticed the
other night in the half-light of Elrod's garage.

Mad-T said to Monk. "Take your jacket off, G."

Monk did so and submitted to a pat-down from the
younger man.

"I've got a gun strapped to my right ankle," Monk volun-
teered.

Mad-T retrieved the rig and the piece, and continued with
his task. He finished his thorough search and straightened
up. "No wire," he announced.

Homburg said nothing nor moved.

Monk said, "What's it going to be, Crosshairs?"

Mad-T whined, "I didn't tell him."

Crosshairs walked past the men in the room and went up
the stairs. Mad-T and Monk remained standing while the
one in the cap sat impassively. He heard the muffled creak
of the floorboards above his head, and Crosshairs and
another man came down.

He was taller than his cousin and his face elastic with expression. Conrad James was dressed in faded blue jeans and a sweatshirt lettered with a Morehouse College logo. He had the shoulders of a wrestler and the hips of a running back. He was a poster stud for a randy sorority house.

"Glad to meet you, Mr. Monk."

He took the other's hand and said, "Ivan."

"Antoine and I have talked this over, Ivan," James began, indicating Crosshairs who stood behind him statue-like. "He thinks you ain't shit, but don't take it personal."

"Oh, I don't. I can name a dozen people who think I'm nothing but shit, so what do you think about that?"

Crosshairs sniffed. James grinned and said, "Anyway, I'm the one that insisted that we talk to you. See what you could do for the Daltons and vice versa. Plus I can't keep this up forever. This ain't my life."

"Can we talk in private, or does the Greek Chorus need to be around?"

James said, "We can talk upstairs."

He started up and as Monk walked past the immobile Crosshairs, he felt a light touch on his arm. "Don't try nothin' slick, slick," Crosshairs hissed.

Monk went on up to the second floor. There was a built-in linen closet next to a small bathroom off the small hallway. On either side of the closet and the lavatory were bedrooms. One of them had three mattresses spread about and several empty bottles of soda and beer. In the other was a couple of folding chairs, a writing desk with a PC and a printer on it, and a set of steel weights. James walked into this room. Monk sat on one of the folding chairs and the younger man sat at the table. A morning breeze blew in from an open window.

"Was that your outline I read at the house near Budlong?"

"Based on some input from Antoine and some others," James said.

"Just so I can get it out of the way, did you kill Kim Bong-Suh?"

"No, I did not. Nor did my cousin or any other gang member as far as I can tell."

"What makes you say that?"

"I saw Bong-Suh twice after he shut down the store."

"About what."

"The first time he got in touch with me was to have me talk to Ruben Ursua."

"About what?"

"Well, Bong-Suh knew that Ursua was into hot cars, and he wanted Ursua to get him a short."

"Kim wanted a hot car?" Monk asked, raising an eyebrow.

"He wanted a car that had a good motor, one that he could pay cash for but that had its serial numbers altered and registered under a false name."

"So he wanted wheels other than his own. And if somebody took down the plate number, the name of Kim Bong-Suh wouldn't come up."

"I guess."

"Where did Ursua deliver this car?"

"I don't know. Once I set it up, Bong-Suh told me to have Ursua be at the Scorpion at a certain day and time and he'd contact him. The Scorpion is a bar Ursua hangs out in over on Figueroa."

"What was Kim's reason for closing the Hi-Life?"

"He said he needed to be moving around, needed to be mobile for the next few months. He couldn't be in one place where they could get him, he said."

"Did he say who 'they' was?"

"No."

"So you and he talked on the phone several times."

"Yeah."

"What happened the second time you saw him?"

"That was in September. Bong-Suh came over to my pad all keyed up. He said he would have something he wanted me to take care of for him."

Monk got excited. "What was it?"

"That's just it. He said he was going to get this thing to me, but that was the last time I saw him."

"You have any idea what he was talking about?" Through the open window, two women could be heard arguing about the fate of one of the characters on the *All My Children* soap opera.

"I'm not exactly sure. Bong-Suh never would tell me outright. But he hinted it had something to do with some of the kinds of people he knew back home."

"You mean like intelligence agents."

James wagged a finger at Monk. "What I remember him specifically saying was that he had something on those bastards, the same kind of bastards who had ruined his life in Korea."

Monk considered the information, then asked. "What made you go on the run?"

"When I talked with Bong-Suh last, he said that if I hadn't heard from him by the end of the year, or hadn't received anything from him, then that would be a bad sign. That I should lay low until things broke."

"He said that, 'Until things broke'?"

"His exact words. Hey, I knew Bong-Suh wasn't a nut, and something else happened that made me think whatever it was he'd been doing was the real deal."

"What happened?"

"My crib got broken into and searched earlier this year. But my TV, stereo, none of that stuff got lifted. My ride, and even the locker I had at Trade Tech got busted into also. And then Antoine asked me to start helping move the truce into a second phase and all, so it seemed the right time to go underground."

"Did Bong-Suh ever mention Jiang Holdings?"

"He could have, but I don't remember."

"Any ideas on where he might have hidden his notes?"

James cocked his head and spread his hands in the air.

Monk stood. "How come he trusted you so much? How come you two were so tight?"

"He was an all right guy, man. Just 'cause he was Korean and I'm Black doesn't mean that we're automatic enemies. Momma taught me to take each one at their word until they do you dirt. And as for why he trusted me, well, I'd like to think it's because we talked for real to each other. Got to know something about the other one. He told me his wife was beaten to death by the cops in some kind of strike at this place called the Dongil Company. I told him about an uncle I had who got sent to the hospital by the cops because he was a garbage man striking for better wages way back during the Civil Rights days in Montgomery."

"Out of curiosity, why did you break it off with Karen Jacobs?"

"I really like her, man. I didn't want her to get hurt in all this mess."

Monk held out his hand and the other took it. "Thanks for your time and the information, Conrad."

"Do you think you'll find Bong-Suh's killers?"

"I'm going to run them to ground, as an old friend of mine says."

At the bottom of the stairs Crosshairs stood, his face in its usual blank pose, but Monk noticed activity in the eyes. As he drew close, the OG spoke.

"You find out something useful?"

"I think so."

Monk started to move past him, but said, "I had a run-in with a couple of Scalp Hunters who said that the Daltons used to deal drugs out of the Hi-Life Liquors." He turned to gauge the other's reaction. "Anything to that?"

"The bums ain't party to the truce. Some of those brothers ain't nothing but stone capitalists, anything for a dollar. I'm not saying the Rolling Daltons are a bunch'a saints, I am saying ain't no Dalton killed Kim over crack profits or any other reason. I've checked, Mr. Detective. If this peace thing is gonna hold, I got to know the for real on everybody who could fuck it up."

"Do you mean that, or are you just giving me a snow job? Make me think you're the gangster with a heart of gold."

"Believe what you want, home. Believe we started this truce 'cause we got a devious plan in mind like the cops say. Believe we did it 'cause some of us is tired, beat down from bangin' and seeing our homies and relatives die. Or believe that some Black men and women can come together and not try and kill one another." Crosshairs went up the stairs, not caring to wait for Monk's reply.

Mad-T dropped Monk off at the Tiger's Den on 48th Street. He assumed that Keys and company were keeping watch on his office and his apartment. And he wanted to be able to move about unfettered at least for the next few hours.

"You look like chewed over gristle," Tiger said, greeting him.

"Thank you, honey." Monk winked at him and walked over to the pay phone. Figuring the tap was still activated on his office phone, Monk dialed the inside line of Hendricks, one of the developer partners he shared space with. She answered, and Monk asked her to get Delilah and put her on the line.

"Where the hell have you been?" she scolded.

"Detecting."

"You better get back over here and detect this."

"What?"

"Ms. Scarn called again. She says maybe you better have your attorney get in contact with her. She says not only is there a question about your failure to file a weapons discharge report, but there is a new allegation of failure to cooperate with the authorities in a murder investigation."

"Goddamn Keys."

"Yeah, well, Special Agent Keys also called and asked in a very pleasant tone that when you had a chance, he'd like to hear from you."

"He's trying to put the screws to me through Consumer Affairs. Did Ms. Scarn say anything else?"

"She said you have to come to her office and talk this matter over."

"She give a deadline?"

"No. But it was pretty clear she wanted to hear from you soon. Like today."

A pause dragged, then he said. "Did you deposit that check I asked you to from SOMA?"

"Of course."

"Okay, don't be so testy."

"You think you're so fucking smooth."

"Everybody keeps telling me that. Call Ms. Scarn and tell her I can meet with her anytime she likes."

"Okay. Oh, Roy Park called you back, too. That is, he called back for the name you gave him on your phony card."

"Did he say when and where I could reach him?"

"He said he'd be out of his office until this afternoon, but that if you missed him he'd be down at his property on Vermont around two tomorrow."

"Good work. Call his office back and tell them I'll meet him there."

"Anything else you need me to do?"

"When I hang up, I want you to priority-messenger a note to Jill's bailiff. His name is Jory, and he knows me. Ask Jill in the note if she will pick me up over at Tiger's place around"—Monk checked the time—"nine o'clock tonight."

"Why all the subterfuge lately, boss? You getting beeps over the phone, rushing in and out of your office, the FBI dropping by, and your fourth call was from Jill. She sounded worried about you."

"There are more things on heaven and earth, my fine beauty, than our petty concerns."

"What?"

"I'll explain soon enough. Put Hendricks back on will you?"

She did and Monk, taking out his notepad and flipping it to a certain page, asked another favor of the architect. She said she'd find out what he wanted to know and Monk hung up. He wanted to call Jill but wasn't sure that her line into her chambers wasn't bugged, so he held off. He went to his locker and changed into his sweats. Mad-T had given him back his .38 and the ankle rig and he placed these on top of his clothes and shut the locker.

For the next hour and a half Monk went through his routine of weights, sit-ups, cals, and some stationary bicycling. He rewarded himself with a stint in the sauna and then, towel wrapped around his waist, laid back on the bench in front of his locker.

"Say man, this ain't no flop house." Tiger Flowers was shaking him awake, laughing.

"How long was I out?"

"A little over an hour. You looked as though you needed it."

Monk straightened up on the bench. "I better get going.

"All this have to do with this case you been on?"

"It's been a bear-hugger, Tiger. Listen, I may be back later tonight, if that's okay."

What passed for a smile creased the folds around the Asiatic eyes of the old champ. He went to his office and returned with a key which he handed to Monk. "You need me to stay?"

Monk clasped him on the shoulder. "Ain't gonna be no rough stuff tonight, chief."

Flowers brushed the hand aside. "Good. Just make sure you turn out the lights when you're through. This damn sure ain't no charity outfit." He rumbled off to find some kid who thought he was going to be the next Sugar Ray Leonard or Riddick Bowe to yell at.

Monk finished dressing, mentally mapping out his moves for the next few hours. As a formality he checked the .38 to make sure it hadn't been tampered with and strapped the ankle rig back on. Emerging into the structured cacophony of the gym, Monk absorbed the sounds and smells of all the agile young men. They were the inheritors of poor and working-class myths, shadow boxing against the Tiger Den's yellowing plaster, jumping rope across her drab floor, or endlessly sparring in the four-cornered ring that would lead nowhere for most of them. Hoping to cash in on their fears and dreams in the great scam as old as the reign of Caesar, the boxing game. And in the process, somehow believing that their magnificent bodies could elevate them beyond the claim that time and death would place on their lives.

The harsh sunshine bracketed Monk's body as he walked out of, then away from, the factory of pugilists. He walked east along 48th until he got to Figueroa, then trudged north along the main throughfare. The El Scorpion was a ticky-tacky joint inserted between a shoe repair parlor and a barber shop in a building which had apartments with fire escapes on its second and third floors. The entranceway was painted in uneven vertical strips of azure and green and a black scorpion—one of its claws pinching the mini-skirted butt of a woman with breasts drawn completely out of proportion to the rest of her body—arched over the open door.

Monk considered walking in and sitting at the bar, but thought better of it. Watering holes, like communities in Los Angeles, tended to be segregated. And judging from the clientele he watched trickle in, the El Scorpion was definitely a gathering place for a Latino crowd. Besides, Ursua's big Caddy was nowhere in sight. He may have already traded it in for something else, but Monk doubted it. That car was meant to be seen in. He waited.

Not having the luxury of a car to hunker down in, Monk passed the time by ordering coffees at the donut stand on the corner and playing a couple of pathetic games of chess with a white-haired man who bore a resemblance to Milton Berle. The location afforded Monk a view of the bar's front door and at a little past four in the afternoon, the metal-flake-blue El-D cruised by and went down a side street.

Monk left the stand in time to see a medium-built, thick-waisted man wearing aviator-style sunglasses in a black polo shirt and white jeans, enter the El Scorpion. As casual as he could make it, Monk entered the establishment after him. The place was dark and there was sawdust on the floor. On its tinny speakers, the juke belted out some woman singer doing heavy melodramatics to a tune in Spanish.

Two men in mechanic's blues huddled conspiratorially over a pitcher of beer and a table. Another man in a UPS uniform sat at the oak bar drinking a martini. Two young Chicanas and a young man in knee-length slack shorts and penny loafers sat at another table, laughing and drinking. It must be some kind of trend, Monk reasoned. College kids, like the ones down in San Pedro the other night, who got a kick out of hanging out in neighborhood dives. Or a grand scheme of organizing the great unwashed into a vanguard of cutting edge culture.

Since the idea of blending in with his environment was not possible, Monk walked up to the man in the white jeans, who also sat at the bar, with one of his boots up on the rail.

"Ruben Ursua," Monk said to the man, standing a little to the side and in back of him.

The other man bestowed a baleful stare on Monk in the reflection of the mirror behind the row of bottles. "Fuck off. I'm not on parole anymore."

Monk laid a business card on the bar for him to see.

Ursua glanced at it and went back to his drinking.

"Usually people whistle and clap when I show them this." Zero.

"How about if I want the same deal you gave Kim Bong-Suh?"

That got a rise. "I know your name, now. You're the one them Koreans hired to find out about his killing. I don't know shit, man."

In his voice Monk could hear the cadence one learned in the prison yard. The code of silence crooks and cops, doctors and lawyers, and politicians and priests used. "Dig this." Monk put two twenties on the bar in front of Ursua, who tried to pretend he didn't notice them. "Just tell me where you delivered the car he wanted, and I'll forget who told me."

"Otherwise the cops might find out, and I get dragged into this thing."

That was the farthest idea from Monk's head, but he said, "And they said you weren't a team player."

Ursua put his squat glass of scotch on the bar and picked

up the twin twenties with the same hand. He folded them deftly with his one hand and placed the bills in his pants. "It surprised me when Conrad called me up, it was him that told you about this. I mean, I ain't mad or anything. I just want to make sure there ain't no leaks on my side."

Monk sat beside him at the bar. "You thinking of supplying cars for the Pentagon or something?"

Ursua sipped his drink and waited.

"Look, the way this works is I gather information from A and that leads me to B, who gives me more information and so on. Now, I don't tell B who A is, and I don't tell C who B is. Know what I'm saying?"

"I'm supposed to be satisfied with that?"

"It'll have to do, Ruben. But just to ease your anxiety a little." Monk produced another twenty and slid it across.

"I guess I'm going to have to believe you're as closed-mouthed as you pretend."

"Like a priest."

The lone twenty joined the others. "I'm going to have to show you. I don't remember the address but I do remember the part of town the place was in. You'll have to follow me in your car."

"I'll go with you."

Ursua's head tilted slightly and he got off his barstool. They removed themselves from the El Scorpion and got into the bad-assed El-D. He fired the big mill up. The V-8 idled with a self-assured purring as the heavy car pulled into the flow of evening traffic.

"Carter 750 Competition carb," Monk said, appreciatively.

"You got good ears. Hey, you must have been the one who came by the house in the Galaxie."

With that, they settled into a lively conversation on cars and the art of rebuilding them. By the time they reached the area where Ursua had delivered the car to Kim Bong-Suh, they both agreed they missed the bygone era of Dodge muscle bangers. It was in the Lincoln Heights section of town, where the houses were neat and tidy California Craftsmen built before the big war, and every backyard seemed to have a dog.

The Caddy slowed to a crawl. "He was standing on the corner, over there." Ursua pointed at an intersection where a dry cleaners stood. "I came with the car, and he gave me the money, in cash."

"How'd you get back home?"

"It was the middle of the day, so I took the bus." Ursua pulled to the curb and put the car in neutral and let the engine idle. "Kim drove off in that direction." He pointed again. "I saw him get to the corner there and make a left on Darwin. After that, he was gone and so was I."

"What kind of car was it? And I guess you wouldn't happen to remember the license plate."

"It was a brown 1988 Volkswagen Jetta. And a man in my profession makes it his business not to know plates. But I do think they started with 2G something."

"You know, it's none of my concern, but you're a pretty bright guy, Ruben. You could make a decent living fixing up cars legitimately."

Ursua looked straight ahead through the windshield, leaning forward, his arms folded along the top of the Eldorado's steering wheel. "That's why I took the job in the liquor store my PO set up for me when I got out. Thought I was gonna settle down and do the straight and narrow."

Monk couldn't tell if he meant himself or if he was referring to his parole officer.

Ursua went on. "Really though, it was something I couldn't escape. It's in my blood, my friend. I don't bash in anybody's head, I don't rape your wife or steal money out of a bank. Hell, a lot of the cars I deal with are right from the owners who want to work a scam on their insurance companies. I like the thrill and, like any junkie, I can't stop until they make me. You know what I mean."

Ursua put the Cadillac back in gear and Monk asked him to drop him off at the Tiger's Den. Tiger Flowers was just locking up as Ursua let him off. "That architect friend of yours sent something over here for you. It's on my desk.

"Thanks, Tiger. I'll shut her up when I leave."

"See that you do." He ambled off and got into his car, an AMC Concord, and drove off to whatever it was that Tiger Flowers did in his off-hours. Monk went in, relocking the door once he was inside. He entered the office and turned on the lights.

It was a spare, functional affair reflecting its owner's personality. There were no pictures from Tiger's past on the cracked walls, only those of young—and some not so young now judging from how their photos had yellowed—fighters. There were two Army surplus file cabinets, a desk of the sort one used to find a third grade teacher behind when Monk went to school, three chairs, a weatherbeaten couch, an ancient clock plugged in over the door and a standing lamp.

On the desk was a packet from a messenger service. Monk sat at the desk and opened the envelope. He read the single sheet of paper twice, then folded it up and put it in his back pocket. Monk got up from the desk and paced around the gym thinking, until fifteen before nine when he went out front. Jill's Saab came into view seven minutes later, and he escorted her inside. She carried two plastic shopping sacks.

"Where the hell have you been?" she demanded, after kissing him on the lips.

"Is that basil and garlic I smell, or a new perfume?"

"Asshole."

They went back into the office, and Monk cleared a space on the desk. Jill sat the sacks down and lifted out two containers and a bottle of wine. "Do you have any glasses around here?"

Monk found a glass with a Texaco emblem on it and one with the logo of the San Francisco 49ers. "There you go, gas station specials." He sat them down and pulled the cork out of the bottle which had already been worked free. Over a meal of linguine and squid in red sauce, Monk told Kodama what had transpired since he last saw her.

"Do you believe Conrad James and Crosshairs? I don't know about James, but Mr. Crosshairs Sawyer is hardly a candidate for the post of monsignor. I had his jacket pulled and since thirteen he's been busted for assault, attempted assault, aggravated assault, robbery with assault, and did some hard time for second-degree manslaughter."

"I know, honey, I read his sheet, too. But who better to teach than someone who's been there? It's certainly something that Malcolm was an example of."

Kodama's lips puckered. "Don't you go pulling your nationalist cloak on me, homeboy. You got the FBI and the Daltons breathing down your neck because they both want you to produce something for them. You can't please both of them, and they both know how to get even. Good and even."

"On the up side, I've got money from the Merchants Group and SOMA burning holes in my pocket." He smiled and took another bite of his meal.

"What makes you think that Ursua and James haven't cooked up this story about the other car just to send you on a phantom hunt?"

"To what purpose?" Monk countered. "If they wanted me dead, they could have easily accomplished that anytime when

I was with them. Don't forget, Stacy Grimes's death figures in this somehow. He and Samuels both worked strong-arm for Jiang Holdings. Their job was to convince the owners of properties damaged after the uprising in '92 to sell."

"Then you believe Jiang is a front for the Korean Merchants Group."

"Let's not get that far down the track just yet, Red Rider. I asked O'Day's office to find out who was really Jiang; here's what they got for me." Monk pulled the paper he had folded up out of his back pocket.

Kodama read the piece of paper and looked from it to Monk, her mouth slightly ajar. "Who gave you this?"

"I had Hendricks look it up for me. She's got friends down in the city planning department who actually produced that information."

Kodama said, "Curious."

"Isn't it. There also seems to be a gentleman with a hunch-back who was seen in the storeroom of Hi-Life Liquors a week after the riots. A so-far unidentified gentleman who has some kind of connection to our Mr. Samuels." Monk didn't add the part about his being at Samuels's apartment and getting a glimpse of the other man before he was knocked out. If he did, he'd have to tell Kodama that he entered and searched Samuels's place illegally. It was times like this that reminded Monk how odd his profession was, to one minute be riding around with an accomplished car thief, and the next eating dinner with his girlfriend the judge.

Kodama was talking. "The first thing you have to do tomorrow is call Keys and tell him everything you know."

"I'm sorry, dear. It sounded like you wanted me to drop a dime on some guys who're trusting me."

"Keys will ask you point blank if you've made contact with Crosshairs. It is a federal offense to knowingly lie to a federal official investigating a crime. If Crosshairs is as sharp as you and I think he is, I believe he's already moved on to another safe house."

Monk rose and stared at the photographs on the wall, his hands in his back pockets. "But how's that going to look to the Daltons?"

"That you're a handkerchief head motherfuckah who would sell out his own momma to save his ass." She paused, watching Monk as he turned to face her. "Or they'll see you had no choice. That if they want you to get them their meeting, you had to give your opposition something."

"I can still lie to Keys, and he'll never know the difference. Left to their own devices, him and Diaz couldn't find Madonna on a bed of coal."

Kodama crossed her legs. "Then you're making me a party to your complicity. Plus Keys can get you locked up on supposition alone. It won't be hard to convince some judge appointed in the Bush era that you surely must have been going to meet with Crosshairs at two in the morning. Or else why the bait and switch with the cars. And even if you stick to your story, he'll probably get this Ms. Scarn to pull your license, the cops will take away your concealed weapons permit, and your bond will be revoked. And then where would you be?"

"Fucked."

"Let's keep our sex life out of this."

"Ha, ha, cute."

Kodama remained silent.

Monk sat heavily into Tiger Flowers's chair. He closed his eyes but the problem wouldn't go away. The words he had said to Ursua in the bar came back to him and a ball of something nasty rolled around in his stomach. "How come small guys like me are the ones that always have to bend?"

Kodama came over and kissed him. "Because guys like you are always there to take somebody else's heat."

"Fine," Monk said crossly.

Monk locked up the Tiger's Den, and he and Kodama got a room at the Bel Age Hotel in West Hollywood. Later in bed, Monk asked Kodama while they were curled up together, "You know things have been jumping since you were shot at and we haven't really talked about it fully. I know you can handle yourself and all, but I'd feel better if you rearranged your court calendar and went down to Dex's place in Lake Elsinore until this thing gets sorted out."

"I've already rearranged my appointments." She wriggled some causing Monk to groan with pleasure. "You're my protection, baby." She dropped off to sleep.

Monk breathed in her aroma, listening to her breathing, his hand cupped under one of her breasts. He could feel the steady drum of her heart and hear the late night growl of traffic not too far away along Santa Monica Boulevard. There they were, safe and warm in their cocoon of plaster and glass, the goddamn FBI and the other wolves circling their lair temporarily abated. But the dam was breaking, and Monk wondered how long he would last in the flood.

SIXTEEN

The woman cop named Bazeco looked at Keys, then back to Monk. She said, "I think's he's up to something."

Kodama folded her arms and spoke. "Mr. Monk has come to you of his own volition. As a licensed private investigator, it is his duty to cooperate with the authorities."

"Then why the fuck didn't he get in touch with us yesterday?" Diaz said, stirring milk into his coffee.

"I was exhausted and needed sleep. And there was a pressing matter I had to take care of," Monk said tersely.

"What was it?" Keys sat at the table with Diaz, his shirt sleeves uncharacteristically rolled up on his forearm.

"That's privileged information, agent," Monk said.

"Which client would that be, Monk? The Korean Merchants or SOMA?" Roberts piped in, leaning along one of the walls.

Monk, who was sitting with his back against the wall, lifted a hand. "Their interests are intertwined."

"How lovely for you," plainclothes detective Haller offered.

"Do you want the information, or not?" Kodama shot back.

"He goes with us," Keys demanded.

Monk laughed without humor. "No, no. If I show my butt around there holding hands with a bunch of cops and feds, how long do you think I'll live after that?"

"How do we know we'll find Crosshairs once we get out to Imperial Courts?" Diaz had stopped stirring his coffee and was now blowing on it to cool it off.

"I never said you'd find Crosshairs, agent. I said I'd tell you where it was that I met with the murder suspect. Now if he's still there, that's his lookout."

Roberts got a drink of water from the Arrowhead cooler in the corner. Bazeco knotted her large, mannish hands. Haller sat down at the table and did nothing. Seguin, standing close to the door to the Detectives' Squad room, looked quizzically at Monk. Diaz leaned over to whisper something to Keys. The other man nodded and Diaz left the room.

Kodama, who had been standing near Monk, also sat down at the table. After a fashion, Diaz returned. He again said something in confidence to Keys, who then addressed Kodama. "Your client draws us a map and he signs a statement that the information he has provided is the truth."

"To the best of his knowledge," Kodama added.

The paper work was typed up and Monk drew a crude map. He and Kodama read the statement, and he signed it.

"You wait here until we get back," Keys said, studying the map.

"No. He's not under arrest and he's not a material witness. We're leaving," Kodama said forcefully.

"Yeah, and call off your lap dog Scarn," Monk put in.

Keys presented Monk with an odd look. "Who are you talking about?"

"You know who I'm talking about."

Keys was halfway out of the door when he turned and

spoke. "I don't know this Scarn or what the hell you're talking about, Monk. Maybe you ought to go home and lie down again. I think running with the big boys is giving you a headache." He walked out, rolling down his sleeves as he did.

"You better not be shittin' on us, Monk," Diaz contributed, walking away also.

"Always a pleasure talking with you too, dear." He and Kodama left the Wilshire Station and went to their cars parked on Venice. "Are you going to be all right?"

"Yes. I'm going out to my folks' place in Gardena for a few days to chill out." She gave him a hug. "Do you think Keys was lying to you about Scarn?"

"I don't think so. He has a big enough hammer with the federal law to hold over me. If I'm busted, then automatically my license is suspended."

"Then who registered the complaint against you with Consumer Affairs?"

"I'm beginning to think I know, Jill. By the way, there's Rolling Daltons in Gardena, too, you know."

"But you don't think it was the Daltons who shot at me, do you?"

"No, I don't."

Something in his face made Kodama take a step back. "You worry me sometimes."

Monk clucked his tongue, kissed her and got into his Galaxie and drove over to Lincoln Heights. Monk cruised the neighborhood Ruben Ursua had taken him to the other day, particularly along Darwin Street where Ursua had said Kim had turned onto. It was a long shot, but one worth playing. For it to make sense, he reasoned that Kim must have walked to his rendezvous with Ursua. Therefore, where he was living, where he must have maintained another place separate from his one on Dunsmuir, had to be in the area.

After two hours of driving around and stopping to look down people's driveways and behind apartment house carports, his search finally yielded positive results.

He found a brown 1988 Volkswagon Jetta whose license plate began with 2G. Monk stood in an alley looking onto the backyard of a dull ocher stucco house. The car was on a concrete patio alongside a two-car garage. From the street it couldn't be seen, and Monk had had to walk down the alley because it was too narrow for a car. There were stairs leading up to a room constructed over the garage.

To complete the pastoral setting, a sleek, muscular Doberman pinscher sat on its haunches, watching Monk. Waiting, he imagined, for him to put one finger on the top of the chain-link fence so he could take his arm off at the base. Monk started to walk out of the alley toward the front of the house when the back door opened.

A young Chicano in his early twenties stepped out of the house. He wore a brown-and-red-plaid Pendleton shirt with the two top buttons fastened. His blue-gray chinos were inspection sharp, their creases clean vertical lines that bifurcated each leg. The butt of the pistol tucked into his waistband was in stark outline to the bright white T-shirt he wore underneath the Pendleton.

"Can I help you?" The dog trotted over to him.

"I want to talk to whoever it was that rented a room to Kim Bong-Suh."

"Who're you talking about?"

"The Korean gentlemen who was living over the garage here last year. The man who drove that Volkswagen."

There was a beat. Then another. Then, "You ain't no cop.

Monk did his license trick, and said. "All I want to do is to go over the room and the car. I'll make it worth your while."

"How worth my while?"

"Forty."

"Sixty."

"Sold."

The studio apartment over the garage had been added by the young man's mother as a way of taking in boarders and making some extra money in these lean times. Kim, Monk was so informed, was a good if strange tenant, going and coming at all hours of the day and night. The young man— he said they called him Frosty—admitted he drove the Jetta on "excursions" several times since Kim had disappeared.

But when he saw the newscast recently about them finding his body, he put the car beside the garage, worried that if he just dumped it somewhere, no matter how good he wiped the car down, the cops would find his prints. He'd already been down once and wasn't about to go back for something he didn't do.

"So you know, I've been in a kind of panic about it ever since then." He was standing in the apartment with his dog as Monk searched the place. They'd had another renter since Kim, but this guy had skipped out on the rent he owed. Frosty said he and his crew were going to find him and request he make good on his debt.

In the closet, where Frosty's mother had put what Kim had left behind—his clothes had been given to Goodwill— Monk found a loose-leaf notebook. Lucky for him, Frosty pointed out, they'd put the stuff in there and hadn't bothered to throw it out. Inside the tablet the writing was in Hangul. But there were several words in English interspersed. Including Jiang Holdings. He took the notebook.

"Hey, man, don't you think if you find something you ought to pay extra for that?"

Monk wasn't about to argue with a man, a gun and a dog.

He forked over another twenty. "Does that thing work?" Monk asked, pointing to a portable TV in the corner of the front room.

"Uh-huh. That's the only thing worth anything that chump who split left us."

Without asking, and trying to avoid another charge, Monk turned it on. He dialed it to the local station that had a midday news show. Kelly Drier, his suntanned face framed by his two-hundred-dollar-styled hair, was talking.

"...Acting on a tip, our news crew arrived several minutes before the combined might of the Los Angeles Police Department and the Federal Bureau of Investigation descended on the Imperial Courts housing project here in Watts." Over Drier's shoulder, the camera picked up several bodies wandering around a cluster of town houses. The camera panned, revealing several residents standing around talking and pointing at Keys and his task force.

Drier began speaking again. "As of yet, they seemed not to have produced Crosshairs Sawyer as he was rumored to be in hiding here. I have it—" Monk shut off the set and looked at his watch.

"Thanks for everything, Frosty."

"Sure, man. Hey, what should I do about the car?"

He wanted him to leave it alone, save it for the cops. But he wasn't about to push it. "I'd leave it alone at least for the next two weeks. If you don't hear different, you can do what you like by then." He quit the room and drove back to his office, pleased with himself.

He'd slipped out of bed last night and phoned in the tip to Drier's station, which had a twenty-four hour hotline. He'd hoped Drier would be eager enough to act on it and he had. If Crosshairs had been in the townhouse, seeing the TV crews would have spooked all of them into running. If and when Keys could get a subpoena for the voice tape, he'd hoped to have this thing blown open.

"Mr. Li called you and he's furious," Delilah said to him as he walked into the rotunda.

Monk waved at her and went into his office and called the head of the Merchants Group. He came on the line fuming.

"Am I to understand that you could have captured Crosshairs and you didn't?"

"Where did you hear that?"

"It was on the news this afternoon, Mr. Monk. One of our members was in his store watching it and called me. This FBI man claimed a private eye had tipped the news media. That this private eye could have done his duty and captured a suspected murderer and didn't."

"That smart-ass bastard," Monk said under his breath. "It's more complicated than that, Mr. Li."

"But you admit you met with Crosshairs."

"Yes, but—"

"Yes, but you didn't inform us. The only thing we have from you is this report which has no mention of you possibly meeting with the murderer of Kim Bong-Suh," Li boomed.

"That was done before I was sure I was going to have a meeting. I can assure you, as things have developed, I would have told you."

"Really."

"Really."

"Then why didn't you tell us you were being paid by SOMA also?"

He wanted to know how Li had found out but he said, "Because it wasn't a conflict of interest. And because it serves their purpose to bring to justice the killer of Kim Bong-Suh as well. And as an entrepreneur, I'm sure you'd appreciate my bootstrapism."

Monk listened to the quiet buzz of the line for several seconds. Then Li spoke again. "Is there anything else I should be aware of?"

"Yes, there is. I'm sending it over to you now."

"What is it?"

"When you get it, I think you'll know."

"Very well then."

Li hung up and Monk laboriously made three complete sets of photocopies of the book. He had Delilah messenger one set over to Li and one to Kenny Yu. If, as he suspected, Li and some others were behind Jiang, the pages would force their hand. He called Kenny Yu's office but he was out. He left him a message telling him about the papers on their way to him, and how he'd appreciate a translation of them. The original he placed in his safe. In the meantime, he had an appointment to keep across town.

Roy Park was chatting with the woman inside the corner store. He was a big man in height and girth. He had on gold-rimmed, red-tinted glasses, and his hair was slicked back in a Vegas pompadour. He wore a pair of tight black-going-to-gray Guess jeans, snakeskin boots and a Raiders jacket over an open-collar Gant dress shirt. He stuck out a small hand upon seeing Monk.

"Mr. Carr," he said, using the fake name Monk had left for him.

"That's not my real name," Monk admitted, shaking the other man's hand. "My name is Ivan Monk and I'm working for the Merchants Group to find the killer of Kim Bong-Suh."

A shroud dropped on the affable act. The creases around the eyes disappeared, and Park said, "I have nothing to say to you."

"Sure you do." Monk showed him the papers tucked under his arm. "This is the information that Kim accumulated on Jiang Holdings. It got him killed. I think you know something about that. I think that's why you're not the president of the Merchants Group anymore. You might also be interested to know that Stacy Grimes is dead, and Bart Samuels is on the run."

"If you're working for Li, then why haven't you given him these?" He fingered the pages Monk held onto.

"I did as a test, Mr. Park. But I want to know what these pages say. I want to know the truth of Jiang Holdings."

Park looked from the papers to Monk, then back to the papers. "I'll do it for Kim Bong-Suh. Let me have them and I'll tell you what they say. But that's all I'll do. I won't go to court, I won't go on TV, or talk to the press. You understand?"

Monk handed him the copies and his card. On the back, he wrote down his home number. "Let me know as soon as you can, Mr. Park." He left and went to Continental Donuts. Elrod was cleaning the coffee maker behind the front counter when he entered.

"I heard through the grapevine you met with brother Crosshairs," the big man said.

"I did."

"I saw on the news that the cops and feds raided some houses in Imperial Courts."

"But they came up empty," Monk detailed.

Elrod wiped his hands on a dish towel. "That's true."

"Is there a point you're getting at here, Elrod?"

"Just people should be careful about what they promise. Sometimes folks take them seriously, and they don't like getting disappointed."

"I know, Elrod. I know." Monk went into his back office and brought up the file of the case on his PC. He entered information, then turned the machine off. He walked toward the front again and right into Maxfield O'Day. He and a bison in a chauffeur cap who looked like he could give Elrod a round or two.

"Good afternoon," O'Day said.

"Mr. O'Day, back in town."

"And just in time, it would seem." An unpleasant lilt was in his voice. "Are you of the opinion that you know more than the authorities?"

"A little bird been talking to you."

"I've no truck with your insolent manner," O'Day said, pulling class on Monk.

"What do you have truck with, Mr. O'Day? Do you have truck with giving me an address to a building near Glendale that's supposed to belong to Jiang Holdings but belongs to you."

"I thought you needed a boost to keep you moving forward. It was a harmless white lie to keep what otherwise appears to be a man operating, if not in collusion with the criminal element, then working aimlessly, which is aiding that element.

"I've been so goddamned aimless, I found the notes Kim Bong-Suh left."

That brought O'Day up short. "You're lying."

"Your momma."

The creature in the black cap flexed, and Elrod stepped up behind him. He turned toward Elrod, and it was as if two locomotives were heading at each other along the same track.

O'Day repeated, "You must be lying. Who have you shown this to?"

"Nobody yet," Monk lied. "They're in Hangul."

"As your client, shouldn't I have a copy?"

"I'll send it to you in the morning."

"I'll pick it up back at your office now, if you don't mind."
The driver and Elrod were still doing the stare down. Monk
smiled languidly. "It's not there," and seeing O'Day's face
brighten, he added, "it's not here either."

"Where is it?"

"You may have a right to its contents, I have a right to
secure the notebook. You can come by my office tomorrow
morning and get a copy."

Imperiously, O'Day intoned, "I don't want to wait until
tomorrow." He held up a finger and the lunk rotated his
muscular torso in Monk's direction.

"If your boy could get past Elrod, what makes you think
he'll get me to do this for you any faster? Or is this always
the way SOMA gets things done in the community?"

"What are you implying, Mr. Monk?" The beast in the
black suit, at another raise of O'Day's hand, went to one side.
An automaton waiting for its master to throw the switch
and set it in a frenzy of destruction.

"I'm recently of the opinion that the work of the late Stacy
Grimes and his missing partner Bart Samuels isn't unknown
to you."

"I explained to you about that number on the back of my
card."

"So you did. And now it occurs to me who might have
put a bug up the ass of the Consumer Affairs Bureau."

O'Day stepped very close to Monk, heavily smelling of
cologne. "Speak a bit plainer, won't you. I'd like to think that
we could be frank with one another after all this time."

"Well, frankly, old son, I think you've been having one on
me. Jerking the chain to see which way I'll jump. SOMA
and the Merchants Groups seem very anxious to lay this
killing at the feet of the Rolling Daltons."

"What of it?"

"So maybe you thought it would speed up the process if I'm not only getting pressure from the FBI, but closer to home in the form of who pulls the strings on my license."

Taking a step back, O'Day breathed. "That sounds like a paranoid fantasy."

Thinking aloud, Monk said, "Well, if you did, it would mean you knew I'd been to Samuels's place that night. Now, how would you know that? And the notebook ain't no fantasy. I'm very eager to see what can be learned from it. And I'm very curious to see what he has to say about you, since there are some English words in it and your name pops up once or twice." It was a falsehood, but it was geared to unbalance O'Day. To Monk's disappointment, it didn't.

"I'm curious, too. But I guess I will have to wait until morning to find out." The lawyer and businessman, and the creature molded in the shape of a car jockey, left.

Monk said to Elrod, "Thanks for the back up, big man."

"I haven't lost faith in you yet, boss." He returned to his work.

Abe Carson came in and Monk waved hello. On the phone, he reached Kenny Yu's office, but they informed him he was still out. No, they didn't expect him back today, probably in the morning, and yes, they received the package he'd sent over. No one answered the telephone at Roy Park's office. Li, he would let simmer.

An anxiousness pounded at him, and Monk hurried away from the Continental shop and back to his office. Delilah was getting ready to leave when he breezed in.

"What's up?" she said.

"Something I don't want lying around, even in the safe." Monk moved into the office and tumbled the safe's dial in the proper sequence, popped it open, and extracted the notebook. Hefting the pages, he considered where he might feel better hiding it. Jill's house, his house, and the donut shop were all out. Dex's place was a possibility, but it was in Riverside County and even then, anybody who had done their homework on him would know about Dex. But there was one place.

An hour later Monk knocked on the door of the house on 76th Street. The door swung inward to reveal a startled Ray Smith.

"What the fuck are you doing here?"

"What, no flowers?" Monk moved past him into the front room. A Rolling Dalton Monk didn't recognize was sprawled in one of the chairs, reading a rap magazine.

Smith grabbed his arm. "How is it that the FBI came crashing around Imperial Courts this afternoon?"

"I told them, Ray." From the corner of his eye, Monk could tell that the Dalton had put down the magazine. "Otherwise, the head FBI boy Keys was going to lock me up. That's why I called the TV station hoping they'd blow it for the law."

"You some kind of sissy?" the Dalton slurred. "Can't stand being in the joint?"

Monk swallowed a reply and kept his focus on Smith. "It's a matter of working the angles, know what I mean, Ray?"

Smith didn't say anything, but looked past Monk's right shoulder at a point somewhere beyond the room.

Monk thrust the notebook at Smith as the Dalton treaded closer. Grinning like a demented clown, Monk hammered at the other one. "Come on, junior, and jump bad with me. I'll pop a cap in your ass faster than you can blink." Monk showed him the butt end of the .45 he'd recently strapped back on under his sport coat.

The young man halted, measuring his youth against the older man's reflexes.

"Sit down and shut up. I haven't got time for the testosterone follies today." Monk's hand hovered near the .45, hoping that once again in his life, he didn't have to shoot someone so young, so redeemable.

"Do it," Smith ordered.

The gangbanger walked out of the room, slamming the door that led to the kitchen.

Monk pointed at the notebook. "I did what I thought I had to do to not get knocked out of the box on this one. And that"—he tapped the notebook in Smith's hand—"names the real players."

"So why you giving it to us? Ain't no Dalton speak Korean. Yet."

"I've got reason to believe that someone, or someones, will try to snatch it."

"You got copies."

"I just made some more. But courts like to see the real thing, in so far as authenticating evidence and so on."

Smith regarded the notebook. "So you're trusting us."

"Let's say it's my way of restoring your trust in me."

The kitchen door opened and Monk's hand went toward his gun. The Dalton emerged, holding a beer. He glared at both of them and regained his chair.

Monk opened the front door, and he and Smith went out to stand on the porch. "This isn't a joke, Ray. That book is going to become more valuable than IBM stock."

"Which ain't worth much anymore." For the first time since they'd seen each other during the last few days, Smith's demeanor momentarily took on the characteristics of his old friend, the bright, gifted student and athlete who was going to set hearts afire and blaze his trail in a furious world. But the world savaged and discarded him as one did a spent match.

Monk shook the nostalgia loose and concentrated on business. "Take very good care of that thing. Look at it as protecting the interests of the Daltons." He got off the porch and stepped across the trimmed lawn. The sun was down and Monk headed the Galaxie 500 into the west, where eventually the land ended, and a vast ocean rolled and crashed.

SEVENTEEN

Monk did a series of sit-ups on the rug in his living room. He worked up a sweat and then did some sets of push-ups and some toning with his chrome dumbbells. He finished and tried to wind down by watching an old movie on TV but couldn't get into it. He opened up Sleeper's book, *The Closest of Strangers*, to the bookmark he'd placed midway in it. Again, he couldn't concentrate. He was too psyched, his mind and body ready for conflict.

Unnecessarily, he took apart and reassembled his gun. Oiling it, Monk looked at it. Looked at it as when his father had shown it to him on his thirteenth birthday.

"This is not a toy, and it's not for settling arguments. And it's definitely not meant to be shown off to make you look big." The words of Josiah Monk echoed back to him over the years. "I know you know that I have this gun. That I keep it in our house for protection should we need it. Your mother doesn't like it, but she's come to accept it. Even though of course, as a nurse, she's seen more bloodshed than I saw in the war where I got this weapon. Go on," his father had said, "hold it."

Quietly, Monk rose from the table where he'd been working on the gun and padded into the bedroom in his bare feet.

He put the automatic on the nightstand, moving the piece of furniture closer to his bed. He went back out into the kitchen and poured himself a neat shot of rum. Just enough for a brace, and not enough to dull his responses. He sat again at the table.

"Aim a little to the right of where you want the bullet to go," his father had instructed him. They'd taken to going out to Needles, in the desert, for the lessons Josiah Monk taught his son in handling a gun. Pulling the trigger; getting used to not blinking at the flash; allowing for the recoil. Later, his father showed him how to care for the weapon, a tool to be maintained like a torque wrench or a good set of sockets.

The first time Ivan Monk had found himself standing in a room with the gun in his hand, it was just like when he and his dad used to watch *Have Gun Will Travel* on Saturday nights. Paladin, the Shakespeare-quoting gunslinger reincarnated in the urban, post-Watts '65 landscape. Only the fantasy ended the day Monk had to actually pull the trigger, not on a beer bottle but on a target the bullet sank into, ripping and rending flesh and bone, changing his and the other person's life forever.

Yet after the initial shock, he became intoxicated with its power. A gun in your hand immediately changed the equation. It took too long for Monk to learn that guns were not the answer to crime, only the end product of flawed social and economic policies.

The phone rang and he answered it. Whoever was on the other end said nothing but they made a point of making their breathing audible. They hung up. The phone rang twice more and each time Monk picked it up to the same effect. It stopped after that.

Inside of his front door, allowing for its arc if it were to be opened, Monk placed some small, cheap, hard plastic toys he'd purchased at the local grocery store. They would make a resounding crunch if stepped on. At the back door in the kitchen, he unplugged the refrigerator and rolled it flush against the door.

He took both of his phones out of their jacks and went to bed. As far as he could tell, nothing happened during the night, because he was alive in the morning.

EIGHTEEN

He made himself a breakfast of three eggs (he had to get that cholesterol rechecked) scrambled hard, three pieces of oat bran toast, five pieces of turkey sausage links, downed two cups of coffee and a large glass of orange juice. He shaved, showered and read the front section of the *LA Times*. The refrigerator was rolled back into place and plugged in again.

The blue serge suit in his closet, which was last worn at a wedding he attended with Jill, was removed and put on. Monk complemented it with a dark burgundy shirt and a gray and green Hugo Boss tie. In his dresser he found a pair of charcoal gray socks with little white clocks on them, and donned them and his brown wingtips. Catching himself in the bathroom mirror, he looked like an insurance salesman with a pocketful of jokers. And his one deadly ace in the hole.

Monk picked up the automatic, briefly weighing leaving it at home. He dismissed the idea as now was not the appropriate time to become a peacenik. The private detective strapped it on using his alternate holster, which allowed for drawing the gun out sideways. He went down to the street, scanning the buildings around his apartment. Would Keys and Diaz still be watching him or sitting in their task force room figuring out what other devilment they could hatch against him?

He beeped off the Ford's alarm and started the car, silently praying there wasn't a bomb attached to it, and smiling at his own bizarre notions. Well-founded, he thought, but illogical. They—whoever the "they" are—would need the original notebook. He'd have to be captured and tortured to reveal its whereabouts. That was probably what had happened to Kim Bong-Suh. His compiling of information about who was behind Jiang Holdings, despite his attempt at hiding out, had no doubt brought their wrath down on him. But he must have been caught away from the garage apartment in Lincoln Heights, otherwise the notebook would have been found.

But torture in the hands of amateurs could go too far, not allowing for the pace one needed to make it work effectively. And, of course, the victim's body had to partially recover and his mind have time to amplify the horror. Or so Dexter Grant had explained to Monk once. He never asked Dex how it was he'd come to that analysis.

Of course, the method of Kim's death meant they intended to kill him all along.

Monk arrived at his office and Delilah motioned him to pick up line one. He did.

"Brother man," a voice Monk didn't recognize began, "got any more hot tips for me?" It was the people's newsman, Kelly Drier.

"What are you talking about, Drier?"

"You know perfectly well what I'm talking about. You set up the FBI to look like a bunch of Keystone Kops."

"They don't need my help to accomplish that. And if you've got Keys and his boyfriend Diaz on the extension, tell them this bad boy is about to bust. Tell them to back off and give me free reign or I'll make it so that their next assignment will be guarding the men's room at Bureau headquarters." Monk softly replaced the handset and went into his office. Forty-five minutes later, Kenny Yu charged into it.

"Do you know what you've got here?" Yu exclaimed, waving the papers before him.

"I have some idea," Monk said.

The other man sank into an Eastlake. He laid the loose sheets on the desk, breathing hard. He rubbed a hand across his clean-cut face. Yu seemed to be having trouble getting his vision in check. "Jesus Christ, Monk, where did you find this?"

Not wishing to answer that question, Monk said, "What does it say, Kenny?"

"I got to my office early this morning and this thing"—he waved a hand at the pile—"was waiting for me."

"It's not a bomb."

"It is and you know it. It's a goddamn box of TNT waiting to go off. I've only skimmed it, but Kim names names, places, and where the money is, or at least how he thinks it's channeled through."

Monk felt a constricting of the muscles in his throat. "Who are the names, Kenny? Who the hell is Jiang Holdings?"

NINETEEN

Tina Chalmers leaned back in her creaky chair. The seal of the City of Los Angeles, the Valley of Smoke, was printed on an aged piece of parchment and framed on the wall above and behind her. A symbolic guillotine that had made many a head roll in the name of maintaining the palace. But the moat was rising, and everybody in local government could feel the water at their ankles, if they didn't act to right this city.

Chalmers let out a long sigh. "Most of the stuff in his notebook is unsubstantiated. It's hearsay from other shopkeepers and small businesspeople, and rumors other Korean Americans and Korean Nationals passed along to him." She closed the file folder of executive summary Kenny Yu had prepared from the translated pages Monk had obtained from Roy Park.

"It's done in a chronological manner. It puts names with dates, and lists various addresses and phone numbers. It raises enough questions, Tina. It got Kim killed."

"What about Grimes?"

"I think he was killed because he got to be too much of a wild card. He was the one who kept getting busted because he was always escalating the strong-arm bit. Samuels seemed to be the cooler head, the one that thinks clearer."

"So it was just him being hotheaded when you had your run-in with him at the Odin Club."

"Maybe he did that on orders."

"But he was on the shit list."

"Yeah. They have him attack me, he gets killed by his pals, and then the obvious suspect is me."

"Why?"

"A magician always uses misdirection. Suspicion on me muddies the waters, and nobody looks beyond me or the other set-up, Crosshairs. The task force tries to keep me on a long leash, hoping I give them Crosshairs. They know Grimes figures in this somehow, but the Rolling Daltons' leader is their main worry."

"That would imply they knew that Ray Smith had made contact, and your name came up in our conversation." Tina said, a daring tone in her voice.

"All wiretaps ain't legal, Tina."

She mulled that over, then said, "If the City Council is going to discuss the matters raised in Kim's notes, I have to supply them with translated copies. What I'm saying is that for us to really discuss it we have to have a closed session. The Council needs a good reason to go behind closed doors."

"But if you pass copies around, sure as hell there's gonna be a leak," Monk said, thinking ahead.

"What if there is, Ivan?"

"Then some of the big fish might swim away."

"Well, what can you do? If you want action, why haven't you taken this information to Keys?"

"I don't want this thing to become compromised."

"Meaning you think Keys or one of the cops is in Jiang's backpocket."

"I don't know what I mean, Tina." Monk got up and paced around the room. "I just know my gut feeling is I need to play this out the way I started it. You, Jill, Dex, Elrod and a few others are all I can trust. Everybody else is a could-be conspirator."

"What about your buddy, Seguin?"

Monk didn't want to formulate an answer. "I think we can force their hand, exposing them."

"I suspect I might know where you're going with this and it's a dangerous place."

"Dig my grave deep, baby."

TWENTY

"I don't care if he's in a meeting with Queen Victoria herself," Monk angrily said into the phone. "Tell him it's Monk, and tell him I've read the notes." Onto the line came one of the soft rock stations, and Monk listened to a Lionel Ritchie number while waiting. The chorus was repeating for the third time when O'Day came on.

"What do you want, Mr. Monk?" He tried his best to sound bored.

"About two hundred thousand dollars," Monk said with equal aplomb.

"Really."

"Really. You, Park Hankyoung, a few others from the Merchants Group and several of your good ol' boy golfing buddies are Jiang Holdings."

"You're in way over your head."

"Then you better throw me a life preserver. Say one that costs about a quarter of a million."

"I'm going to hang up," O'Day said, without much conviction.

"Go ahead," Monk challenged. "I'm itching to send my story around to the papers. Oh, and not the *Times*, I know you and the publisher both take breakfast at the Odin Club.

But the folks over at the weekly alternative in town, and the Black paper *The Sentinel*, and hey, maybe somebody at *The Nation* or *Mother Jones* might think it's worth a few inches of ink."

"Everything is spelled out in Kim's notes." There was a crack in the veneer, a sliver of desperation in the silky voice of the lawyer and power broker.

"You know it, slick."

"I thought you were a standard bearer, Monk. The postmodern, hip-hop private eye operating in the Land of Nod. The city-state trapped forever between the sea and the desert. The perfect metaphor for lives born in the womb of wetness only to dry up and blow away in the harsh unforgiving arid landscape."

"Nice imagery there, M.O. Did you have something similar in mind when you sent your goons on their errand to scare Jill? Sent them on a bogus drive-by so I'd be all hot and bothered to go after Crosshairs."

"You're swimming a little deeper."

"Sure I am, big boy. Like you were the one who succeed the Consumer Affairs Board on me so I'd jump more, and Keys and I wind up chasing phantoms rather than the real crooks. Hiring me so you could keep an eye on what I was doing, and because you think you're the lord of the manor, and can do anything you want. Even flaunt Kim's death by burying him at Florence and Normandie. Knowing then it was going to be the sight of a SOMA groundbreaking. A not-so-subtle warning for the other shopkeepers to keep their nose out of the business of Jiang Holdings."

In a measured manner, O'Day said, "Grimes was fucking up. We had to make some good out of a bad situation."

"Right. Like Kim really believed you were going to let him live."

"How much was that amount again, small change?"

"You know goddamn well what it was. And I just tacked on another 50 Gs 'cause your breath stinks."

"And you give me back the original. Not, I might hasten to add, that there's probably anything in there to legally indict me. But it might stir up unnecessary concerns."

"The right of conquest has no foundation other than the right of the strongest."

"You mock me with Rousseau, Monk. But you don't mock my money. Stay by the phone, my greedy friend, you shall hear from me soon."

Monk stared at the phone. He doubted if Keys and Diaz were still listening in, but what if they were? Would they intervene, or were they in O'Day's pockets, too?

The door to his office moved inward and Dexter Grant, carrying a cup of coffee, entered. That unmistakable gait of his took him into one of the Eastlakes.

"What the hell's wrong with you?"

"Nothing."

"You look worried."

Perturbed that his old mentor could read him so well, Monk went on the offensive. "Dex, is there something I can help you with today?"

He crossed his bandy legs and slouched in the seat. As was his custom, he put the cup on the floor next to the chair. "I was watching the news yesterday, and there was this reporter talking about how the special task force had blown an arrest."

"I told you about Drier, so what?"

Grant gulped down some coffee. "So I got to wondering who might have tipped off Crosshairs and why."

"Of course," Monk said noncommittally.

Grant folded his arms and waited.

"I suppose you won't be satisfied until I tell you everything that's happened since I last saw you."

Grant took another leisurely sip of his coffee.

Reluctantly, Monk filled him in.

"Sheeoot, as granny used to say." He was about to go on when the phone rang.

"Hello," Monk said into the receiver.

"I'll have your money tomorrow. But how do I know you won't try something with one of the copies you've made?"

"That's your lookout, O'Day. The deal is for the original."

"And your silence," he added flatly.

"Three-thirty at the sports store on the second floor of the Baldwin Hills Mall. And it has to be you."

"No."

"Bye." Monk hung up. He and Grant looked at one another, then the phone went off again.

"I guess I've got little choice."

"See ya."

THERE WAS a throng of teenagers milling about the mall. They were raucous and demi-god self-confident in their powerful, graceful bodies, larger and taller than Monk remembered being at their age. Decked out urban slick in their Air Jordans, Cross Colours, Guess Jeans, NaNa boots, Champion sweatshirts, X watchcaps, Bronze Age shirts, and cuffed and rolled 540 Levi's.

A passel of them—girls reeking of knock-off Giorgio and boys with shoulders wide as Kenworth cabs—sauntered past Monk. He leaned on the rail in front of the popular sports store owned by an ex-NBAer on the second floor. Maxfield O'Day, walking stiff-legged and looking straight ahead, appeared at the other end of the walkway a minute ahead of schedule. With a deliberate pace, he approached

Monk. A soft leather attache case hung straight down from his arm.

"Good afternoon, Mr. Monk."

O'Day had a smirk on his face and that made him nervous. Monk looked around, being careful not to linger on the young Black woman Tina Chalmers had sent to surreptitiously take the picture of his handing the notebook over to O'Day. Back some paces from where he and the SOMA president stood, there was an Asian man in an expensive suit. What made him stand out was the tilt to one side of his body and the lift of his shoulders as if he wore football pads under his jacket. Kyphoscoliosis, curvature of the spine, an M.E. acquaintance of Monk's told him once. Robinson was wrong, he was handsome with close-cropped black hair, and a noticeable five o'clock shadow dominated his lower jaw. His hands were clasped before him butler fashion.

Near the man were three teenaged girls laughing and goofing on one another. Ostensibly they were looking into the display window of a woman's clothing store, but that was just an excuse to slyly watch the boys go by. The man, aware that he had Monk's attention, tipped his hands slightly forward. The overhead track lighting gleamed off the knife he held.

Monk snarled at O'Day. "What if I gat you while you stand there laughing up your sleeve at me?"

O'Day said, "I believe you have something for me."

Kim's notebook for a stranger's life. Did the man with the hunchback think he could get away once he did his deed? What did it matter? If one of those girls went down, the blood would stain Monk's soul. He held up a loose-leaf notebook.

O'Day calmly took it out of his hand. He put down the attaché case and paged through the notebook. Satisfied, he

placed the notebook in his attaché case. The hunchback
melted away. "Thank you for all your good work, Mr. Monk."
He looked around. "I wonder where my associate has gotten
off to." He turned hard eyes on Monk. "He can be so capri-
cious at times. Stay right here while I look for him, will you,
Mr. Monk? In case he comes back this way."

"Sure."

O'Day walked away and Monk remained by the rail for
a long time, wanting to be certain that the handsome killer
wasn't prowling around the mall, watching for Monk trying
to follow O'Day and lashing out at some young throat.
Eventually, he left the spot and went down to the Sears on
the first floor. Back where the catalog department used to
be before it was dropped due to the recession, there was still
a bank of pay phones, and Monk stood by one in particular.
Thirty minutes later it rang.

"They're at a building out here near Glendale."

"Off of Riverside Drive?" Monk asked Grant.

"That's the one, Hemlock."

"I'm on my way."

"I'll be parked behind a building with the name Macdon-
ald Family Heirlooms on it."

Monk arrived and pulled his car in next to where Grant
had parked. The car the retired PI was in was a two-door,
late-model Grand Am. The older man got out as did Monk.
"This must belong to one of your daughters," Monk said,
pointing at the vehicle.

"I think we're going to have to build up a special reserve
of ordinary cars. How the hell did Spenser on TV in that
cherry Mach I Mustang follow people?"

"Thanks for your help, Dex." Monk started to move off.

"Thanks for your help, Dex, my ass." He came up beside
him. "I'm with you, old student, till the bitter end."

Monk halted. Somewhere a dog barked, and a truck rumbled by over on the main street. "I can handle it from here, Dex."

"Look, I may have lost a step or two but I ain't blind, I don't need to wear a diaper yet, and my hand don't shake, much." He unlimbered his dated Police Special .38, a natural extension of his large knuckled hand. "I was going through skylights and busting down doors when you were still throwing your strained carrots at your mom."

Monk was inclined to give him an argument but knew that would only result in the both of them shouting at each other and alerting O'Day. He shook his head in surrender. "Come on."

Monk tried the door but it was locked. Grant gently pushed him aside.

"What, you thought they'd leave breadcrumbs for you?" Grant produced a lock pick kit from the pocket of his windbreaker. Expertly, he undid both locks and turned the knob. The door went in on darkness. They both listened but could hear no voices.

"The young before the restless," Grant invited.

Monk went in, gun out, thankful that the light was failing outside and therefore his body less of a silhouette in the doorway. Silently, Grant came in behind him, closing the door. The interior of the building was a large warehouse space. Various types of machinery, scattered around haphazardly, were covered in tarps tied down with steel cables. Both men wore rubber-soled shoes, and they went along quietly in the gathering gloom of the place.

Off to the right, cut into a far wall, was a lighted archway. A railed catwalk rose along the south wall. Metal stairs led up to it. Grant pointed up and headed for the stairs, Monk toward the archway. Getting closer, Monk heard a noise. He looked to his left and thought he saw a shape detach itself from next to one of the bulky tarps. He went in that direction and something caught him in the middle of his back, and he went down on both knees. "Dex," Monk hollered.

A dampness spread on the back of his shirt like a hawk unfolding its wings. His arms were getting numb. The figure shifted in front of him, the light from the archway highlighting someone raising something overhead. It was a woman, the woman from the picture in Samuels's room. Grant fired his gun. The bullet went past her. But it was enough to momentarily stop the downward arc of the iron bar she held.

Feeling returned to Monk's right arm, and he brought his gun up. "Throw that thing away." He got his feet under him.

Her hair was tied back, and she wore black Spandex tights, white tennis shoes with white socks over the ankles, and an armless sweat top that displayed the bunched muscles in her arms. Aerobics to murder by. The iron bar made a loud noise as it met the concrete of the warehouse.

"Come on, let's see what our other playmates are up to."

The archway went black and the woman jumped him. She was strong and her hand wrapped around his right wrist while her other one drove into his rib cage. Monk gasped, letting go of the automatic. Rather than try to fight the motion of her pushing him backwards, he went with it and dropped to the ground. His knee sought purchase in her body, but she was already thinking ahead of him. She blocked his leg and caught him on the side of his face with her fist.

Pain pulsed inside his temples, and Monk countered with a blow that managed to find her washboard of a stomach.

"Shit," was her reply.

Monk couldn't tell if she was expressing contempt or actually felt his blow. He got out from under her, and the two got to their feet. She rushed forward immediately, and her arms encircled his torso. They were driven back in the blackened room and Monk crashed into something hard. One of the covered machines. He got an open palm under her chin and shoved upward.

The beam of a flashlight pierced the room, and Monk and the woman were briefly illuminated in it. Suddenly the light jiggled, and Monk was aware that it dropped to the floor and blinked out.

There was the flash, then the retort, of a gun blast. As if on a dance floor where moving bodies are seen only in the glare of a throbbing strobe light, Monk had a nanosecond glimpse of Grant and Bart Samuels. They both had guns in their hands. There was another burst of light and a retort, and someone yelled.

The woman spun Monk around and hit him solid in the stomach, doubling him over. His knees went weak, but it was Monk's turn to think ahead. Instinctively, he'd raised his forearm and it blocked the fist she was bringing down on his head. He felt the rush of wind as her knee came up. Monk grabbed it in both hands, and forcefully yanked on the leg. It straightened, and the body attached to it must have reared back straight as a plank. Because the next sound Monk heard was a sharp wet thud and the leg went limp. Monk released the limb, guessing that the woman's head must have hit one of the large slabs of machinery.

"Dex, Dex," Monk yelled, not caring if Samuels and the other man heard him.

"Over here, by the archway," a quiet voice replied.

Monk stumbled to it and knelt down when he felt a hand on his leg. "How bad is it, Dex?"

"Hard to say, youngster. I'm feeling dizzy in the head and my left leg has a cramp in it."

"Is it the leg?" Monk said hopefully.

"No. His bullet caught me a little above the midsection." His breath was becoming ragged and Monk had to fight down a feeling of helplessness. "Finish the job, Ivan. Or they'll for sure finish us both. I'll crawl off somewhere so they can't find me and use me as a hostage."

Monk wanted to say something else but knew Grant was right. There was a another sound, and suddenly Monk felt the Police Special pressed into his hand.

"I think I clipped him, too." Monk could hear Grant, heaving in and out large gulps of air, slide his body away.

He straightened and found that as his eyes became adjusted to it, the warehouse was not totally black. Light from the street filtered in from the frosted windows set up high in the walls. With the hulking, unused machines lying about, it gave the place the quality of a mist-covered land full of tombstones and grave markers waiting to be used for dead dinosaurs. Off to one side, Monk could perceive the inert form of the woman. The archway was just before him. Grant had disappeared. He went through the arch.

Entering the area on the other side of the archway, Monk stood still, trying to orient himself. There seemed to be partitions in this part of the warehouse that at one time had probably been the office portion. Stepping more into the space, Monk strained to somehow extend his other senses in an effort to detect Samuels. He went down on his stomach and slowly sent himself forward as a soldier might slither under barbwire.

He halted his forward motion but he wasn't sure why. An undefinable feeling touched on a nerve and he stopped and listened. Listened hard. Monk reached his free left hand out to his side and it landed on cold metal. He felt more of it. A secretary's chair on casters. Monk swung his body toward it, grabbed the chair, and quickly shoved it along the floor in front of him.

A gun barked like a German shepherd in heat. Its bullet pinged off the floor near where Monk had been. He sent a .38 round up and to the left of where he'd seen the flash.

"Goddamnit," Monk heard Samuels yelp. The ponytailed man cranked off another shot where he'd seen Monk's gun flash. But the private detective had secreted himself behind the desk the chair had been at. Frantically, Monk felt in his pockets and produced a book of matches. Another slug tore into the top of the table. Careful to shield the light as he struck one of the matches, Monk set the whole pack ablaze and threw it into the air like a rookie trying his best for the quarterback position.

Briefly, Samuels, one of his legs leaking vermilion, was caught in the hot burst of light as he leaned against a far wall. He recovered from his surprise just as Monk grouped two in his chest. The matches went out, and Monk could hear the body tumble forward onto the floor. He got up running. There was a closed door next to where Samuels had stood and Monk could still see it in his mind's eye. He found the knob and got the portal open. A hand lashed onto his ankle and he kicked his foot loose.

"Help me, man."

Monk ignored Samuels's plea and found himself in a hallway. It was so narrow that he could touch either wall by stretching out his arms. He turned and went in that direction. Suddenly a wall rose up to meet him and he could feel the rough hewn surface of its bricks. He turned around and went in the other direction. He passed the doorway he'd just entered, and could hear Samuel's labored breathing. He went cold because he had to. "Where are they, Samuels, what room are they in?" Monk said, whispering close to the other man's face.

"You'll get me a doctor?"

"Yeah," Monk said keeping his bile down.

"Down the hall, last door on the right."

Monk stood to the side of the door. A high window at this end of the hall bathed the space in a soft yellow light. Monk tried the knob but it was locked. Where the hell was the man with the curved spine?

"Samuels? Myra?" came a voice on the other side of the door.

Monk waited. The voice said, "Kyung?"

The other man. Suddenly, Monk felt vulnerable standing in the hall, and his first impulse was to shoot off the door's lock and rush in and get O'Day. But he checked himself. There was something about the pause between when O'Day had said the first two names and then calling Kyung's as if it were an afterthought. Maybe Kyung wasn't prowling around the warehouse.

The area of the doorjamb that held the lock mechanism gave way as the second blast from the .38 ripped into it. The door was kicked and then there was a discharge of air, like someone spitting. The silenced .32's bullet was spent on the door opposite the one that Monk had kicked. But he wasn't standing in front of it, but to the side, where he had shot from. As he'd guessed, O'Day had tried to sucker him in the room. Kyung, and his small bore gun with the sound suppressor, was also in the room.

Monk had retreated down the hall and was now crouched at the doorway that led back to the partitioned office.

"You're a smart man, Monk," O'Day boomed. "I'm sure we can come to some agreement."

Monk didn't reply.

"The phone's in this room, Monk. The only one that still works in this building. Is Grant dead or wounded, Monk? Will you let your old partner die?"

"What's the deal, O'Day?" Monk could wait it out from his position, since it was obvious the only way out of the room for the both of them was past him. Yet the head of SOMA's hole card was Grant's life, ebbing from him as they dickered.

"Throw your gun out. No, wait, Kyung has made it clear that the .38 is spent, but we want your .45 and the gun you probably have from Samuels."

"I lost the automatic on the warehouse floor. Here's Samuels's gun." Monk made a big production of sliding it down the hall toward their door.

"That won't do, Monk. Get the other one and slide the .38 down here also."

He did as ordered and said. "You'll have to wait, I've got to look for the automatic."

"I've got time," O'Day said, some of his old charm returning.

Back out in the warehouse, Monk found the .45 near Myra's unconscious form. He slid it down the hall.

"Now come out and stand perfectly still in the hallway, hands so we can see them."

"Okay," Monk said and did so.

The overhead light came on and Monk squinted to see. O'Day and Kyung, a .32 Beretta with a suppressor in his hand, appeared. Not a powerful handgun, it required up close and personal use. Clearly, Monk concluded, Kyung enjoyed his work. His hands hung loose at his sides, the backs of them facing the other two.

O'Day was back in form. "You were right about most aspects of the case, Monk. I've got to hand it to you, I didn't think you were that capable."

"Thanks."

"Kim wouldn't tell us where he'd hidden his notes and so

I saw it was to our advantage to make an example of him. I had him buried at Florence and Normandie"

"Why'd you have Kyung kill Grimes?"

O'Day was an actor playing to his audience. He worked his hands like an orator. "On that, you were correct, too. Mr. Stacy was getting a bit too obstreperous for our needs. His attack on you at the club, thinking that would put him in good graces with me, and some of his other antics were calling undue attention to our work. It seemed convenient to deal with him when we did." With that, he waved a hand in the air and Kyung raised the Beretta, taking a step toward Monk.

Monk's left arm jumped. The small frame hidden hammer .38 was in his hand. He got off two as Kyung squeezed off one. The assassin's head snapped back, his face contorted with disbelief. Something gurgled in his throat, and he sank to the ground. Monk charged forward.

"How, how . . . ?" O'Day said to him open-mouthed.

Monk grabbed him hard by the throat. "There better be a phone in there." He hated the lawyer for all that had happened; the machinations, the avarice, the killing and the blood. And that one, if not two, men were dead by his hand and his gun. He'd done it to protect his and Grant's lives, but the act of eliminating a human existence was a malignancy too many in the world shared. And if there was anything Monk was sure about, it was that guns didn't cure the disease.

He dialed 911.

TWENTY-ONE

Samuels died after an hour in surgery. Grant made it to life support and for the next week and a half stayed in intensive care. Monk spent several sleepless nights camped out in the older man's semi-private room, the retired cop's HMO plan picking up the tab.

"It's not your fault, Monk," Seguin told him.

"Neither one of you are kids. And what the hell were you thinking taking an old man along for your backup? Jesus, Ivan, sometimes I think the two of you believe you're Butch and Sundance. That nothing can happen to you as long as you got the luck. Well honey baby, anybody can die by a bullet," Kodama had said to him. Later she apologized for berating him. She realized he felt bad enough.

"Cute trick, Monk. Tying your shoelace around your left wrist and the other end around your little .38 you had on your ankle. Then hiding it with the back of your hand facing them. You're lucky the light wasn't better in there or they would have seen the lace around your wrist," Keys had begrudgingly told him.

"The old bastard's tough. The bullet traveled down into

the muscles of his back rather than an organ or the spine. He'll be walking again. Oh, he may slow down a step or two, but which one of us hasn't?" the young doctor with the chubby face told Monk.

TWENTY-TWO

The epic of *Gilgamesh*, originating in third millennium Mesopotamia, BC, told of the hero and his friend Enkidu who do battle with the gods. As a result, Enkidu is slain and Gilgamesh wanders the earth searching for the secret of eternal life. The object of his quest eluded him.

In 1460 BC, Queen Hatshepsut of Africa sent expeditions to foreign lands to bring forth the wonders of the known world, and discover what lay in the unknown lands. Though she longed to know the meaning of life, none of her explorations was able to produce the answer she sought.

Crosshairs Sawyer and Conrad James arrived at the Main Street steps of the Los Angeles City Hall in a caravan of chopped and channeled cars piloted by members of the Rolling Daltons, The Swans, and the Del Nines, modern disaffected nomads, returning from the barren regions. Their grail mere words on paper, a truce among battling factions. The object of their quest was nothing as cosmic as eternal life or its meaning. It was peace, and if it didn't elude them, it could be as devastating as a swath laid down by napalm.

As one, the carloads of young men and women exited their vehicles and escorted Sawyer and James onto the steps and to their appointment with Councilwoman Tina Chalmers inside City Hall. Reporters pressed forward as cameras and videocams recorded their arrival.

Monk, waiting in Chalmers's office, watched with her from her office window as the phalanx of gang members formed a semicircle across the steps. This effectively stopped the progression of the media and allowed James and his cousin to enter the building unobstructed.

"Maybe this will be, at least for some of the gang members, their *moksha*," Chalmers said.

"Their what?" Monk said.

"It means liberation. A release from the bondage of endless reincarnation. In this case, a release from the endless warring and cycle of self-hate and self-destruction. It is good karma, and one creates it by living a good life."

Monk believed you made your own luck, what little there was to be found in this rapacious world. He didn't tell her that, but he did give her a hug around the waist.

TWENTY-THREE

The impact of the translated notes of Kim Bong-Suh reverberated all over town. The seventy-five members of the board of directors of SOMA held press conferences ad infinitum in board rooms, press clubs, City Hall and street corners denouncing the ruthlessness and venality of Maxfield O'Day who sought to make millions from his shady land deals, and tarnish the image of Save Our Material Assets.

FOUR OTHER Anglo Fortune 500 CEOs mentioned in Kim's notes, in what was quickly dubbed SOMAGate, were forced to resign from their respective positions. Subsequently one of them went into a famous detox hospital up in Montecito—blaming his years of inebriation for his bad judgment in being part of the Jiang Holdings scheme. Another one opened a pottery shop in Santa Fe, another got a job as a consultant to prisoners in halfway houses, and the fourth wrote a book and sold the movie rights.

Of the three Korean men who were in on the Jiang fix among the Merchants Group, two of them left the United States for parts unknown, and the third attempted to make restitution to some of the land owners who had been forced to sign over their property.

One of the men who left the states, Park Hankyoung, was revealed in an article in the *LA Weekly* to have ties with the Agency for National Security Planning, formerly called the Korean Central Intelligence Agency. There were allegations that certain officers of the military hierarchy in South Korea, which now enjoys a civilian-led government, had knowledge of Jiang, but this was never proven.

Ultimately, Jiang was a consortium of capitalists whose binding contract was not race or nationalism, but the making of money.

Linton Perry and Luis Santillion held a summit on Black and brown relations. And Conrad James, Crosshairs Sawyer, and some other Rolling Daltons started a nonprofit economic development corporation. Some on the board of SOMA, in an effort to clean up their image, provided grants and technical assistance to the ex-gang members. There was even a meeting held between Crosshairs and some of the OGs and the Korean American Merchants Group in an effort to arrive at strategies to staunch some of the violence in the inner city.

O'Day, who had been subpoenaed to testify before a grand jury, died at home. It appeared he'd slipped in his shower/ sauna and cracked his head open on the tile imported from Greece. The coroner ruled his death an accident by misadventure. Nobody hired Monk to look into it.

DESTRUCTIVE ENGAGEMENT
Gary Phillips

Originally published in 2002's *Geography of Rage:*
Remembering the Los Angeles Riots of 1992

A South African friend of mine was visiting Los Angeles
a week before the city immolated on the fires of neglect
and rage. He'd lived here while attending the then Graduate
School of Urban Planning at UCLA, and had returned to
Johannesburg to head the urban policy section of the Urban
Foundation—a liberal-to-left think tank plotting economic
strategies and tactics for a new South Africa.

Over some Cuban food and a few beers, we kicked it as
to how in the fifteen months since he'd last seen L.A., the
city seemed to be fraying more. Not from the edges, but from
the center outward. He also reflected that JoBurg was not
so different than the City of Lost Angels: whites ensconced
behind high walls shrouded in webs of electronic security, a
growing chasm between those who want and can get and
those who go wanting, an exploited immigrant labor force,
and recession and crime at an all-time high.

Yet like the promise of a shiny mansion on a distant hill,
the allure of a coming economic boom seduces both cities:
JoBurg positioning itself to become one of the centers of

finance capital, which will infuse the whole of southern Africa; and Los Angeles waiting to reap the rewards as the center of Pacific Rim finance. The city is building huge skyscrapers and massive office complexes on spec—allowing for numerous vacancies against future returns—while in some areas of town African American and Latino males suffer double-digit unemployment.

We talked of those economic matters, films we'd seen, books we wanted to write, and of course the pending verdict in the trial of the four cops who beat Rodney King. My friend, who is white, left Los Angeles a day before The Verdict and the whirlwind it unleashed. He and I made commitments to keep in touch as the uncertainties of our respective hometowns played themselves out.

Wednesday afternoon, the 29th of April, all of L.A., and certainly other parts of the country, awaited the jury's decision in the courtroom located in east Ventura County. In particular this was the bucolic Simi Valley, site of the Ronald Reagan Library.

I hadn't been that anxious about a news report since I was in high school and couldn't concentrate on homework and kept turning on the TV to see who'd won the first Ali–Frazier fight. But this outcome would have a far greater impact than the arena in Madison Square Garden.

This arena of Simi, thirty-seven odd miles to the north and west of Los Angeles, was, and is, more than just another bedroom community begun by white flighters. It is a community, like Mission Hills, Manhattan Beach (Shaq who lives there notwithstanding), or Newhall, where the cops, as civilians, interact with people in the supermarket, the bowling alley, and on front lawns. Not like the inner city where young Black and Latino men more than likely deal with cops who prone them out

across a police cruiser's hood on Martin Luther King Jr.
Boulevard.

And so a few minutes after three that afternoon, the radio
played the measured tones of the sixty-five-year-old forewoman, who said that the jury had found the four cops
innocent of all criminal charges, save for a secondary count
against Officer Lawrence M. Powell (the man who struck
Rodney King the most times) for abuse under color of
authority. The jury was hung only

on this count. Post verdict. And in the wake of the massive
reaction to it, the then L.A. District Attorney Gil Garcetti
requested a retrial of Powell on this charge. But that afternoon, relatives and supporters of the cops celebrated in the
courtroom, while Black folks throughout L.A. watched their
televisions like Regis just pimp slapped a contestant for
messing up on *Who Wants to Be a Millionaire*.

Sitting in my office at that time of the Liberty Hill
Foundation (a progressive funder of grassroots organizations in Santa Monica, California), I wondered abstractly
if the work of Reverend Cecil Murray, Congresswoman
Maxine Waters, City Councilman Mark Ridley-Thomas,
and others would go for naught. Since the previous Thursday, when the jury sequestered itself, these community
leaders had been putting the word out that people had to
be cool no matter what decision came down. There would
be organized rallies and speak-outs for the populace to vent
their frustration. But the acquittal came a week and a half
after an appellate court upheld the ruling of Judge Joyce
Karlin in the Soon Ja Du case. Mrs. Du was a Korean
storeowner convicted by a L.A. jury of second-degree murder in the death of Black teenager Latasha Harlins. Karlin
gave Du five years' probation rather than the sixteen years
maximum in prison others had received under similar

convictions. The judge said Mrs. Du's going to jail wouldn't serve justice.

And so unanswered anger and blind fury collided at the intersections of Florence and Normandie in South Central. By dusk of the 29th, rioting and firebombing and looting had jumped off. Like Watts in '65 when I was a kid, you could watch the action on TV. Unlike Watts in '65, where shit was confined to a specific area, the anarchy spread from South Central to Koreatown, to Pico-Union, the edges of Silver Lake, Mid-City, and on into Compton, Long Beach, Pasadena, Inglewood, and even the gilded confines of Beverly Hills. Not only could you see it live and in color, but you were part of the action too.

Yet on Thursday morning we thought the worst might be over—psychologically tricking ourselves into thinking that one night's blowout would equal years of injustice. I went to work but my wife wisely decided to keep our, at the time, small children home from their preschool. Sure enough, Thursday afternoon the descent into the "riddle of violence" as African liberator Kenneth Kaunda phrased it, began again.

I rushed home midday from the office to find my neighborhood of Mid-City poised to go under the knife. The family gathered at a friend's second-story duplex with others, feeling as though we were in a nameless land experiencing an ill-conceived coup. People were clamoring in the streets, darting here and there as gun shots whined through the air, cars slammed into each other and buildings, sirens screamed, and police and news helicopters swarmed about pyres of flame like giant mechanical moths. Shit was happening all around, the neighborhoods were a torrent of rip and run, yet all you could do was watch out your window, unsure of who was in charge and who wanted to be.

Stores not five blocks from us blazed red and gray into the darkening sky as the local Vons at Pico and Fairfax was looted. Three middle-aged women, one with a pistol in her apron pocket, stopped a roving band of gangbangers from torching the Texaco station at the corner of our friend's duplex on Ogden. When night arrived, my wife, Gilda, drove our children, Miles and Chelsea, out to another friend's house in Van Nuys in the Valley for relative safety. But being the proud, petite bourgeoisie homeowner, I decided to stay at our crib so it wouldn't be empty. So on a small table next to the live drama on my TV set rested my loaded Smith & Wesson .357 Magnum and a half-pint of courage-in-a-bottle Jack Daniels—a volatile combination in the best of circumstances.

Well, the house didn't burn down nor did anybody, fortunately, try to bust a cap in my dome. But two personal things happened to me as a direct result of the civil unrest. It turned out our kids were incubating chicken pox because at the time it was going around their preschool and you're supposed to let them get it to develop the immunity. But at my then thirty-plus years I'd never had the disease and subsequently got it 'cause of that Thursday afternoon being cooped up with them in our friend's apartment. And my dad, Dikes, who was alive then and seventy-nine, had also never had chicken pox and subsequently got it from me (he was living with us but in Kansas City visiting relatives when the riot erupted). We were both miserable.

And that summer of '92, I started to write my second book, which would become the mystery novel *Violent Spring*. I'd already written a previously unpublished book with the main characters—donut-shop-owning private eye Ivan Monk, Superior Court Judge Jill Kodama, retired LAPD cop Dexter Grant, et al.—but knew using the backdrop of the siege and its aftermath as it shook out racially and politically would make for a compelling story. Ten years later, I'm still writing about Monk's travails and other stuff. And Los Angeles is still the sexy beast you can't help but look in the eye now and then and write about.

Continue reading for a preview
of the next Ivan Monk Mystery

PERDITION, U.S.A.

CHAPTER 1

S ay, brother, I ain't runnin' no newsstand where you stop and browse for hours. You gonna buy or what?"

The other man, an older gentleman in a plaid vest and a pair of doubleknit slacks in dire need of a hot iron, massaged his chin between thumb and index finger.

Scatterboy Williams let out an exasperated growl. "This is a genuine Cartier chronometer, my man. Stainless steel band with gold trim and a two-carat movement."

The man chewed his lip and looked at Scatterboy, then back to the watch in his outstretched palm. "Two carats, huh?"

Scatterboy nodded. "That's right. You go to any one of them stores where them Jews and them Iranians shop up in Beverly Hills and you see this fine timepiece goin' for no less than three thousand dollars."

"How'd you get one?"

"You really want to know, or you want a good deal on a handsome watch?" The salesman grinned, because he knew the answer. People were so predictable.

"Two-fifty," the man mumbled as he grasped the watch, turning it this way and that to determine its authenticity.

That was okay with Scatterboy. He doubted if the man

had ever seen another Cartier to compare it to. "It's gonna be three hundred in a minute, reverend, if you don't make up your mind."

"Very well, brother Williams. I wouldn't be doing this, only the beautiful Omega my dear wife bought me some twenty years ago is just too beat to be fixed again."

He droned on about the need for a preacher to keep up appearances before his congregation and what not. But Williams wasn't paying much attention save for the twenties the baritone-voiced healer extracted from his cracked-leather wallet. The money and watch were exchanged, and the holy man strapped the timepiece around his bony wrist.

"Is this band alligator skin?"

"That's illegal, reverend," Scatterboy said without a trace of irony. "It's snake, dyed to look like that."

"Yes, of course," the other man responded as he rose from the booth in the King Lion barbecue restaurant. "Well, thank you, Mr. Williams. I hope I see you in church soon."

He didn't wait for an answer and exited the establishment. Scatterboy leisurely finished his order of links, greens and potato salad. He also downed another can of Shasta cola, and sat working particles of gristle from his back teeth with a toothpick. The booth was next to a window which afforded a view of Ludlow Street, the main drag of Pacific Shores, and Scatterboy gazed out as the sun set.

Once upon a time, or so the old-timers would tell you, Pacific Shores was a going concern. Chiefly a town erected around the shipyards, the Shores enjoyed a solid, if limited, economic base for decades. Following Pearl Harbor, there were ships needed for the war. Following the war, there were ships needed to stem the red tide. By the '60s, a steel plant and a GM factory supplemented the shipyards. The working-class residents of the Shores—Blacks, whites and Latinos thrived.

In those days, most everyone owned their own home and worked twenty to thirty years at the same job, got a pension, and hung out at the VFW or B.P.O.E. hall when it wasn't bowling night. Not that the Shores was a model of an ethnic utopia. Like most of America, the various races tended to congregate in their own churches and shop in their own stores. But a standard of civic harmony prevailed.

By the tail end of the '70s, harsh changes came to this city located some thirty miles south of Los Angeles. Ship orders were down, "outsourcing" became the new corporate buzzword, and the GM plant moved to Mexico to cut costs. The outmoded steel plant closed for good. The two shipyards reduced two shifts to one, forced some workers into early retirements and laid others off. Eventually one moved to a "right-to-work" state whose legislature believed things like employees' rights originated in *The Communist Manifesto*.

By the mid-'80s, the only heavy industry left in Pacific Shores was one shipyard operating with a skeletal crew. The smaller businesses, dependent on a healthy workforce, withered and blew away in the recessionary winds sweeping the Southland.

Robert "Scatterboy" Williams, who had once worked as a shipyard welder, watched his second prostitute saunter by the King Lion. With a deft thrust, he freed the last piece of meat between his teeth. He rose, burped, and left the barbecue place.

A cool breeze coming off the ocean greeted him as he made his way along the street. Walking aimlessly, he turned over several options in his mind. All in all, he was about seven hundred dollars richer than he'd been two weeks ago. The seven hundred was the net from what he'd paid the sly Swede for several of the questionable Cartiers.

Whether they were genuine or not didn't matter to him. That they'd been stolen was a certainty. What really mattered was that others wanted them.

Problem was Swede wasn't the most easygoing guy to deal with. He was always cautious, always wondering if you'd slipped up and would lead the cops to him. But, Scatterboy allowed, there was a lesson to be learned from that sort of thinking. Which was why Swede'd never done time when guys like him found themselves marking the days in Deuel, Folsom or—the Lord help his homeboys—Pelican Bay.

Scatterboy drifted along a residential street with rundown Craftsmen and Spanish bungalows in need of paint and patching. A few of the lawns were trimmed but most were brown and shaggy. A tired street in a worn town.

Passing by an old Riviera parked at the curb, he noticed shapes moving in its darkened interior. He tensed, considering how fast he could gain some distance. Fortunately, the barrel of an Uzi wasn't suddenly erupting in his direction. Peering closer in the fading light, Scatterboy was relieved to see the windows were up in the vehicle.

He was no gangbanger, but given the vagaries of drug turfs, one never knew what real or imagined line of demarcation you were crossing. As he got closer, he could see two teenagers inside the Buick. The boy was sitting in the driver's seat, and had his arm around a girl next to him. The youngster gave Scatterboy a challenging look, and the girl sipped on a beer.

A thin trail of vapor was rising from between the two of them, down where the boy had his other hand. Scatterboy grinned wolfishly and walked on. Weed and pussy were about all a man could ask for these days. He got to the corner of Creedmore and Osage and stood there, thinking.

The watches were a good hustle but they took a lot of time to sell and required a lot of exposure. The seven hundred wouldn't last forever and he'd promised the mother of his baby girl he'd do better at supporting the kid. Slangin' product was not his forte. He could never score enough crack on his own to make any real money. And if he wanted to be big, he'd have to be beholden to a gang lord. The thought of being in the pocket of some kid with a 9mm tucked in his belt, and malt liquor fueling his thoughts, was not his idea of upward mobility.

Well, he reasoned, something would turn up. He crossed the street and started in the direction of his apartment several blocks over. As he got mid-block on Creedmore, an open-air Jeep rounded the far corner.

The driver crept at a slow pace then pulled to the curb. A light came on under the dashboard. Scatterboy could see that the man at the wheel was dressed casually, and he studied a map spread out on his knees.

"Maybe something's turned up already," Scatterboy happily intoned to himself.

He got closer, rehearsing how his next moves might go. Slip close while the lost chump looked for his route. The man wasn't wearing a seat belt. Perfect. Just ease up, yank the square out of the car by the elbow and slip an arm around his throat. Grab the wallet and run off before the mark could react.

The other man wasn't too big and Scatterboy, standing over six feet, had worked out daily on the prison iron yard. He gloated inwardly and drew closer, trying to control his hurried breathing.

"Do you know how I can find Terminal Street?"

"Wha?" The man's head had come up so suddenly it caught Scatterboy off-guard. Shit, now this punk could ID him. He turned sideways and pointed back the way he'd just come. Scatterboy figured to give him his directions, then as he looked that way, jump him. Fuck it, he needed the money. He better not resist. "Yeah, man. Go to the end of this block, make a left and go down another four or five blocks, you can't miss it."

"I don't plan to."

"Huh?" Scatterboy said as he pivoted back around.

The bullet entered his head on the right side of the bridge of his nose. It angled up and left the rear of his skull near the top of his close shaved head. The Jeep did a vicious U-turn and sped off as Robert Williams, aka Scatterboy, fell dead to the pavement.

CHAPTER 2

The small single-family house was the second from the end of the block. The grass was brown, and a low hedge bordered the driveway. A baby swing rested on the enclosed concrete porch. A cat leapt onto the balustrade and curled out on the warm stone railing.

"Are you Ivan Monk? Are you the man I need?"

Assuming the questions weren't meant to be existential, the private eye said, "Yes. Are you Clarice Moore?"

The screen door opened outward to reveal a teenaged girl with long strands of thick cornrowed hair. She was holding onto a baby. The kid had three of its fingers jammed in its mouth and drooled as it eyed the stranger. "Do you have some kind of identification? Mom says I should ask to see that."

It occurred to Monk that Clarice Moore should have listened to her mother when she'd told her about boys. He produced his photostat and the young woman took it from his hand.

She consumed it with a fierce glare. The baby began to cry and Clarice bounced the child gently and continued to peruse the private investigator license. Finally she handed it back. "Come on in."

He entered a room that reminded him of his mother's house. The home was lived in but cared for like a favorite shirt. Hanging from the walls were prints—a Charles White, a Rome Bearden, and an artist Monk didn't recognize.

"Come on in the kitchen. I've got to get Shawndell's formula."

Monk followed Clarice Moore into the back of the house. She retrieved a baby bottle warming in a saucepan and leaked a few drops from the nipple onto her slender forearm. "Can't give this child cold formula, no sir. Little Shawndell wants it toasty." She held up the child and giggled at her. "Isn't that right?"

She gave the baby her nutrition, and put her in a high-chair. She sat at the kitchen table but didn't offer Monk a seat.

He remained standing in the doorway, his arms crossed. The young woman looked at him, then down at a few letters and a folded newspaper on the table. She shifted the letters around but didn't speak.

Monk broke the silence. "You said over the phone that your boyfriend had been murdered."

For an answer she unfolded the newspaper. Monk got closer to read it. The paper was the *Press-Telegram* from two days ago. Clarice's thin finger hovered over a five-paragraph article relating the street shooting of twenty-six-year-old Robert Williams. Who, the report stated, had been on parole for assault and robbery from Solano State Prison. It went on to say that he'd previously done time at the California Youth Authority for second-degree manslaughter. Police sources said the investigation was continuing.

"Do you think someone he knew from Solano did him in?" Monk took a seat at the table and watched her face and body movements.

She looked at him and for the first time Monk noticed her light-caramel eyes and the tiny freckles that dotted her fine boned coppery face. "I don't know anything about that. I just want you to find out who killed Scatterboy."

"Scatterboy?"

"Yeah."

She didn't seem inclined to explain the root of the nickname so Monk said, "How'd you find out about me?"

The baby threw her bottle on the floor and smiled a toothless grin at her mother. Clarice put the child over her shoulder, and walked out of the room patting her back gently. Several minutes later she returned alone.

"My mother remembered hearing about you on the radio. Something to do with the mayor of L.A. killing Koreans," she said earnestly.

Monk blinked. "It wasn't the mayor, Clarice. Was it your mother's idea to have me look for Robert's killer?"

"No, that was my idea. Matter of fact, I kept on about Scatterboy's death until finally she said if I wanted to do something so bad, I ought to get a detective. I told her I didn't know no detective and that's when she got smart like she do and said if I listened to more than Ice Cube and Yo Yo I'd know about you and how you was a Black private eye and famous and all."

In the face of unassailable logic. Monk moved onward. "This is not a game, Clarice. The father of your child wasn't a candidate for a Nobel Prize."

"That mean he deserved to get killed like he did?" There was a sternness in her voice but the eyes were calm as they locked on him.

Monk tapped the paper. "This seems to infer your Robert was out doing something he shouldn't have been doing at that time of night."

Her lip curled upward but she fought to get it under control. "I know he wasn't out seein' no other woman. I know Scatterboy was loyal."

"That's not what I'm talking about, Clarice. Anyway, how do you plan to pay me?"

Peeved, she leaned close to Monk. "I ain't on welfare, man. I work part-time at a Radio Shack. I can pay you for your time and effort."

Monk continued to humor the headstrong girl. "Fine. Do you have a list of Robert's friends and acquaintances?"

"I told you, none of them had anything to do with this."

"The investigation has to start somewhere."

Her brows bunched in that absorbing countenance she'd used on Monk's license. Abruptly, she got up from the table and left the kitchen again. The sound of a drawer opening and shutting forcefully filled the empty moments as Monk waited.

Clarice returned and put a single piece of white lined paper on the table. She sat and began to laboriously write on the sheet. At various intervals she would pause and study her output. Then she would resume in her slow, steady pace. Finally she slid it across to Monk.

Listed in compact block letters were individuals with names like Li'l Bone, Two Dog, and an Angel Z. There were no addresses for these and the others written down. But she had indicated where a particular individual might hang out. A Junior's Liquors, a place called the King Lion, and so on. Lines were drawn from the names to the places.

Monk said as evenly as he could, "I could spend a lot of time looking for these people you put down here just so I could talk to them. Don't any of them live somewhere? Didn't Robert have a mother or father, some relative somewhere?"

Clarice snatched the paper from Monk's hand. "Why you got to be askin' so many smart questions? Look, that's how I know where to find them. Ain't none of them got an office, man." She began to jiggle her left leg and slap the table quietly with the back of her hand. "I mean you acting like you don't want to help and all."

"Come on, Clarice," Monk said, allowing exasperation to color his voice. "Robert, Scatterboy, or whatever you want to call him probably got done in by a homey he'd stiffed."

She pointed at the doorway. "Then why don't you leave, Mr. Headlines."

"All I'm trying to say, Clarice, is that you know perfectly well what kind of dude Robert Williams was. Be realistic. I bet if you thought about it, you could come up with one or two people on this list who might have done him harm."

She was having none of it. The determined teenager cocked her head and bounced her leg again. He waited for a few minutes, but all he got was the sound of her foot tapping against the patterned linoleum.

Monk got up and headed for the front door. He looked back at her sitting in the kitchen, head cradled in her hand, fuming. He clucked his tongue, feeling like he was casting her adrift. Slowly, the big bad detective went back into the afternoon air.

RONNY AARON sold his next-to-last dub of crack to a blonde woman whose license plate frame read: I only tan in Newport Beach. The Infiniti roared away and Aaron took his lanky frame along Ludlow. He was tired and he walked without much of a destination in mind.

It had been a long night of mostly haggling with money-poor crack heads. But the two or three sales to upscale clientele—Pacific Shores was less than a half hour drive due north from the Orange County border—who paid the rate and split, made up for the hassles.

Aaron adjusted his Fila so it rested more fashionably on his head and drifted into the Zacharias corner market on Osage.

"Give me a half pint of Seagrams," he said to the middle-aged Latina behind the counter. Hefting his purchase, he walked back outside and ran into one of his customers, an addict named Herbert who was always short of cash.

"My man," Herbert effused.

Aaron kept walking but Herbert wouldn't take the hint.

"Say, bro', how 'bout a little something on credit?"

Aaron gritted his teeth and marched on.

"You can't speak, motherfuckah? Can't say shit to one of your best customers?" Herbert shoved Aaron from behind and the drug seller stopped, then turned to back-hand the man.

"What the fuck's your problem, Herbie? You don't want me to get in your ass right here in the street, do you?" Though he knew Herbert could be violent, Aaron also sensed he was too strung out to cause him much damage.

Self-contempt or anger contorted the crack head's face. He spat red on the pavement between them. The contempt overtook the anger, tightening the slack skin around the pin-prick eyes. "I got to have some, man. I've got to."

"Fuck you, punk." Aaron strode off, triumphant. He left Osage and went east along Kenmore. He felt good having stood down Herbert. Word would spread and those that inhabited the depths of Pacific Shores would know he was not a man to be fucked with. Hell, he was a man of respect.

"Yo," a voice said from somewhere behind him.

Feeling immortal, Aaron turned. "Yeah," he said, Napoleon addressing a lesser. He grinned crookedly. "What?"

The first bullet tore into his left kneecap and he sunk to the sidewalk on his good leg. "Motherfuckah," Aaron screamed, grabbing for the .32 tucked in his back pocket. The second bullet entered his open mouth, busted out his new fillings, and continued to travel downward. The slug exited his back below the shoulder blades. Ronny Aaron was already dead when his body gently crumpled to the earth.

CHAPTER 3

There was no mention of Ronny Aaron's shooting in the *L.A. Times*, nor any coverage of it on the nightly news. There were three paragraphs in the lesser-circulated *Press-Telegram* out of Long Beach, but it was a dry summing-up of an insignificant life. He was just one more penny-ante drug dealer the sheriff's deputies in Pacific Shores were glad to be shut of.

Even if there had been banner headlines about Aaron's killing, it probably wouldn't have been the topic *du jour* at the reception for California's new Senator, Grainger Wu, at the Sunset Orchid Hotel in L.A.'s Chinatown.

Jill Kodama stepped out of the ladies room just as Walter Kane was placing an empty glass on a table in the foyer. "Jill, I saw you come in earlier. I meant to say hi but you know how it is when you get cornered by ass-kissers."

"Not that you're opposed to that in certain circumstances."

"Yeow." Kane did a Groucho Marx with his eyebrows. He was over six-two and rapier sharp in a grey double-breasted suit. Underneath the jacket was an aqua-hued shirt with a spear-point collar and a black tie. A crimson pocket square completed the look. His auburn hair was cut modishly long, and he sprouted a thin, Errol Flynn mustache.

Standing close to him, Kodama was greeted with the aroma of vodka mixed with Obsession for Men. "Yeah, it's a tough job being the senator's chief aide, running interference with the oil lobbyists, the aerospace industry, and the tourist bureaus. Helping them figure out which political action committee to dump their next ten thousand on."

Kane grinned and the two walked back toward the room where the reception was taking place. "What a cynic, and you're not even old enough to drink."

"You can quit the flattery, Walter. I've already voted."

They crossed the threshold into the reception area, called the Autumn Lounge. A jazz sextet played a low samba from the raised stage off to one side. Kodama plucked a white wine from the hosted bar and took a sip. "Seriously, Walter, Grainger's got a hard row to hoe and we both know it. A freshman senator from California who won in a tight race."

"And standing on liberal legs," Kane added. "'Course it didn't hurt he has sound fiscal programs that appealed to the older, whiter electorate."

"Despite a campaign where the racial mud-slinging flew fast and furious in the last weeks."

They both turned to the new voice as Ursala Brock walked up. She was a large-hipped, small-waisted, handsome Black woman who handled urban affairs for Senator Wu. The two women kissed one another on the cheek.

"Yeah, the mailer Jankowsky put out in the last month ran with the headline, 'A Peril from the East,'" Kane said. "So of course he gets a lot of attention for it. Then the old cocksucker goes on talk shows and claims it referred to the fact that Grainger had been an assemblyman from the East Bay—Oakland." Kane winked broadly.

The band began a version of a Cedar Walton tune called "Midnight Waltz." Kodama asked rhetorically, "So with less than a three-percent margin of victory, does our favorite son have a chance to do anything in the Senate?"

A toupeed white man in a pin-striped three-piece suit, his vest straining against an ample belly, grabbed Brock aggressively from behind. "Ursala, when the hell are you going to forget about politics and come work for me?" He quaffed a healthy amount of the drink he was holding.

Brock smirked. "I lay awake nights thinking about the good the advertising council does, Harry." She removed the ad man's hand from her body, giving Kodama a sidelong glance.

"Fuckin' A," Harry agreed and wandered off to cop a feel on some other woman.

Momentarily a silence descended on the trio. A reflection on the forces that created men like Harry, and an understanding it was his universe they were operating in, not the other way around.

Eventually, Kane spoke. "You're right, Jill, we ain't got shit in the way of a mandate, but I'll be damned if we won't fight for the high ground." Somehow the aide had obtained another vodka tonic and was sampling it steadily.

Brock put her hand around Kodama's waist. "Before we take Pork Chop Hill, sarge, I want to know how's that brutally handsome Black man of yours?"

Kodama bared her uppers. "How come every time I see you, you got to be asking about my man, honey?"

"Girls," Kane intoned. He leaned into them like a schoolyard leech, "I'm serious, you guys," he pointed the rim of the glass at Brock. "Tell Jill about the kind of mail we've been getting."

She eyed him curiously. "Well, what else do you expect to get in the office of the first Chinese-American, hell, the first Asian from the mainland to become a member of the U.S. Senate?"

"Meaning there's a certain level of racism and intoler-
ance we must accommodate," Kane said, baiting her as the
sextet swung into a rendition of Herbie Hancock's "Can-
taloupe Island." Several people bobbed their heads to the
jaunty beat.

"Meaning we have to push to accomplish some goals,"
Brock responded testily, "'cause we may not get a second
go-round."

"All of us are well aware of the limits of politics," Kane
slurred.

"My point, Walter, is that we need to do something about
these groups," Ursala replied aggressively.

It seemed to Kodama this was getting to be an old argument among her two friends. "How do you mean, Ursala?"

"I mean, your honor, that I don't think the goddamn nazis,
the Posse Comitatus, gangsta rappers calling for bashin' their
hoes, the Jewish Defense League, or the fuckin' War Reich
have a right to exist, let alone exercise their poisonous free
speech."

Kodama was used to being grilled for being a cardcarry-
ing member of the American Civil Liberties Union. "I
suppose I don't need to remind you our chapter broke with
the national and didn't go along with the nazis' march that
year in Skokie, Illinois."

"I'll give you that," Brock conceded.

Kodama said, "Now before you expect me to go into my
patented 'The Constitution is nothing if it's not for all of
us,' who the hell is the War Reich?"

"A group of skinheads who started in the Pacific Northwest," Kane contributed.

"An all-too-typical group of young disaffected whites who
see it as their Aryan destiny to create a homeland for their
race." Brock waved a silent hello to a passerby.

Kane said, "They're connected to that fire bombing of a Puerto Rican family in Port Huron."

"No question these are serious times, Walter. This state passed the anti-immigrant 187 and that goddamn three-strikes 184."

"Which takes even more discretion away from judges," Brock observed. "Further demonizing Black and Brown youth."

"Which," Kane said, sipping more vodka, "is right in line with the thinking behind Colorado's gay-bashing Proposition M measure. The lines are being drawn in this country just like in Bosnia."

"I hope you're wrong, Walter," Kodama said.

Wu called to Kane from the stage and the chief aide polished off the last of his vodka tonic. He placed the glass in the dirt of an urn next to a twisted thick-trunked cactus. "But we can only do what we can to make the system work," he said, his breath heavy with drink. He jogged to the stage.

"Enough of this depressing shit" Brock took Kodama by the arm, leading her to one side. "So what's going on with you and Ivan?" Her eyes glittered mischievously.

"Cool, cool. How about you and Terry?"

"We spent last weekend up in Monterey. Got away to talk about the future. You know Terry, he had champagne sent up to the room and took me on a balloon ride."

Brock took delight in her stock broker boyfriend and his doting on her. "And what does the future hold, Kreskin?"

"Love or ruin, baby. But Terry and I will face it together."

"Ivan and I have a good thing," she said defensively. And surprised that she felt the need to blurt it out like that.

Brock perceived it as a challenge. "Four years is enough time to make up one's mind."

"We're comfortable, Ursala."

"My shoes are comfortable, girl. But I walk on them."

Kodama got hot. "Ivan doesn't take me or our relationship for granted. We both have careers."

"So do a lot of us. Maybe it's you who likes the status quo."

"What if I do?" Kodama replied tersely.

Brock drew close. "Jill, if you're happy with where you're at, so am I. We've known each other too long to fall out over some silly men." They hugged and Brock went off toward the stage where Wu beckoned her.

The wine glass was in her hand, but Kodama had suddenly lost the taste for the stuff.